INDIA-PAKISTAN NUCLEAR WAR

Munir Muhammad

ISBN: 1539024571
ISBN 13: 9781539024576
Library of Congress Control Number: 2016916139
CreateSpace Independent Publishing Platform
North Charleston, South Carolina

All men dream, but not equally. Those who dream by night in the dusty recesses of their minds wake in the day to find that it was vanity: but the dreamers of the day are dangerous men, for they may act their dream with open eyes, to make it possible.

—T. E. Lawrence, *The Seven Pillars of Wisdom*

Bruce Riedel claims, "There is probably no worst nightmare for America, for Europe, for the world in the 21st century than a Pakistan that is out of control, under the influence of extremist Islamist forces armed with nuclear weapons."

In May 2011 American military units flying in two helicopters penetrated deep into Pakistan's top military city, Abbottabad, headquarters of one of its key army divisions, the Baluch Regiment. The city also housed the elite military academy Kakul.

To reach their target, American forces invaded Pakistani air space from Afghanistan, flew over large parts of Frontier province, all the way to Abbottabad, carried out a successful operation of killing Osama Bin Laden (OBL), capturing prisoners and taking loads of data and computer equipment.

Throughout this operation, from the time Americans entered Pakistani air space till they left, a total time span of over two hours according to some estimates, there was zero, nil, no response from Pakistan's air defense or ground forces located within a kilometer of OBL's compound.

The attack carried out by Indians in the following pages is based on this state of Pakistan's response time during the Osama Bin Laden capture.

THE INDIAN ATTACK—
PAKISTAN'S NIGHTMARE

PRESENT DAY

On the first day of the holy month of Ramadan, the moon had been sighted, and most people of Pakistan were getting ready to close their first fast of the month, when the attack began.

The objective of the attack was to fragment and eventually destroy the Pakistani Air Defense Systems (PADS). The strategic attack plan, which had been in place since the attacks in Mumbai in 2008 and upgraded after recent war exercises carried out with the Israeli Air Force and Navy, called for a four-phase attack.

In the first phase, helicopters were to penetrate, flying low into enemy territory and destroying their advance-warning radar systems. In the second phase, AWACS (Airborne Warning and Control Systems) aircraft were to carry out massive jamming operations to disable the communications and electronic capabilities of the enemy forces. In the third phase, fighter jets were to inflict maximum damage on the enemy defense systems, and in the fourth phase, as many secondary targets as possible were to be taken out. The operation was called Agnipath, or "walk on fire."

The Indian Air Force enjoyed a massive advantage, having invested ten times more money than their enemy forces over the past two decades. The technology at the disposal of the Indians was decades ahead of that enjoyed by the Pakistanis. In addition to that, through carefully planned terrorism acts, India previously had managed to destroy and/or damage the advance-warning capability of Pakistan's Orion spy planes. These acts were carried out with the help of the Israelis, using Pakistani militants in various false flag operations—that is, Pakistani militants thought they were working for their own cause, but in effect they were recruited and deployed by Israeli and Indian agents who had deeply infiltrated most militant organizations operating inside Pakistan, some of which were even patronized and actively trained by Pakistan's own intelligence agencies.

Precisely on the stroke of midnight, one squadron of Dhruv Mk4 helicopters equipped with a turret guns, rockets, and various air-to-air and air-to-ground missiles such as the antitank Helina missile, took off from Jamnagar. The air distance from Jamnagar to Karachi was outside the combat radius of the helicopters, so after taking off from Jamnagar, the helicopters had to make a short refueling stop at Dwarka airport before moving on to targets in Karachi, Pakistan. The helicopters, traveling at 250 kilometers per hour, completed the long, earth-hugging flight and sighted the assigned targets: early-warning radar sites inside Pakistan. The objective was to blind the Pakistani air defenses to the attack that was to follow shortly after.

Another squadron of Dhruv Mk4 helicopters took off at 1:00 a.m. from Ambala on a mission into Lahore and was ready and positioned at the same time as the squadron flying from Jamnagar to Karachi.

At 2:00 a.m. the attack began with the opening blow of Indian helicopters destroying the radar sites with missiles. The helicopters were followed by Advanced Warning Aircraft Systems, which were specially equipped to jam the radar and communications of the Pakistani air force. Thus, Pakistani forces were denied both visibility and communications at the most critical moment. As soon as the helicopters and AWACS had done their jobs, they were followed by the attack squadrons, which moved in to inflict maximum damage.

At 1:30 a.m., one squadron consisting of twelve Jaguar SEPECAT fighter planes, also known as *shamsher* or *sword*, took off from the air force base at Jamnagar in the Southwestern Air Command. The squadron was led by Group Captain Mehta; his mission was to destroy Karachi's sea and air ports, as well as to attack PAF bases Masroor and Faisal.

The second squadron, led by Group Captain Browne, took off from Halwara air force base in the Western Air Command.

The job of this squadron was to penetrate deep inside Pakistani territory and take out Pakistan's three nuclear installations at Kahuta and Chashma. The third squadron, flying MiG-21s under Captain Singh, took off from Ambala air base in the Western Air Command. The target for this squadron was a suburb near Lahore where the terrorist group was headquartered. After the attack the squadron was to inflict maximum damage on key military and infrastructure installations.

The fourth squadron, captained by Anup Jalwa, took off from Jodhpur in Mikoyan MiG-29s, known as *baaz* (Hindi for hawk). The Jodhpur squadron was to attack military installations in what was known as Pakistan's soft underbelly, the area between Pano Aqil and Multan, to soften it further.

By the time the first squadron, led by Captain Mehta, entered Pakistani air space, the forward force of attack helicopters and AWACS had already "blinded" the targets.

⊫⊣ ⊢⊨

Mehta's squadron approached the port city of Karachi; the lights of the city could be seen from the sky. The city, even at 2:00 a.m., seemed to be alive. The squadron split into three groups. One group, led by Captain Shukla, headed for the air force base at Masroor. The second group, led by Captain Sukh, approached PAF base Faisal; and the third group, led by group captain Mehta, stayed on course for the Karachi port.

Mehta was first to reach his target. Carefully selecting one end of the port, he started dropping bombs. Within a matter of minutes, Karachi port was ablaze. The next targets were oil storage depots scattered around the port area. His team carefully started taking out the targets, one after another. Soon the whole port area was like an inferno. Next they started targeting naval installations, some of which had already been wiped out in the first wave of the attack. Within fifteen minutes the mission was over. But Mehta wanted more, so he looked at his secondary target list and turned west toward a beach area known to locals as Paradise Point. Close to Paradise Point was an atomic power plant, KANUPP. Mehta and his team took out KANUPP and turned to go home, their mission accomplished but the thirst still unsatisfied.

Captain Shukla's attack group was the next to reach their targets. Without much ado over identifying the target, they proceeded to carpet bomb the place. Within a matter of minutes, Pakistan Air Force Base Masroor in Karachi was no more. Shukla too wanted more, so he went for a secondary target marked a little further up on the map as "Sonmiani." This was a hidden navy installation in the mountains off the Baluchistan coast. As Shukla approached Sonmiani, he suddenly realized that the enemy forces were on alert.

After the Karachi port attack, the whole defense structure in Karachi had gone into complete panic. The corps commander, head of the army in Karachi, was woken up. The naval chief, who happened to be present in Karachi and was enjoying a late-night party, was dragged to soberness, and the air force local command all came into panic action. Their first response was to call up army headquarters in Pindi and the Joint Chiefs of Staff based in Islamabad, the capital.

The man in charge in Sonmiani was an old veteran, Captain Nazir. When he picked up the report of the attack on Kemari port, he immediately knew from experience that the Indians were retaliating against the Delhi terrorist attack. Without waiting for any orders, he went into battle mode. He ordered antiaircraft guns to be readied and had radar on high alert. He tried to contact Base Masroor but failed, and his attempts to contact naval air support units also failed. As soon as the attacking planes were within sight, he ordered the firing of ground-to-air missiles that had been installed at Sonmiani just for such an eventuality. But it was too little.

The enemy was ready; they saw the incoming missiles, dodged them successfully, and dropped enough bombs to put Sonmiani out of action. With that, Captain Shukla and his team also headed for home.

For Captain Sukh it was the toughest, because when he arrived over PAF base Faisal, he realized that the base was surrounded by a civilian population, and there would be a huge number of civilian fatalities. But that was not something for him to think about, he realized with a heavy heart, and proceeded to drop bombs at his prechosen targets. Two fighter planes from his team had gone across to other navy installations, PNS Karsaz and PNS Mehran, to destroy them. That done, they proceeded to Karachi's international airport and completely destroyed the runway to ensure it was not functional anymore. Sukh saw that right next to the airport was Malir Cantonment, and he decided he had enough time to do some more damage, with no resistance from the enemy, so he proceeded to bomb the cantonment area.

Group Captain Singh's squadron from Ambala was the second one to reach their targets. Just about the time Singh's squadron was entering Pak air space, Mehta's squadron had started raining hell on Karachi, but Pakistan's defense forces were still in deep slumber. Captain Singh and his team reached their target, a suburb of Lahore known as Muridke, and wiped it out off the face of the earth with their bombs. Muridke was, according to Indian intelligence, the training, recruitment, and headquarters of the group that had launched the attack on Delhi. That done, Singh and his pilots started picking targets off the list around Lahore and let hell loose on Lahore. Singh and his team, having used less than half their firepower, decided to head for Rawalpindi, the headquarters of the Pakistan Army, which was only thirty minutes away.

Singh divided his squadron in three: One unit, led by Singh, was to target Rawalpindi. A second unit was to target the capital city of Islamabad and the oil refinery there. The third group was to break away and go deeper into Pakistani territory, first attacking KAMRA aeronautical complex and then striking various military installations in the area.

By the time they entered the air space of Rawalpindi, Pakistani air force planes were waiting. A dogfight ensued, in which three Pakistani planes and one Indian MiG-21 were shot down. The Indians succeeded in dropping enough bombs on Pindi to do serious damage. But as time was passing, the Pakistanis were beginning to launch an air counteroffensive.

Singh realized that the chances of him and his team returning to India were running out fast. He turned on his secure communications with his fellow pilots, of whom only two remained, and ordered them to turn around and head for home base in Ambala.

The second group, led by Captain Charlie, reached Islamabad and took out the Islamabad airport and the air force base in Chaklala before the Pakistanis knew what hit them. He then turned to the oil refinery and took it out, thus crippling the oil supplies for the army and air force. Next he decided to flatten the Pakistani parliament, the president's house, and the prime minister's secretariat. In the process, in the first major mistake of the attack, Captain Charlie mistakenly bombed the American embassy and some other NATO country missions, which happened to be in close proximity to the parliament. But before he turned around, he had to take out another target that was of symbolic value: the headquarters of Inter-Services Intelligence, which was thought by India to be the criminal mastermind behind all the terrorism directed against India. That target was easy, as it had been picked and identified well in advance, but here too, because of the target's proximity to civilian populations, the bombs dropped by Charlie left a lot of civilians dead.

7

With some satisfaction, Charlie and his team turned around to head for home base in Ambala.

The third group, led by Captain Arudhna, daughter of a retired air force chief, was heading for Kamra, but by now the element of surprise was lost, and Kamra was one of the most defended targets in the country because of its importance as a key manufacturer of weapons systems. Arudhna and her team encountered heavy resistance; her wingman was the first to receive a fatal missile. She and her remaining team maneuvered and fought Pakistani fighter planes, but there was no letup by them. Arudhna and her team managed to discharge most of their bombs, but these were not precisely delivered. One by one all her team members were brought down by the Pakistani air force. Arudhana was the second of her team to be shot down.

Group Captain Anup Jalwa was thirty-six years old and had only recently gotten married to his long-term sweetheart, who was now pregnant with their first child. Anup had gotten the call as he was just heading home from his in-laws' house after a family reunion. He dropped his family at home and immediately left for the base, where his team was already waiting. He was part of the squad that took off from Jodhpur, headed for the area between Pano Aqil and Multan.

Anup and his team were right behind Mehta's squadron, and by the time they entered Pakistani air space, Karachi was already ablaze, so there was very little element of surprise. However, what worked in Anup's squadron's favor was the fact that Pakistan's air-defense capability in this sector had largely been deflated.

Anup led the front team and went for the farthest target, the forward positions of the Pakistani army in the Multan sector and military and air force installations in the vicinity. His squadron met no resistance—it was a walk in the park; the Pakistanis were simply not expecting anything. It surprised Anup, who had been a student of military history, to see that after so much hype about Indo-Pakistan enmity, his enemy could be so ill prepared.

The other two units of Anup's team also had the same dream-like experience of going through the enemy's air space, dropping their load on the targets, and returning without even being challenged.

⟫⟪⟫⟪

Group Captain Browne's squadron out of Halwara entered Pakistan about the same time as Singh's squad bombed Muridke in Lahore. Thus, any reaction Pakistan had was focused on Karachi, which had already been bombed, and Lahore. Browne knew that this was a potentially "no return" mission, but this was war, and this what they were trained for.

PAF base in Sargodha, which is the largest air base and practically an air force home city, is closest to Pakistan's nuclear installations. On hearing of the Karachi bombings, Base Commander Butt had set in motion standard operating procedures for such eventualities. Thus, a squadron of Chengdu F-7s was already giving air cover to the nuclear installations.

Browne was in front and realized that the element of surprise was no more; further, he and his squadron were potentially entering a death trap. But before his thoughts could conclude, his radar detected incoming missiles fired by Pakistani fighters. Browne fired two decoys and turned the nose of his plane upward to evade further attacks, with two Pakistani fighter planes on his tail. This was pretty much the fate of all the other fighter planes in the squadron over Kahuta. But two fighter planes, flown by Ravi and Ganga, managed to drop to low altitude just long enough to avoid enemy fire and drop bunker-buster bombs over Kahuta.

The Pakistanis launched a second squadron of Chengdu fighters, and after that the sheer numeric strength of Pakistani planes gradually brought all of the Browne squadron down. But Browne had realized this, and had ordered his team to discharge as many bombs as they could regardless of the accuracy, before they were trapped.

No one from Browne's squadron survived; Pakistan also lost one full squadron of Chengdu fighter planes.

Kahuta and the areas around it were turned into rubble. No one knew the extent of the damage caused to the atomic plant, because most of the critical facilities were buried deep underground.

The speed and the ferocity with which the Indians had attacked had left the Pakistanis in shock, but as the shock wore off and anger set in, there were calls by demonstrators for Pakistan to launch a nuclear strike against India.

The Morning after the Delhi Attack—3:00 a.m.

The Indian cabinet meeting at the defense bunker in Sonepur, Orissa

The prime minister was given a full briefing of the damage inflicted by the Indian Air Force on Pakistan. Out of four squadrons of twelve fighter planes each, thirty-two had returned to their home base, and sixteen had been lost, succumbing to enemy fire.

Damages on the Pakistani side were much greater, because most of their planes were still on the ground. Damage to the military installations was substantial, but the full extent was not easy to determine just yet.

The air force chief unveiled the second wave of air attacks, which was already underway. The planes had taken off from their bases, and this time the targets were forward Pakistani positions along the border.

By 6:00 a.m., according to the air force chief, Pakistan's defenses would be crippled.

The army chief took over and briefed the meeting on how the Indian Army had been mobilized, and five armored brigades were already beginning to roll toward Pakistan. Their main target was Pano Aqil, Bahawalpur sector, and the mission objective was to sever the country into two parts.

HOW IT ALL STARTED

April 2007—Karachi, Pakistan

It was 8:30 a.m., and the alarm was shrieking. Sultan pushed the silk sheets aside and stepped naked onto the cold white marble floor, stretching his lanky, almost-six-foot-tall frame before lumbering to the bathroom. The bathroom was an elegant affair, made with Italian granite and accessories; it was one of the few luxuries Sultan truly enjoyed. While he shaved and showered, his mind went back to the lead story he had edited last night for his own newspaper, which was published this morning. The story related to the return to Pakistan of Benazir Bhutto (BB). BB had been elected twice and dismissed twice on charges of corruption, and she was now negotiating her return to the country and to power through the Americans. Sultan's stomach turned at the thought of BB coming back into power. Every time he saw her on the TV, his blood boiled.

"You took longer today, honey," his wife commented as he approached the breakfast table, where she was already seated, reading the newspaper. He gave her a kiss on the cheek and sat down, picking up his orange juice and one of the newspaper sections.

"Yeah, just had too much going on in my head," he replied.

"Let me guess—you were thinking about BB returning to Pakistan. I know you said we would emigrate to Canada if she ever returned to power, but, honey, don't worry. What difference does it make to us? You know things will go on as usual, so why worry?"

"I worry because this is my country, and there are two hundred million people who are suffering because of outside interference in our country. We are suffering not because we are incompetent or illiterate, but because we are a Muslim country and a nuclear power."

His wife interjected as he took a mouthful of his breakfast. "But, honey, people elect these leaders; if BB comes back into power, it will be because the people elect her. Don't you agree?"

"It is the same old story over and over again. In 1977, the Americans orchestrated the overthrow of the first elected government of Ali Bhutto because he initiated the nuclear program, and instead they gave us the gift of Army Chief Zia, the dictator who ruled the country for eleven years. When he started going against the American agenda, he was killed with the connivance of our own security establishment. In 1999 the Americans supported and allowed the army to take over after overthrowing Nawaz Sharif, to punish him for carrying out nuclear tests. Mind you, Nawaz was elected with the biggest-ever majority in the history of the country. He too would have been hanged, had it not been for the Saudis interfering. And now the Americans are arranging for another politician who will do their bidding to take power, even though she has been tried twice before, and her party has a reputation for corruption and incompetence. But her return to power is more or less certain, because in Pakistan the two most important factors deciding political fortunes are the army and America." Sultan took a deep breath to calm down.

"Well, I intend to change that," Sultan added quietly. His wife looked up in surprise; this was the first time her husband had expressed his intention to go into politics.

"Honey, you just told me that two of the elected prime ministers were hanged or nearly hanged. What makes you think, if your argument is correct, the same will not happen to you?"

"What will be will be. *Que será, será*," replied Sultan. His wife knew the old Doris Day song and had a sinking feeling in her stomach.

What she didn't know was that this resolve had come a few days ago, after discussions with a young trainee who had been crabbing about the fate of the nation and the dismal state of affairs. Sultan had asked him, "Are you prepared to die for your country?" The young man was stunned at this question. "The change will only come if we are prepared to sacrifice, and my friend, none of us are prepared to sacrifice," Sultan had said, concluding his short talk.

Later that night his own words kept echoing in his head. The short talk with the trainee had clarified Sultan's own thoughts, and this is when he had decided that he would sacrifice in whatever way was needed to bring change his country.

After almost a decade of writing, editing, and publishing, Sultan had realized that no change was likely to come through writing; he had to do something more. Today, if all went well, he would be launching his political career. And in a few years, he should be in a position to bring meaningful change to the lives of hundreds of millions of people in this country.

Karachi University Auditorium, Later That Day

The auditorium was filled to capacity. Most attendees were students in business courses, but there were also some from other disciplines and a few outsiders. As Sultan entered the room, his eyes settled on the other occupants on the stage; one was the professor who was hosting this debate, and the other was a medium-height, stocky man in his early seventies. The man had a bushy mustache and a full head of hair that was dyed black, except for the sideburns, which were showed gray. Sultan knew this man; well, everyone in the country knew this man, but this was the first time Sultan was going to meet him face to face. This man was the reason Sultan had accepted today's invitation to speak.

The man was General Masoom Bhaya, considered by many to be the chief architect of the Afghan jihad against the Russians. As chief of the influential Inter-Services Intelligence, he, under the guidance of his mentor, General Khan, had navigated the war to its ultimate victory, bringing down the Soviet empire. He had been in line to become chief of staff of the army but was forced to quit the army, which had been his life, career, and passion ever since he had grown up, because the Americans didn't want him to be the army chief. Every Taliban leader and most senior al-Qaeda operatives were on his speed dial, and none would ignore his call because he was the ultimate secret keeper. Equally important, from Sultan's perspective, was that the general was instrumental in setting up the political movement called "IJI"—Islami Jamhoori Itthehad (Islamic Democratic Alliance). The IJI was a coalition of religious parties and right-wing politicians, and it had catapulted Nawaz Sharif into power in 1990. However, Nawaz had not delivered and over the years had become another traditional politician interested in the perks of power, forgetting his earlier promise of an Islamic state. Ever since then the general had lacked political influence, though from his media interviews, he still had ideas he would like to see put into action.

The clock chimed 4:00 p.m., and the elderly professor took the podium. Gradually, silence fell in the hall.

"Ladies and gentlemen, it gives me great pleasure to introduce to you Mr. Sultan. As you know, Mr. Sultan has created a career over the past twenty-odd years that is a success story that many of you would like to emulate, and all of you certainly want to hear about. So without further ado, I present to you Mr. Sultan."

"Good afternoon, ladies and gentlemen. Let me start with the good news: I am not going to make a speech! I am just going to share with you my thoughts, and you can ask questions." After ten minutes of speaking about his experiences, Sultan decided the time was ripe to start the dialogue he had come here for, which he hoped would set him on the course for his destiny. He selected a young woman in her early twenties in a yellow sunflower-print dress.

"Sir," she asked, "why publish a newspaper? What do you know about journalism?"

Sultan chuckled. "Well, because no one would publish what I wrote, so I decided to buy a newspaper!"

The audience burst out laughing and clapping. Good, thought Sultan; if I can get a few more responses like this one, I will be on my way to political stardom.

"But it is true I wrote a few articles and found no one would publish them, and then this opportunity came along. The workers' union of this newspaper had published an appeal to the president and everyone under the sun, because they had not been paid wages for six months. So I went to the owners, negotiated a buyout, saved the jobs, and ended up with the newspaper. Thus, I discovered my passion for writing, and I could start putting my ideas and vision into writing for the public to read."

Another student stood up. "Sir, my name is Shehzad, and I am a student of journalism. What do you think is Pakistan's biggest problem?" he asked. This was good, thought Sultan; this meant media coverage.

"Are you prepared to sit here for another week while I go through the list?" Sultan replied with a smile, and the audience started laughing and clapping again.

"But truthfully, we have too many problems. However, if we were allowed to work though these problems without foreign interference and took decisions in the national interest, then things would start falling into place. For example, we hand over our citizens to the CIA without any due process of law; they are sold like a commodity to get a few million dollars in aid. I am referring to the fate of Dr. Aafia, a young and brilliant physicist, one of the finest minds this country ever produced. She went to the top American school, MIT, and now she has become a 'missing person' who, according to my information, is being held captive without due process of law by the Americans along with her young and infant children. If we do not respect our own citizens, if we do not protect our own citizens—and let us not forget that is the fundamental responsibility of every government—then no one will respect our citizens.

"I am not against Americans; they have always done what suits them and they always will. In 1949 they convinced our first prime minister to not engage in hostilities with India, assuring us that the United States would prevail upon India to settle the Kashmir issue. Late PM Liaquat fell for their false promises and was later assassinated by the extremist elements within our own security establishment, as he was deemed a traitor. That, ladies and gentlemen, sowed the seeds of instability and led to the first martial law. In 1962 China opened a window of opportunity for us to grab Kashmir while India was dealing with the Chinese intrusion. Once again the Americans intervened and promised General Ayub Khan, the military dictator and ruler, that India would be brought around to settle the Kashmir issue; once again we were let down, and that led to the 1965 war. America had signed a treaty with Pakistan to supply us with weapons and help in times of war, but when India attacked us in 1971, causing the breakup of the country, the Americans never lifted a finger to help Pakistan. As a result of American friendship, we didn't get Kashmir, and we also lost East Pakistan—half the country.

"In 1977, Prime Minister Ali Bhutto initiated a program to build nuclear bombs. For that crime he was hanged, because he went against the Americans' wishes. It was the security establishment of our country, under General Zia, who did the dirty work for the Americans. Then we were embroiled in a war with the Russians at America's behest, turning our country into a sanctuary and nursery for militants of every shade and color from every part of the world, trained and funded by the CIA. The CIA used weapons and drug-smuggling to fund its operations. Today we have tens of millions of drug addicts, millions of Afghan refugees and innumerable small and large weapons freely floating around the country, thanks to the American CIA.

"Americans sponsored and supported General Ziaul Haq, who created sectarianism, ethnic divides, and religious militancy in the country. All our problems today can be traced to those policies. Then they supported General Musharraf, who teamed up with the religious lobby to keep himself in power, while the same religious lobby was working with the Taliban." Sultan paused to take a sip of water.

Another hand went up in the audience. "Sir, but what about all the money the Americans have given us?"

"Let me ask you, where is that money? Tell me, where have those billions of dollars gone?" Sultan fired back.

The audience waited eagerly to hear more.

"I will tell you: we have been led into a debt trap. In the 1960s, before the Americans and their donor institutions started giving us money, the country was on a path to development. Ever since we have started receiving their money, we have just gone downhill. Today every house has power breakdowns, and the factories are shut down because the Americans will not let us build a gas pipeline with Iran, because that is not in America's business interests. Today, the Americans will not let us build a transnational highway from Gwadar Port to Central Asia with China's help, because that is not in America's national interest. All the money the Americans have given has either gone to the American contractors, or to the corrupt politicians, and our country has to foot the bill for it. There is no money; it is just a complex accounting entry with net credit going to the Americans and net debit coming to the Pakistanis, while our establishment is a giant brokerage house making money in the middle.

"The only way this country can ever hope to develop is by not taking money from the Americans and their lackeys—the World Bank, the IMF, the lot—and to do that we must break free from the Americans."

Another hand went up in the audience. "Sir, are you going into politics?"

"When I was younger, I used to listen to a song by a famous singer that went something like this: 'What will be will be, *Que será, será*.' Thank you all."

And with a quick wave, Sultan got off the podium. He smiled inwardly at the last question; the boy who asked the question was very perceptive and would make a good political analyst, because this was precisely what Sultan was about to do. After writing in the newspaper for seven years, some two thousand editorials, he had concluded that change cannot come from writing in the newspapers. It required more.

He needed to enter politics, and to do that he needed a party organization, a network of contacts, and financing. But all those things were irrelevant unless he could galvanize the masses to a cause. For the past decade, anti-Americanism had been running high in the country, and now it was reaching a feverish pitch. Sultan wanted to cash in on these sentiments. He wanted to set himself up as the savior who could deliver Pakistan from the clutches of an imperialist America. He needed people who could provide him with the party organization, network, and financing, but they must also be sufficiently anti-America to subscribe to Sultan's ideas. This is where the general came in. He was now seated on Sultan's right, exactly where Sultan wanted him, and Sultan hoped he would remain there in the years ahead.

As the proceedings of the debate concluded, Sultan turned to the general. "General, this is an honor and great pleasure, to finally make your acquaintance." The general smiled politely and shook Sultan's offered hand. While his one hand was still clasping the general's, Sultan produced a visiting card in his other hand and presented it to the general, who accepted it. But before they could further engage in small talk, both were surrounded by eager students asking more questions.

Sultan was disappointed as he saw the general slowly moving away in a throng of students, while he himself was caught in the middle of another group. He decided he would have to figure out another way to get in touch with the general, or maybe find another patron.

The general got into his car, took out his cell phone, and made a call. "Sabir here, sir," came the crisp reply from the other end. Sabir was one of the general's assistants; he had served under the general in ISI and still retained many of his contacts there.

"Sabir, get me all the information you can on Sultan. He owns an English daily newspaper."

"Right away, General," replied Sabir.

While the general was making his call, Shehzad was rushing with his laptop to the cafeteria.

Shehzad found himself walking with another student from his class, Aslam, who had also been at the debate. "So what do you think of him?" Aslam asked Shehzad, as they walked through the garden in the shade of tall coconut trees.

Shehzad looked at Aslam and decided to instead gain some insight from his friend. "You tell me, Aslam; your family is in politics, and you are studying journalism. You are also constantly on social media. What is the buzz?"

"He is hot right now—everyone loves him, and we are all tired of the same old farts sitting in the parliament getting rich and fat while we don't have chairs or fans in our classrooms, or light in our houses, and can't afford to buy petrol for our bikes. If this guy goes into politics, I will certainly join him." They arrived at a crossroads. Shehzad turned toward the cafeteria, while Aslam waved good-bye and headed in another direction.

Shehzad needed to send the text of the speech and questions and answers to his journalist friend and employer Charles Madden, who paid him US$200 for each worthwhile story.

Charlie Madden's real name was Mark Bloomberg. He worked for the CIA, and his job was to analyze terrorist threats and terror groups by tracking the money trail left by terrorists. He was based in Hong Kong, where he was working under the cover of a journalist. This had required him to travel to Pakistan, where he had recruited Shehzad as a potential source of intelligence.

Mark was still at his desk in his office when he received the email from Shehzad in Karachi. After reading the email, he called his supervisor in Langley, Virginia, at the CIA headquarters.

"Simon, Mark here. I have just forwarded to you an email I have received from one of my sources in Pakistan. I think we should put this guy Sultan on our watch list, and maybe someone in our Karachi consulate can start monitoring him."

"I hear you, Mark, but you know with our own man in the presidency"—he was referring to the president of Pakistan, General Musharraf—"we have very little to worry about on the political side. Our resources are stretched thin on the ground looking for people who are on our top-ten list. So why don't you follow it up at your end and keep me posted?"

"Simon, I really don't have the resources or budget at my end, and this guy Sultan could become important down the road. Look at the things he's saying—we may have another Fidel Castro or Kadhafi, or worse still, an Ahmadinejad in the making. And remember, none of those people were leaders of a nuclear power with the seventh-largest army in the world. We need to penetrate this guy's inner circle right now, before he grows too big."

"Mark, we have so many willing recruits in Pakistan at every level, you cannot even begin to imagine. And you know what they all want in return for working for us? A green card. They would even settle for an employment visa or just a five-year multiple-entry visit visa. We can pick and choose as we go along, so buddy, don't you worry about 'getting in there.' As and when the need arises, we will get in there. Hell, we might even recruit Mr. Sultan himself—it's not like we haven't done that before! You're doing great work. Keep at it and continue working on this guy. Sounds like you already have the resources on the ground covered."

Mark stared at the phone as the line went dead. His boss had landed the problem right back in his lap.

It was the early hours of the morning, and Islamabad, the capital of Pakistan, was dead at this time of day. There wasn't a soul anywhere. General Bhaya had gotten out of his car two kilometers before his destination and had sent his driver back. The last two kilometers the general would cover on foot. The air was still, and the mountains in the background were like giant spectators watching the general as he briskly walked through a maze of streets. Finally he arrived at his destination and entered the house through the front door, which had been left unlocked.

Bhaya walked into the garage and down the stairs into the basement. The basement was connected with another house that was behind the house Bhaya had entered. After crossing the basement, the general climbed the stairs into the other house and gave three short knocks on the door.

The door was opened by an elderly man who peered through the darkness at his visitor. General Bhaya entered the house and found himself in the bedroom of one of the most famous nuclear scientists in the world, who was under "house detention." Effectively, his home was a prison, and he was not allowed any visitors.

Dr. Q had built Pakistan's nuclear capability, even though every powerful country in the world opposed it. Traitors in his own country had betrayed the project many times, but he had stayed the course and eventually delivered nuclear capability to the country in 1998. But in 2004 his world fell apart when, under pressure from his American masters, the general publicly humiliated him by forcing him to confess to alleged wrongdoings on national television, and he was put under house arrest. The only reason he had not been murdered was because he had sensitive information safely tucked away in Europe that could implicate many powerful people, institutions, and governments. He had given his life to his country, and in the end he was disgraced and treated worse than a common criminal—all because of one man who wanted America's support to stay in power. Dr.

Q thought of his mentor, Ali Bhutto, who had brought him back to Pakistan—the prime minister who was overthrown in the 1977 coup and was hanged for conceiving the idea of a nuclear program for Pakistan. And it was not the foreigners, but this country's army generals who, at the behest of America, had carried out the deed in connivance with the judiciary of the time. The Americans wanted Pakistan's nuclear program rolled back and had punished Dr. Q for his involvement in building the Islamic bomb.

But presently on his mind was something else. A childhood friend from India who was now settled in Islamabad, not far from where the doctor now lived, had sent him a letter narrating his family's ordeal. His friend's niece, Aafia, had been picked up some time ago from her parents' house in Karachi by Pakistani agencies and made to disappear, along with her three young children. His friend swore that Aafia was innocent and all the charges against her were trumped up. He begged Dr. Q to help get his niece released.

General Bhaya and Dr. Q embraced. "Doctor, how are you?" the general asked of his old friend, who was looking tired and seemed to have lost weight.

Dr. Q looked at General Bhaya and smiled, but it was a sad smile. "General, you know how I am; I cannot have visitors. I cannot take walks. I am not allowed access to a computer. There are policemen inside my house—one is sitting right outside this bedroom, and you can hear him snore while he guards me! I am a prisoner, and all this after I served my country for thirty years and developed nuclear weapons technology. Hell, you know all that: you were there. And what did I get in return? Disgrace and house arrest! I was forced to accept the whole blame in the name of national interests and national security. All because another general wants to suck up to the Americans so he can perpetuate his own power. These people, your colleagues, have turned the military into their personal fiefdom. The army is deployed to kill our own people, and to add to all this misery is the guilt I feel for my very dear friend's niece—a brilliant girl I encouraged to go to MIT. I got her American visas and helped her with money, and now she has been abducted by our own intelligence agents and handed over to the Americans for her alleged links with terrorists. You know Aafia is innocent, General, and yet she is being held without any due process of law. You know what is worse? Her children, too, have been kidnapped along with her, by the same people."

General Bhaya thought that a few years ago, Dr. Q would have perhaps not been so moved, but having undergone such a humiliating experience at the hands of his own country's establishment, and knowing how these conspiracies were engineered, the situation enraged the good doctor all the more.

"But even if she were not known to me, I'd still be outraged as a Muslim and as a Pakistani; a woman has to be treated with great respect and dignity, and it is the responsibility of every Pakistani and every Muslim to defend his women. And this was not just a woman, but her three young, defenseless kids who were also abducted.

"You know, if Aafia had been arrested like a common criminal and charged with treason by the Americans, that would perhaps be acceptable because she would have gotten the benefit of due process of law. But to abduct her and her children was inhuman, and should not be allowed to pass without retaliation."

The general knew from the newspaper reports and media coverage that a vast majority of Pakistani people felt the same way as Dr. Q did; they hated America because of what its government had done to a defenseless Pakistan Muslim woman and her children. The general could feel blood boiling in his veins at this grave injustice, in which his country's government had been an active participant for a few million dollars from Americans in aid.

The general decided to update Dr. Q on the political developments. "Doctor, we are working on a project that will rid the country of the yoke of enslavement to America. I have found a man who is dedicated and visionary and has great leadership qualities. He is in the process of floating a new political party."

"General, I sense a donation call coming," said the doctor with a chuckle.

General Bhaya burst out laughing. "That's a good one, Doc. I had it coming."

"General, you know the Americans cannot be simply asked to leave—they don't leave, and will not leave. Do you remember what happened with Japan and the Philippines? At different times they tried to ask America to vacate bases in their countries. Once the Americans are in, they don't leave. And if they do leave, they make sure they leave behind carnage. I am sure a military strategist and expert such as yourself has not forgotten the aftermath of the Vietnam War."

Dr. Q continued, "When you cross the Americans, they will come after you with everything they have. First they will try to strangle the economy. If that fails then they will try to bring down the elected government as they did in the 1950s in Iran and many times after that in many other places, including in Pakistan in 1977. If that fails, then they will try to kill the leadership, just as they orchestrated the hanging of Ali Bhutto and as they tried (and failed) with Saddam and Fidel Castro. And if all else fails, then they will bring boots on the ground; the American troops will invade on false excuses like they have done in Afghanistan and Iraq.

"They went into Afghanistan knowing the Afghans could not really do any serious damage to the United States or the Allied forces. They went into Iraq once they were sure Iraq had no weapons of mass destruction, because they could not risk Saddam firing such a weapon at one of their allies or on the American forces.

"General, we need to restore the dignity of this country, and we need to send a clear message to the Americans: 'No more, and certainly no more do more,'" concluded the doctor.

"I am aware of the dangers you speak of, Doctor. What do you have in mind?" The general sensed Dr. Q had a game plan of his own.

"Well, General, you must have a deterrent to stop the Americans from doing any of those things I mentioned, and the only thing Americans fear is the deaths of their own people in their own country. You must present them with a challenge, but it must be a credible threat for them to not come after your country. You need a dirty bomb inside the United States, to make sure they hold back, or you detonate."

General Bhaya waited patiently, because he sensed there was more. Dr. Q said, "You convince your guy to make it an election agenda and a key deliverable to bring Aafia back to Pakistan. Free her from the Americans, and the Pakistani people will rejoice; they will hold their heads up high. Every Pakistani knows that American assassins kill Pakistani citizens in broad daylight in front of witnesses, take pictures of their dead bodies, and upload them to their headquarters, but no action is taken by our government, while innocent Pakistanis are thrown in Guantanamo Bay prison on mere suspicion, without any due process of law. This needs to stop."

So this was it, thought the general: bring Aafia back, and Dr. Q will help us get a dirty bomb into the United States, to prevent the United States from turning Pakistan into Iraq or Afghanistan.

After General Bhaya left, Dr. Q sat back in his reclining lounger, lit his pipe, and thought about his meeting with the general. He knew the general was a zealot and would fall for the offer, and would also convince others. Dr. Q had no doubt that he had the means to deliver what he had offered. He had asked for Aafia's freedom, but that was really not his ultimate objective. His ultimate aim was to exact revenge on the army who had disgraced him and the Americans who wanted him tortured and dead. To do that, he needed to create an incident that would drive the Americans into retaliating against his country, which would inevitably force the army into the middle of it. He had sacrificed everything for his country not once, not twice, but three times during his life—but no more. Now he would get his revenge.

Sultan had hoped that after his brief meeting with General Bhaya at the Karachi University auditorium, he might get a social call from the general, but nothing of the sort had happened. And as the general had not offered his own contact details, Sultan had no way of contacting him. So he decided to try another approach to get the political organization he needed to carry his plans forward.

Sultan got in the back of his car; the driver knew where he had to go. He arrived at Shakaib's house, which was in the posh middle-class locality of Karachi called Nazimabad, named after the second prime minister of the country. Shakaib was an old friend and, over the years, had moved up in the local organization of one of the best-organized Islamic political parties in the country.

Sultan was received at the door by his friend and ushered into the living room, which was nicely furnished. As they sat down, Sultan asked, "So, Shakaib, what's the news from your party chief Maulana?"

"I told the Maulana that you wanted to discuss a political idea, but that put the Maulana off instantly. The only people he likes to discuss political ideas with are either the Americans or the army; no one else really matters in this country, according to him. The Maulana wasn't impressed with the request. His exact words were 'After all, what was there in meeting an out-of-work stockbroker, unless he wants to donate a few million rupees, or better still, a few million dollars, which does not appear to be the case.' But I have been pushing him, and he needs my support in the *shoora* [inner cabinet], so he has agreed to a brief audience. He is in town, and we are meeting him in forty-five minutes, so we'd better leave."

Sultan knew the Maulana was an old player; he had been in politics all his life and chief of his party for twenty-five years. He had seen it all, and nothing surprised him anymore, so it would not be easy to entice him. But Sultan needed the Maulana, without whose help there was going to be no game plan. The Maulana's party strength at the workers' level, and his organization, were the most important elements for Sultan's plan to succeed. The money was not going to buy it; it might rent the party for a few demonstrations, but what he wanted was to effectively take over the Maulana's party without him realizing or resisting it.

Sultan guessed the Maulana had agreed because he thought Sultan could be manipulated to serve a greater purpose, and the greatest purpose, to the Maulana's mind, was to keep himself in the position of perpetual power and his party as a power broker in the fragile political system of the country.

Sultan and Shakaib arrived at the meeting venue, the house of one of the party leaders in the Federal B area of Karachi. It was another nice middle-class neighborhood, which was once a bastion of the Islamic party's power, but in the past two decades had become the main constituency of an ethnic party, MQM. It was an ordinary house built on an area of two hundred square meters, with a small, well-cared-for lawn in the front. He was shown into the living room, which too was simply furnished, with pictures of the professor, the owner of the house, spread all over the walls. It was interesting, thought Sultan, for a man who believed photography to be un-Islamic to have so many photographs around. Many were with the military dictators. This gave him some satisfaction; he was at least in the right shop! These people would do business with anyone.

Much to Sultan's surprise, the Maulana walked in within minutes of his arrival. Given the Maulana's lack of interest, according to Shakaib, Sultan had expected to be kept waiting.

Sultan rose and smiled as the Maulana walked toward him. The Maulana was in his late sixties, with a flowing white beard. He was around five feet four inches, with a protruding belly that seemed to push him forward, and he was dressed in traditional white shalwar kameez (a shirt and baggy trousers), wearing a karakul cap (also known as a Jinnah cap) on his head. Shakaib made perfunctory introductions, but the Maulana showed no reaction or interest; he just stared into space in front of him. Once Shakaib ceased his narrative, he asked Sultan to say his piece.

A little bit put off by the cold and indifferent attitude of the Maulana—though given Shakaib's briefing this should not have been unexpected—Sultan took a few moments to think before opening, and he decided to go for the jugular. "Maulana saheb, thank you for meeting me. I know you are very busy and don't have much time, so I will get straight to point." Still no visible reaction from the Maulana, as if he couldn't wait to get up and leave. Sultan pressed on, "Maulana, your party has never won an election majority, and sadly it never will. I have a plan that can get you real power, the power to bring real change in this country, which will put your party in the driving seat and allow you to drive the Americans out of the country, once and for all."

The eyes flickered, and a smile, more like a sneer, almost appeared on the Maulana's face. A question popped out from the jungle that was the Maulana's beard. "And what magic have you found that no one has found for the past sixty years?"

Sultan relaxed. He knew he had scored a victory—a small one, but nevertheless a significant one.

"Maulana, with your help and guidance, I want to create a new political party, which will have no religious affiliations, to bring new order to Pakistan. This party will especially target young people between the ages of eighteen and thirty. We will use the Internet and modern technology as our tools to recruit them. Each member will be given a small target, which will earn their membership subscription if they reach it, and they will be given a commission so this will not just be unpaid social work, but something that will put bread on their table as well. In return for your help, I will offer control of the interior ministry, under which all the police and public prosecution fall, to be staffed by members of your party. I will do that because I know the workers of your party are the most honest and disciplined people in the whole country, and this is what we need in our law enforcement. Once we have law and order restored in our country, other things will start falling into place. But to achieve that, we need to win elections, and your current party cannot win elections on its own platform. You will be a key, but unofficial, member of the new party's executive board and will have a say in the final selection of the cabinet members." The sneer was gone, and the Maulana's eyes shone.

Maulana whispered to Shakaib, who respectfully got up and left. Sultan smiled inwardly; the Maulana was hooked and was probably already fantasizing about becoming the prime minister himself, and of ways to get rid of Sultan at a later date, but that was to be expected. Sultan laid out the rest of his plan. The meeting lasted for two hours. Shakaib had been sent out to cancel the Maulana's other engagements and to make sure the meeting was not disturbed.

Sultan left the meeting satisfied that the Maulana would fully cooperate, and his plan was in motion. Sultan had offered the Maulana the post of the president of Pakistan, a largely ceremonial post, and administrative control of the most important ministry in the country—the home ministry. This was much more than the Maulana's party had ever achieved.

After Sultan left the Maulana called his old friend General Bhaya. He was now retired, but the Maulana was well aware that men like Bhaya never retired. He informed the general of his meeting with Sultan. General Bhaya encouraged the Maulana to go forward and suggested that they should offer manpower to Sultan to move things along. The general offered to send one of his trusted men to the Maulana, and it was agreed that that man would be planted as a close confidante of Sultan.

The next day Shakaib came to see Sultan with another man in tow. Shakaib introduced him as Mohammad Abdullah or Mohammad Bin Abdullah, as the man himself said. Sultan realized that the Maulana wanted to put someone close to him to keep tabs on him, but that was not a problem because Sultan had no intention of double-crossing the Maulana. According to Shakaib, Mohammad had recently retired from the army and would be invaluable to the cause Sultan was pursuing.

Over the next month, Sultan engaged Mohammad on various occasions for discussions, and eventually decided to take him on as his personal assistant.

"Mohammad, we need to have a senior military figure as our defense and foreign policy advisor. I have been reading analyses presented by General Talat and have seen him speak on many TV shows. I would like to meet him to explore further if he is someone we can work with," Sultan said to his newly appointed PA.

"General Talat is a good man, but my sense of him is that he is very happy being a retired intellectual. I don't think General Talat would want to get involved in any political movement. This is also the sense I have gotten from various meetings I have had with retired military personnel over the years. The reality of life in Pakistan is that ISI, is the supreme institute in the country and formulates, through various means, Pakistan's internal and external policies. Therefore, we need someone who understands the ISI, commands respect with the rank and file of the ISI, and shares our vision for Pakistan. General Qazi is considered a brilliant man, but in some quarters it is believed that post-retirement his interests are more focused on business and investment. General Durrani is another great general, but he too has become more like General Talat, and seems to confine himself to being a commentator rather than an active player. However, there is one man who is revered in the ISI and military, has a great vision, and is still very active politically. We can perhaps talk to him." Mohammad paused.

"Who do you have in mind?" Sultan asked.

"General Bhaya," replied Mohammad.

Sultan was pleased that Mohammad had zeroed in on General Bhaya's name, as he had already decided on Bhaya and was thinking of asking the Maulana to arrange a second meeting (after their somewhat disappointing first encounter at Karachi University).

"Okay, Mohammad, your logic is sound, and everyone knows General Bhaya and his track record. But how do we bring him around to our side?"

"Leave it to me; I have met the general a few times and even did an assignment for him a few years ago. I am sure I can get him to meet us," Mohammad replied, smiling inwardly. The general was right as always; the hook was in, and it was now just a question of reeling in the catch.

Sultan thought about this. It was public knowledge that on a personal level, the general had suffered because of Americans by missing the opportunity to become the army chief of the country. And under General Musharraf, he had been put on America's list of people who were considered a threat to American national security. To add insult to injury, the lucrative public transport business the general had established had been driven into bankruptcy by hostile policies of the current government. Most importantly, General Bhaya saw America as the evil that needed to be contained, and this was precisely what Sultan was selling.

Sultan's meeting with General Bhaya came a week later at the farmhouse of a friend of the general, in the outskirts of Attock on GT Road between Islamabad and Peshwar. The farmhouse was located on the riverbank of the Indus, which flowed all the way from Afghanistan, and overlooked terraced wheat fields.

After they had sat down and been served tea, General Bhaya started the discussion. "Sultan, I like your thinking, and you are right about many things you have told me. But you perhaps do not realize what you are up against. What you are proposing to do is take power away from the politicians, the military, and the religious groups, and deprive America, Britain, Iran, and Saudi Arabia of influence. In essence, they all will come after you and will do everything in their power to thwart your plans, derail your party, and maybe even kill you. The most likely outcome of your adventure may be more violence inside the country, or worse still, a war with India. There is also another flaw in your thinking: you think the people want change, but in fact people are so used to this corrupt and decadent system that they will not be able to deal with a system that is not corrupt. We have a whole generation that has grown up without any respect for law or governance. The country is run by an assortment of mafias: the drug mafia, the arms smugglers' mafia, the kidnapping mafia, the extortion mafia, the land-grabbing mafia, the intelligence agencies mafia, the police mafia, the transport mafia—the list is endless. These are not just criminal gangs; they are deeply entrenched in our political and social system. No change will come peacefully, and if it comes it will bring with it a heavy toll of human misery and suffering." The general paused, giving Sultan an opportunity to put his reasoning forward.

"So what do we do, General? Shall we just immigrate to Canada or Australia like so many in this country are doing, and put a sign at the airports saying, 'Will the last person to leave the country please switch the lights off?' I know this country is a big mess, and I know this process may cost me my life, but we are all going to die anyway. The greatness is in choosing how you live your life and how you die, and not running away from it. I have been blessed that I have done everything I wanted to in life and have been successful. Now it's time for me to do something for others. And the question really is, General, are you willing to help me do something good for this country, or do you now prefer to wage your war from the TV screens?"

The general's eyes hardened at this insult, and he rose, offering his hand to Sultan. "I wish you luck with your mission." And with that, General Bhaya was gone, leaving Sultan somewhat dumbfounded.

Mohammad, who had arranged the meeting and had been present throughout, watched in amazement as the general played Sultan by walking out. General Bhaya was indeed master of the game, he thought.

Shehzad had not heard anything from Charlie since the email he had sent, and he was beginning to wonder if his goose laying $200 eggs had lost interest. So he was astonished when his phone buzzed and he heard Charlie on the other end of the line. The caller ID was blocked, as it often was in the case of international numbers.

"Hey, Bud, how you doing?" Mark asked, and continued, "Haven't heard anything from you lately. Is there no news of interest, or have you simply become too rich to care about money?"

Oh boy, how do I wish that was true, thought Shehzad, but aloud he said, "Hey, Charlie, there are a lot of tidbits but nothing of real importance, and I didn't want you to feel I was feeding you crap just to milk you for some more dollars."

Charlie smiled at this friendly rebuke and carried on. "Well, my man, we need to continue gathering information, building profiles, so one day when I write my Pulitzer-winning book, we are not found lacking. I was thinking, why don't you take a closer look at the new political players and parties that are emerging on the scene, and let me know if something of interest comes up?" He added, almost as an afterthought, "In fact, why don't we start with writing a piece about that guy Sultan you mentioned in your last email. Maybe you can do an interview of him for some local newspaper. But let us get to know the man. His ideas are certainly interesting."

"Sure, Charlie, I will get on to it right away," replied Shehzad. Shehzad was only too happy for the work and the prospect of making some money. He quickly dug up contact details for Sultan and placed a phone call to his office number. On his third attempt, he was connected to a secretary, who informed him that Mr. Sultan was traveling, and he should write an email stating the purpose of his request for a meeting, which would be forwarded to Mr. Sultan. Shehzad would be informed of Mr. Sultan's reply.

Great, thought Shehzad with dismay. We may have not achieved much in this country, but we certainly excel at bureaucracy.

Nevertheless, he quickly drafted a short email requesting an interview with Sultan for a local newspaper he freelanced for. Shehzad knew full well that his editor would assume that Shehzad was being paid by Sultan to get the interview published and would not publish it unless the editor got something out of it. He decided to worry about it when and if he needed to publish the interview.

Sultan had begun to feel that perhaps General Bhaya was not the right person for what he was planning, and a few days after the meeting in Attock, he raised this issue with Mohammad.

"Mohammad, General Bhaya doesn't seem all that keen on our plan, so we need to find someone else. What do you think?"

"I think we should meet with him again. Let us not forget, General Bhaya is a very senior military man who played a key role in bringing Soviet Russia down, has been a behind-the-scenes kingmaker for many politicians, and has a network of contacts no one else in this country has. Besides, we need to find money, and only General Bhaya's contacts can open those doors for us. But this time, we should perhaps treat him with a little bit more respect."

"Okay, see if you can arrange another meet with the general."

Much to Sultan's surprise, the general was willing to meet the next day.

⊨⊰ ⊱⊨

This time the meeting took place at Sultan's house in Karachi. The venue had been suggested by the general himself, so Sultan really had no choice but to accept.

General Bhaya arrived at Sultan's house exactly on time. As the general climbed out of the Jeep, driven by Mohammad, he noted that Sultan lived in a relatively small house; it was built on a five-hundred-yard plot, which was considered small by Pakistan's upper-middle-class standards. Bhaya also noted that the interior of the house was modestly furnished, and the cars parked outside were not outlandishly expensive. Interesting, thought the general. Sultan obviously didn't like to flaunt money, or maybe he didn't have all that much to flaunt. The general wondered if, behind all the facade, Sultan was really in it to make big bucks.

"General, welcome to my humble abode." Sultan led General Bhaya to a big, imposing chair. Sultan usually sat in that chair himself; it was designed to make every other piece of furniture in the room look smaller, thus giving the occupant a sense of superiority. Sultan had decided that if the general's ego needed to be massaged, so be it.

"Sultan, I have seen more blood and death than you can even dream of, so I am no stranger to wars, and believe me, you don't want to be in one. What you are proposing—the change, usurping power from the mafias, and enforcing governance—these are all great ideas. The idea of ridding the country of foreigners is also a noble one, but all these elements—the foreigners, the mafias—will come together to defeat you. In the process, they will not hesitate to push you into a war with India." General Bhaya paused. Sultan was listening intently, waiting for the general to go on.

"You know very well Ali Bhutto stood firm against the Americans and was hanged by our own security establishment in connivance with the judiciary," Bhaya continued. "President and Army Chief Ziaul Haq was assassinated along with five top generals and the American ambassador when he attempted to change the course of this country's foreign policy. Nawaz lost his nerve after the Kargil war, and the army punished him by overthrowing him, and the Americans were all too happy to see him go because he had rejected the American president's request that we not test our nuclear bomb. In the end it comes down to two things: one is preparing for all eventualities, and the second is not to lose our nerve when the pressure comes. General Musharraf, for all his bravado, buckled under pressure when US Secretary of State Colin Powell called him after 9/11, and the rest, as you know, is history."

Sultan took a sip of the green tea that had been placed in front of him by a servant.

The general said, "If you want my support, then there is one condition, and that is when the going gets tough you will not cut and run like Nawaz did after the Kargil war, or buckle under pressure like General Musharraf did after 9/11. There may come a time when we are forced into a situation that may threaten the loss of millions of lives. Maybe circumstances will call for the use of nuclear weapons, but only by standing firm can we achieve the goal. No matter what the threats and pressures are, we must see it through," the general concluded and looked at Sultan for his response.

He is trying to scare me and wants to see if I will turn and run, thought Sultan. He needed the general, though, so he decided he would play this game until he got real power as the prime minister of the country. After that he would be able to call the shots; right now it was all talk, and talk is harmless and costs nothing. "General, I firmly believe in—and only fear—God, Allah. I am not afraid of America, the army, or death. Sometimes death is better than life. Sometimes we have to destroy to rebuild. I assure you, you will not find me lacking when the time comes to take truly difficult decisions."

General Bhaya decided, given the lack of any other potential candidates for the job, he would have to be content with Sultan. He smiled warmly, expressing his willingness to join Sultan in his venture.

Sultan knew that no plan could succeed without money, and no bank or financial institution was likely to finance his venture. He had to look at a different set of players, people who had the money and wanted power. After some research Sultan had identified Dalbadin as the most likely candidate. The general knew Dalbadin well and agreed to arrange the meeting.

⇢+ +⇠

Mohammad arrived at Sultan's house in his black Honda city car and told Sultan that the meeting with Dalbadin was on. They were to go to a location just outside the city limits, called Sohrab Goth, where they would receive further instructions. One hour's drive from Sultan's house in the Defence Housing area of Karachi to Sohrab Goth brought them to a small café, where they parked and disembarked, sitting down for a cup of tea while they waited. Another hour passed, and then two Toyota Hilux pickups, vehicles very popular with landlords and tribal chiefs, arrived with gun-toting guards. Mohammad needed no invitation. He immediately walked toward them, and Sultan followed him. They got into the car, and within thirty seconds they were speeding away on a dirt road. The journey down the dirt road was deliberate, to ensure there were no tails. After fifteen minutes of driving around, they arrived at Al-Asif Square, which was only a few minutes' walk from where they had been sitting for tea.

As Sultan walked hurriedly behind the Afghan guards, he sensed many eyes following him. The buildings were a combination of shops, apartments, and offices. The shops ranged from butchers and cobblers to currency changers, all sitting side by side. There was no concept of cleanliness; in fact, the place stank. There were Afghan women shopping, wearing their shuttlecock burqas; everything was available here, from basic necessities of life to stacks of Afghanees, the Afghan currency, to a load of drugs and weapons. You just had to have the money. This was Afghan land—no outsider was welcome here, and those who ventured in uninvited usually ended up with their throats slit, dumped at some garbage camp in nearby North Karachi.

The guards walked them down the street—two in front, and the other two behind them. Sultan could feel the eyes of the two behind him boring into the back of his neck. He walked quietly, carrying nothing but a brown envelope containing a very special document, one he planned to use to persuade the Afghan to do what he wanted—that is, if the man's thugs didn't shoot him first.

The guards paused at a dilapidated building, or rather, at one of many equally dilapidated buildings. The front of the building was chipped and cracked, bits of masonry littering the ground at the base of the walls. There was an arched entrance with an iron gate across it, hanging a bit askew on its hinges. It squeaked loudly when the guard opened it.

Inside was a small courtyard littered with trash. As they crossed the courtyard to a flight of stairs leading to a balcony, a feral cat slunk out from behind a stinking pile of refuse and snarled at them. The guard in front of Sultan pulled out his pistol and shot it. Mohammad slowed down, and Sultan heard him give a slight hiss of disapproval. One of the guards behind them poked him in the back with his rifle. Sultan tensed, anticipating trouble, but Mohammad simply shrugged and moved on.

They went up the stairs to the balcony, which opened off a first floor apartment. Before they could knock, the door was opened by a small, slight man in a shalwar suit. He offered no greeting, just moved aside for them to enter. The guards motioned Sultan and Mohammad to go inside. They stayed outside, ranging themselves across the balcony, two on each side of the door.

Sultan stepped inside. It was dim compared to the sunlight in the courtyard, and it took a moment for his eyes to adjust. The apartment was like a well-to-do man's living quarters in a poor neighborhood: the walls were painted in bright colors, but the paint was chipping off in many places, and there was a stain down one wall where a water pipe had leaked. The ceiling had an old-fashioned fan, turning slowly, and a cheap chandelier.

In the middle of the room was a desk with a computer, set in front of the entrance to the next room so that one had to go around it to enter. Seated behind the desk was a bearded man in his late twenties, completely engrossed in something on the computer screen. Next to him was a table with a phone and fax machine on it. The only other furniture in the room was a three-seat wooden sofa. The cushions were tearing at the corners, and their dark maroon color could not hide the dirt and grime that had accumulated from years of use.

The man in the suit asked Mohammad to wait in the outer room. Sultan didn't care for that idea—he would have no protection and no witnesses to his meeting, and he had no idea how many men the Afghan had inside. However, he said nothing. Inside these walls, he was totally at the Afghan's mercy. It was his mission to bring the Afghan to his side, and he would do it, with or without Mohammad. Mohammad sat on the sofa, staring into the middle distance, his expression showing nothing of what he was thinking or feeling. The man in the suit politely asked Sultan to take his shoes off and then ushered him into the next room.

This one was completely different from the outer room. It had ethnic Afghan furnishings—curtains of red with a yellow-and-blue motif adorned the windows, and the floor was covered from wall to wall with a hand-knotted Afghan carpet. Cushions lined the walls, and seated around the room were six men, all armed, bearded, and wearing black turbans, some chewing a wooden stick known as a *miswak*, supposedly a habit of the holy prophet Mohammad that many devout Muslims copied. Others chewed a traditional Afghan tobacco, Naswar. They were dressed in traditional Afghan clothes of baggy trousers and shirts, with big shawls wrapped around their shoulders. An air conditioner whirred in the window, but it did little to dissipate the heat of so many bodies.

Sultan recognized the leader of the pack from his photos taken during the Afghan jihad era—Dalbadin Maarmatyar, the man he had come to see. He was much older now and had put on a lot of weight, but he was unmistakable. Dalbadin was a warlord who had worked with Pakistani intelligence agencies in defeating the Russians and was supposed to have been the major beneficiary of the billions of dollars in aid that had found its way to Afghanistan during the 1980s. He was rumored to have a personal security force of five thousand men and commanded the loyalty of almost fifty thousand warriors from southern Afghanistan. His weapons dump, a lot of which was buried in the White Mountains of Tora

Bora, could let them fight an army for years before running out, and was rumored to include dozens of Stinger missiles. He was the biggest importer of goods under the Afghan Transit Trade agreement, which allowed duty-free import of goods through Pakistan into Afghanistan. In reality, 90 percent of his imported goods ended up back inside Pakistan without paying any duty or taxes, but more important, the trade allowed him to launder his money effectively through the banking system. He was involved in traffic of any goods where there was handsome profit to be earned; that was the bottom line. He had four current wives and seventeen children; the youngest child was only six months old. He had a wife (the youngest) who lived in the posh Defence area of Karachi, one in the Landi Kotal area on the Pakistan-Afghanistan border, one in Kandahar, and one in Madina, Saudi Arabia, where he regularly visited for business and religious reasons. He had four passports, all genuine—Afghan, Pakistani, Saudi, and Iranian—and had a permanent arrangement at all key border posts to cross through without any checking or reporting. All of this information had been dug up by Sultan's men to prepare for this meeting, which was yet to start.

There were a pot of green tea between them and some dried fruits in a bowl that was being passed around. He was asked to sit down, but there was no hand shaking or any other form of welcome. As soon as he sat down, a cup was placed before him and warm green tea poured into it by one of the younger Afghans in the group. The chattering among the Afghans continued, and Sultan started feeling that he had made a mistake coming here. He felt like a piece of carpet, and he toyed with the idea of making excuses and leaving, but he knew that could prove fatal. These people didn't take well to insults. Some fifteen minutes passed, during which no one spoke to him, but they were scrutinizing him, sensing his emotions and reactions. If he got too twitchy or uncomfortable, they would quietly show him the door without another word and set people to watch him to make sure he wasn't working for some foreign intelligence outfit or rival group. If he was, his throat would be slit and his body packed into a jute sack to be deposited at a garbage dump in North Karachi.

Finally, the Afghan, Dalbadin, spoke. "So are you going to sit there all night, or do you have something to tell me?"

This was mighty rude, thought Sultan, but decided this was not the time or place to get aggressive. He smiled, bowed his head briefly, and then looked the Afghan straight in the eye and told him, "I can help you become president of Afghanistan." The Afghan stared back, not saying a word. It was difficult to fathom what he was thinking because most of his face was covered with hair and his forehead was covered by his turban. Only his intense dark eyes were fully visible, but they did not share any secrets. Sultan decided to continue. "I have a plan to start a new political party in this country. In three years, when the next elections are due, my party will fight and win the elections. We will then force America out of Pakistan and Afghanistan. That will open the door for you to grab power in Afghanistan, and you can become the president of Afghanistan."

"The only reason you are allowed in here is because General Bhaya and the Maulana, both good friends and long-time associates, have asked me to meet you and have taken your guarantee. So tell me, what do you want from me?"

This attitude was completely unexpected, but Sultan smiled broadly and said, "Thank you, Khan, I understand your concerns. Only time will prove my credentials, and I am not in the least bit worried about it, because I know I can deliver. I need ten million dollars over the next four years to finance my party organization."

Still no emotion from the Afghan "And what do I get in return?" The question was spat out.

"We will force the Americans out and help you become the president of Afghanistan."

"Mr. Sultan, my patience is running thin; do you take me for a fool? The Americans have already announced their pull-out; they will leave Afghanistan one way or another."

Sultan was waiting for this opportunity. He pushed forward the envelope he'd brought with him, which had been sitting on his lap. "This is a secret CIA report that has recommended to the president that the pull-out should be delayed by two years. The same recommendation has been given by the Pentagon, and even when they leave they will make sure that someone of their choice will be running the Afghan government. You know it would not be you. Without our help—the help of the Pakistan government, ISI, and the army—you cannot get into power in Afghanistan. I can deliver all of that when I win the elections."

The Afghan had clearly run out of patience and was gathering himself to rise, but he paused and said, "I will make you a simple offer. I will finance you for ten million dollars, but I want fifty million dollars back and a few other things. Think about it, and my people will contact you in one week." With that he rose and left the room. Sultan tried to follow but was gently restrained by another Afghan, who told him to stay there until he was told otherwise. So he sat down and waited. After one hour he was told he could leave. Mohammad told him that the reason they detained him was to ensure that there was no ambush waiting for the Afghan after the meeting. If there had been, then both he and Sultan would have been tortured and killed.

A week passed, and then another. After two months, during which Sultan had the sense of being watched by some Pashtuns who acted as drivers and security guards, he was approached by an Afghan man one fine December evening when he was about to drive to his home from his office. It was one of the men who had been present at the previous meeting with the Afghan, and he told Sultan to ride with him in his four-by-four Toyota Hilux pickup. Sultan was told to leave his mobile phone in his car. He did as he was told. He knew that Mohammad was waiting in a car down the street and would follow at a distance; this was the security protocol they had established. Sultan's office was located in Clifton, a posh and relatively new residential and commercial hub. The escort headed toward the port area, which was in the opposite direction from Sultan's house in Defence. Within a few minutes, they arrived at Shireen Jinnah colony, a stronghold of the Pashtun people, many of whom were truck drivers. The driver negotiated through a narrow maze of streets and stopped outside a nice house in a narrow street. Sultan was ushered into the living room, which was also furnished with wall-to-wall Afghan carpet and cushions on the floor. Seated in the center of the room, leaning against two cushions, was the Afghan. This time he acknowledged Sultan's arrival and was almost warm.

"So, Sultan, are you ready to accept my offer?" asked Khan.

"Thank you, Khan, for inviting me again. This is an honor, but I cannot accept your offer. I will make you another offer. After winning the elections, I will pay back your ten million dollars and set up an oil refinery and an oil marketing company in Pakistan for you. The government will arrange 80 percent of the financing through the banks and will help and support you. You could own hundreds of petrol pumps, and you could list your company on the Karachi Stock Exchange and make twenty times your money within two to three years. We will help you get into power in Afghanistan and become the president." Sultan knew that tribal people loved to own petrol pumps; in their psyche this was some kind of statement of wealth and power, so he was playing on that. He also knew that the Afghan had billions and needed a legitimate business plan to grow. He added, "Once you become president, your oil company could become a monopoly in Afghanistan, and you can just print money through petrol stations."

The Afghan stared into space. A sixth sense told Sultan the Afghan was hooked. He motioned Sultan to have some tea and nuts, which had been placed in front of him. Finally, the Afghan spoke. "Okay, we will do it your way, but remember, I know where each member of your family and your parents' families and your wife's family live, and if you try to run away with my money or breach our agreement, then I will kill all of them, each and every one. Do you understand?"

Sultan looked the Afghan in the eye, held his gaze level, and said, "I understand perfectly."

Sultan left the meeting feeling elated. Without serious funding, his dream of turning the country around would have been a pipe dream. Now, with the funding in place, it was a real plan with a real chance of success.

Shehzad was sitting in his favorite spot in the Karachi University cafeteria, surfing the net looking for something newsworthy, some story, some angle—anything. He was sipping a cup of tea. He had paid ten rupees for the same cup of tea he had paid two rupees for when he joined the university four years ago. The cafeteria was bustling with students. A group was sitting in the corner singing some Indian movie song, using the table and cutlery to create music. Another group was engrossed in a heated debate. Shehzad looked up at the noise, as did many others; one bearded student had just banged his fist on the feeble table made of aluminum and tin, and it had risen from the ground and wobbled, its feet in the air. The student kicked his plastic chair aside and walked off in anger. Shehzad smiled and went back to his net surfing; this was mild in comparison to what other students resorted to when they were angry, he thought. Others might have resorted to open gunfire; this was Karachi, probably the small illegal weapons capital of the world. You could buy any kind of weapon here, from a handgun to a rocket launcher. Rumors were, you could buy armored personnel carriers (APCs) and even tanks. Shehzad shook his head in dismay.

His email pinged—there was a new message. It was from Sultan's office, asking him to come for an interview with Sultan next week.

Finally, Shehzad thought, and relaxed.

⚔ ⚔

Shehzad arrived at Sultan's office in the posh residential area of Clifton, which was quickly being converted into commercial and official buildings. Sultan found the address, a bungalow that had been remodeled as an office. Well, Mr. Sultan doesn't seem to care for building violations, thought Shehzad, and yet he wants the world to believe that he will change the country. It was an interesting contradiction that told Shehzad a lot about the man he was

52

going to meet. As Shehzad entered the building, the front gate was open, and he noticed that the old house had been converted tastelessly and perhaps in some hurry.

As Shehzad entered the office, a young man in his early twenties asked him the reason for his visit, and when he mentioned his appointment, the man escorted him to the second floor. As Shehzad emerged, huffing and puffing from climbing two flights of stairs, he noticed the difference between this and other corporate offices he'd seen. The decor was tasteful, and there were calligraphies on the walls, but the furniture was all functional and inexpensively mass produced. As he entered the meeting room, he noticed more differences. Unlike the usual meeting rooms Shehzad had seen in corporate offices, this was arranged more like a drawing room in a house; the furniture was more tasteful then that in the outside office, and custom made. There was a large TV on the wall that was tuned in to a local news channel, there were fresh flowers on a table, and the wooden floor had a lovely Baluch rug sitting in the middle. Shehzad was ushered to a set of twin chairs set against the window and asked if he wanted something to drink. Shehzad asked for coffee, which arrived within minutes with some biscuits, and immediately afterward a door on the side of the room opened and Sultan walked in.

Shehzad noticed Sultan was dressed in a dark business suit, carried himself upright, and was sporting a well-trimmed beard. This was the kind of beard people of the Shia sect usually preferred, whereas Sunnis tended to prefer long, flowing beards. Shehzad also noticed Sultan's eyes. For a very successful man, the sadness in the eyes didn't make much sense. Something was off about this guy, Shehzad mused; he preaches reform but is happy to violate every building law. He is a successful businessman yet has so much sadness inside him. Shehzad pushed these thoughts away and rose to greet Sultan, who had walked right up to him and had extended his hand in greeting. Shehzad shook his hand firmly and sat down.

"I remember you, Shehzad," Sultan said. "You were at Karachi University the day I spoke there, and you asked me a question about the problems this country is facing." Shehzad was surprised that Sultan remembered him and the question he had asked. Sad eyes or not, Shehzad decided to be more careful.

"Yes, sir, thank you for remembering me and giving me time. I'd like to ask you a few questions for the newspaper."

"Shehzad, the newspaper you work for will not print an interview with the editor's own mother, unless some money changes hands. I have my own newspaper, so I really don't need to do that, but the reason I agreed to meet you was to offer you a position with my newspaper. How would you like to join my team as a political analyst?"

Shehzad sat back, not sure how to respond. He had come here to gather more information about Sultan for his employer, Charlie, but suddenly he was finding himself in a job interview.

"Sir, with all due respect, your newspaper doesn't command that much of a readership audience, so I am not sure this will be such a great move on my part," Shehzad replied cautiously.

Sultan laughed heartily. "You know, you are right, but the newspaper is just a means to an end. I am now launching my own political party, and in effect you would be working as part of a sort of think tank for my office, and for the political party. Once the party organization is set up, you will be made part of the party's policy wing. Now, how does that sound?"

Shehzad's heart was racing. He was getting the scoop needed by Charlie, and he could be inside Sultan's party, get paid by him, and get paid by Charlie, and soon he would be able to buy himself that Suzuki Alto car he had been dreaming about. No more shuttling around in the scorching heat on his motorcycle.

But for now he needed to focus on the present assignment, so he asked, "Sir, can you please tell me a little more about the party, and how will it be different from all the other parties?"

"We are going to be working on a single-point agenda, and that is to eradicate foreign interference in our country. Today, most of our problems are rooted in that failed policy that involved Pakistan in a war that we should never have gotten involved in. After 9/11, when the Americans called General Musharraf, he should have simply refused. But he was a military general, and all generals are the same; the last thing they want to do is to fight a war, especially if it is a war against a powerful enemy. Give them a bunch of un-armed civilians and they will crush them in an exemplary fashion, but when it comes to a real war, they will surrender without negoti-ations. That's what happened with General Musharraf; he surren-dered to the Americans because he was afraid they would impose a war on Pakistan, and a war the general didn't want. So instead, he jumped in with the Americans, and we now have an insurgency in our country that is destroying us from within. We have lost more soldiers and more money in this war on terror than we lost in all the wars we fought with India!

"Ten years or so before Musharraf, it was General Zia who made Pakistan a staging ground for training militants—then 'freedom fighters'—against the Russians in Afghanistan. Anyone could join in as long as they were prepared to fight the American war against the Russians: Saudis, Egyptians, Jordanians, Yemenis, and Pakistanis all were given training by the CIA, funded by Saudis, and housed by Pakistanis. These soldiers fathered what is today the Taliban, and now we are fighting them!

"General Zia wanted to export these Mujahidin to Central Asia for strategic depth and use them in Kashmir. Well, now the tables have turned, and India is training militants in Afghanistan and sending them back into Pakistan, and the Americans are helping the Indians because they want to contain China. So we are once again caught in the middle.

"Then we have our beloved Saudis, who are fighting a proxy war with Iran by funding a host of Sunni groups against Shia groups who are funded by Iran. And we are providing them the playground.

"Therefore, my young friend, unless we eradicate foreign influence from Pakistan, we cannot hope to get our house in order. And we need to start with the Americans. For sixty years they have betrayed us by giving us false promises. So we are going to bring an end to this: no more American interference; no more American slavery. That's how and why we will be different." Sultan stopped.

Shehzad thought Sultan was mad, because these were the ravings of a madman. No politician in his right mind could ignore the realty that it was simply not possible to take America on or throw them out of any country unless they wanted to leave. Countries like Japan could not get a military base vacated by Americans, and Japan was the second-largest economy in the world. And Sultan is talking about Pakistan, a bankrupt country living on the IMF's generosity, talking about throwing the Americans out. But even more foolhardy was the thinking that Pakistan's army wanted to break up with the United States, or indeed would allow that to happen. Without American dollars and their flow of defense equipment, the Pakistan Army would not be able to sustain itself and certainly would be in no position to fight the Indians. Therefore, the army would not allow anyone to change the course of the country's foreign policy.

Shehzad made up his mind he was going to join Sultan and his party, because he didn't want this man and his group of madmen to hijack the country. So he would join him, while continuing to work for Charlie and doing whatever he could to save his country from the destruction that was inevitable if this man was to succeed.

Shehzad put on his best smile and, pretending to be impressed, he bowed to Sultan. "Sir, it will be my great honor to serve this country by working for you."

Sultan smiled at his own ability to motivate and command the loyalty of the younger generation.

That evening, Shehzad called Charlie on Skype.

"Hey, my man, what's up?" Charlie asked chirpily as the connection was made.

"Charlie, I have met Sultan, and I am sending you a full report, but I wanted to tell you, sort of face to face, that he is a madman. He sounds like Ahmadinejad on steroids, and blames the Americans and the Pakistan Army for everything that has gone wrong in this country. He wants to start a political party with the agenda of throwing the Americans out of the country, or, as he calls it, 'ending the American and foreign interference in the country.' He even hates the Saudis, and thinks they are also the bad guys. I am afraid if he succeeds in his plans, then there is no telling what might happen." Shehzad paused.

"Who else is with him? Who are the other people in his party?" Charlie asked.

"I have heard rumors that he is teaming up with an Islamist party and maybe some former military men, but I am going to get in there and find out more," replied Shehzad.

Charlie smiled. Shehzad was set on the course Charlie wanted him on. "Okay. Good work, Shehzad; keep it up, my man, and let's talk more frequently." With that, Charlie hung up.

"I have General Bhaya on the line. He wants to meet tonight; what shall I tell him?" Mohammad asked Sultan, who was sitting next to him in the car on their way to Sultan's office.

"Sure, when and where?" asked Sultan.

"He has offered to come to your house later today?" Mohammad looked askance at Sultan.

"Okay," Sultan replied, concealing his annoyance at the general insisting on meeting at Sultan's home. Sultan wanted to keep his personal life and political life as separate as possible, and the general wasn't helping.

Later that evening Sultan met the general at his house at the appointed time. As soon as General Bhaya had sat down and the servants left the room, Bhaya said, "I was invited by Dr. Q to discuss the current developments in our country. Dr. Q thinks that the only way we can realistically force the Americans out of Pakistan is by having some kind of a powerful deterrent." General Bhaya paused.

Sultan guessed the general had more to say. He also realized that Dr. Q had a score to settle with Pakistan's military generals and the Americans, for disgracing him and putting him under house arrest for delivering nuclear capability to Pakistan. Given this background and the doctor's technical background, Sultan figured this "deterrent" would involve the use of nuclear technology, but he patiently waited to hear it from the general.

"Dr. Q thinks the Americans will come after us with everything they have, and the only way to stop them is to have a nuclear deterrent, a dirty bomb, in place inside the United States, in time to check any aggressive plans the United States may put in action," the general concluded.

So there it was, thought Sultan. The general and Dr. Q wanted to smuggle a nuclear bomb inside the United States to prevent them from doing harm to Pakistan.

"General, you realize the Americans never give in to blackmail," observed Sultan, while his mind was racing through all the combinations and permutations of various ways this thing could play out.

"We will never tell the Americans that we are planning to use it, nor will we make any public demands or seek anything from them, so it is not blackmail. We will simply convey to them to leave us alone, and if the time comes, we will show them enough of our cards to make them realize what is at stake. But this will be done directly with the president of the United States, at the highest level, without getting others involved. We will never risk this getting out in the American media; otherwise the US president will be forced to act against us."

Sultan wasn't convinced, but he realized that for now he would have to play along to ensure the continuation of General Bhaya's support. There was no harm in Dr. Q working on a contingency plan, which Sultan could either use as planned, as a possible deterrent, or if the need arose, to gain favor with the Americans by handing them Dr. Q and his plans.

"General, I like the idea," Sultan said.

"Dr. Q also wants us to commit to freeing Dr. Afia from American detention. He is concerned about the treatment of Dr. Aafia by the Americans. She is known to him personally, and her uncle has approached him and asked him to help her," concluded General Bhaya.

"I am all for freeing Dr. Aafia and every other Pakistani wrongly imprisoned by any other country; this is our duty. But we must plan carefully, and we must examine all the angles before we take any final, irreversible steps. So let us develop this, and review it when the time comes for a final decision," Sultan said.

Mark Bloomberg, a.k.a. Charlie, had just moved to Islamabad from Hong Kong and was now head of the CIA's Islamabad station. In Hong Kong, Mark had been responsible for tracking the money pipelines of terrorists. Mark had been closely following the reports made by Shehzad. During his assignment Mark had tracked some funds moving from a company owned by people fronting for an Afghan warlord to Sultan's party, and this had spiked Mark's interest.

Today, finally, Mark had nailed Sultan down for a meeting. He was on his way now to meet him at the Islamabad Golf Club.

The Islamabad Golf Club was a short drive from the American embassy, in the diplomatic enclave area of Islamabad. Islamabad was one of the greenest cities in Pakistan, and in the last few years the population in Islamabad had increased exponentially, so it was no longer "as big and as dead as Arlington Cemetery," a quote attributed to a former American diplomat. Mark entered the lush green gardens of the golf club. He didn't have to stop at the entrance, as his car number plate was registered with the security service for unhindered access, being part of the diplomatic car pool of the US embassy.

Sultan had booked the Rose Room, which overlooked the eighteenth hole of the golf course. He had been briefed by General Bhaya that his guest was a CIA spook, under the guise of a diplomatic attaché.

"Mr. Bloomberg, it's a pleasure meeting you. Please sit. What would you like? Some tea perhaps?" Sultan asked affably.

"Thank you, Mr. Sultan; I will just have some still water," replied Mark. "Let me thank you for finding time to meet me. I know with all your political engagements, you are a very busy man."

Okay, Sultan thought, so you are watching me and monitoring my activities. Outwardly he smiled and said, "It is always a pleasure to meet our guests who are in our country for a short period."

Mark realized he was being told his stay in the country was short, probably a reference to his tenure, which normally lasted three years. Also, he was being reminded that he was a guest in this country, so he should behave like a guest. Mark surmised that Sultan knew of his CIA position and was letting him know that.

Mark decided to cut to the chase. "Mr. Sultan, the United States is not Pakistan's enemy. We are on the same side; our countries want the same things. You want the Taliban contained in Afghanistan, and you want militancy not to spread to Pakistan; we want the same thing. The United States is the biggest financial supporter of Pakistan, and we are fully committed to the development of your country and her people." Mark paused.

After a moment, he continued. "I can understand the Pakistanis' disillusionment. All the money in the country is being stolen by corrupt politicians and the establishment. Debt service is eating into most of the government's income, and after that it's the army that is getting the lion's share of the budget, with nothing left for the welfare of the people or to invest in building infrastructure. Pakistani politicians have diverted public anger by blaming the Americans for everything; the religious political parties have only survived by fanning anti-West and anti-American sentiments, and the masses have fallen for it hook, line, and sinker." Sultan listened passively, so Mark pushed on.

"The underlying problem is a perception gap; many Pakistanis perceive the Taliban as their friends and think the Taliban are devout Muslims who could somehow usher a new era of prosperity into this country and the world. The Pakistan Army understands the Taliban for what they are—armed gangs of militants who want to capture power and cash it in for everything they can get—but the army is using them to further their own agenda. For Americans, the Taliban is the source of all the terrorism currently directed at our country and our allies. Thus, Americans see it fit to eliminate the Taliban wherever they are found, using drones. This policy, though condoned by Pakistan's military and the civilian government, is nevertheless used to fan anti-Americanism by many vested interests inside Pakistan."

"Mr. Bloomberg," Sultan said, "it is an illusion you and your people suffer from, that we want the same things. You want India to be the regional policeman; you want to contain Pakistan and use India to do that. We want India not to be the regional policeman, and we want to resolve the Kashmir issue, which you have refused to help us in resolving. In fact, your government, for the past sixty years, has made one false promise after another in this regard.

"You want to prevent China from gaining access to Central Asia using Gwadar Port, which we have built with them, and the transnational highway we want to build with them. To prevent that, you are funding insurgency in our country in Baluchistan, turning our own people against us, and you are helping India do the same.

"We want to build a pipeline with Iran to overcome our energy shortages, but you won't let us do that. You want us to wait for a pipeline you may build from Turkmenistan, which is but a pipe dream. You want India to occupy Afghanistan and thus encircle us; we want you and the Indians out of Afghanistan.

"You want to control our economy and keep us on drugs—drugs like USAID, IMF funding, and so on—but we want to break the addiction. We want better trade access to your country, but you will not give it to us. We want to get rid of corrupt politicians and overbearing security institutions, but you support them and nourish them because they do your bidding. Every military coup in the history of this country has been supported by your government, which has not allowed institutional building in this country, and that is why we are in this mess.

"So you see, Mr. Bloomberg, we want exactly the opposite—and the problem is you are too powerful for us, so we are stuck, rather like in a bad marriage where a husband beats the wife regularly and mercilessly," concluded Sultan.

Mark noticed the smirk of satisfaction on Sultan's face. Ego, thought Mark. This man was an egomaniac. "Mr. Sultan, as a policy of national interest for my country, we have sanctions against Iran. Those sanctions are not against your country, but obviously if you want to do business with Iran, you will face difficulties. That is not because we are against your country.

"As for India, we have always supported your country. With the Indians, our friendship is more recent, but let us be honest here: India is a country of over one billion people, and the opportunities she offers, no other country does. So yes, we are more business friendly with India, but that doesn't make us anti-Pakistan. And India is a big country; she will, regardless of what we think, do what is in her national interests, and you just have to deal with that realty.

"As for Baluchistan, forty years ago Pakistan lost half the country because your army committed atrocities against the Bengali people and your government deprived them of their basic rights. It had nothing to do with us. The same thing is happening today in Baluchistan. Baluch are killed every day; they are kidnapped, allegedly by security agencies, and then turn up dead. That is what is feeding the insurgency. You fix that, and the problem will go away, but if you don't, who knows what will happen?

"I can understand the frustration of the Pakistani people and them lashing out at the United States, but your country's problems can only be solved once the people take ownership of these problems. They are living in denial, and it is convenient to blame America for everything. For example, we didn't put the present set-up in power; it was people of Pakistan who elected the current lot—whom you describe as the most corrupt—in free and fair elections. For God's sake, all your political parties have been sharing power for the past five years! How can we be blamed for that?" Mark realized he had gotten carried away and decided to pull back. He smiled and said, "We can debate this all day and all night."

Sultan smiled back and said, "That, my friend, you are right about. So tell me, what can I do for you?"

"I wanted to meet you, Mr. Sultan, and tell you in person, on behalf of my government, that we are not the bad guys. We can work together; we want the people of Pakistan to have clean government and strong institutions, we want you to have a vibrant economy, and we are happy to work with you guys to do that. But it is the people and their leaders who have to take the initiative. We are here to help," said Mark.

"Thank you, Mr. Bloomberg, but as you know I am a nobody. I have no political office, and I am not a military general. I am but a humble political worker vying for change, like the majority of my countrymen. I hope when the time comes, your country will do what you say you will do. But anyway, thank you for your visit and your perspective on our problems." With that, Sultan rose and extended his hand to Mark. Mark was surprised—even though the room was warm, Sultan's hand felt like it had been on a slab of ice.

As Mark drove out of Islamabad, he realized that the meeting had achieved little, except for him to meet the man and develop his own sense of him. It was early yet to predict how things would go in the next elections, but this man would have to be watched. He was certainly a wolf in a sheep's skin.

Sultan sat back after Mark had left. So the Americans are sniffing around, he thought. They want to know what we are thinking and planning, and they are telling us they want to help. Well, that's Americans—they will do business with anyone, and this is the message he had received from this meeting: you get into power, and we will be happy to do business with you!

Sultan's reverie was interrupted by General Bhaya, who had just come in after finishing a game of golf. Sultan briefed him about the meeting with the American spook and gave his own take on it.

After getting back to the American embassy in the diplomatic enclave area of Islamabad, Mark called his boss at the CIA headquarters in Langley.

"Peter, Mark here. I have just returned after meeting Sultan—he is the guy who is heading the new party that is a grouping of Islamists, Afghan Mujahedeen, and former military generals. I have extended to him our support and willingness to work with his party, but he didn't seem to care much about the idea. I think we have hit a brick wall here."

What came next was a bit of a surprise to Mark, because he had assumed that Pakistani politics was not at the top of the agency's agenda. "Mark, I want you to meet this man Sultan again, but this time lay it out for him without any ambiguity. We will pour money into his election efforts, but he has to ditch the Islamists, the Mujahedeen, and most certainly General Bhaya. In fact, if we could get him to ditch the general, the whole thing might just fall apart. And if he doesn't agree, than we go to Plan B." Peter hung up.

Mark decided to try a different approach this time.

"Ambassador Suhaili, it is a great pleasure to speak you again. I wanted to thank you for the lovely dinner party you hosted last week; the food was exquisite and the company was charming as always." On the other end of the phone, Saudi Arabia's ambassador to Pakistan squinted, trying to figure out what the CIA wanted now. Mark ploughed on. "In fact, the dinner was so great that I have called to request you host another one and invite Mr. Sultan, head of the Islamic Inqilabi Party also. And, Excellency, I will require a little time alone with Sultan in a secure room. I hope that is not a problem." A lot of profanities sprang to the ambassador's pursed lips, but he managed to keep his lips tightly shut while he quickly weighed his options.

Pakistanis, both the people and the government, would do almost anything for Saudis; such was the strong bond between the two countries (though the same could not be said of Saudis' sentiments for Pakistan), so arranging the meeting was not a problem. But Americans tend to act like a bull in a china shop, much as the CIA goon was doing now by tactlessly putting the ambassador in such a delicate position. But they were Americans, so allowances had to be made for their misbehavior. Wrestling with these inner thoughts, the Saudi ambassador came up with a solution "Mark, I think I have a better idea. The UAE ambassador has invited Sultan and some other businessmen and politicians this weekend for a dinner, so why don't I ask my friend to invite you also? This way, you can achieve what you want without making it look like you engineered the whole thing just to meet Sultan." Ambassador Suhaili was pleased with himself for his quick thinking, and for dropping the ball into the Emirates' court.

Mark realized the Saudi diplomat was getting out of inviting him and Sultan but, at the same time, had offered him a graceful way out that solved his problem. He smiled and said, "Thank you, Your Excellency; this will be perfect. I knew we could always count on our best friend in the region."

The ambassador said a quick "You are always welcome" and got off the phone lest he say something to the CIA man that could affect his own diplomatic career.

The UAE ambassador's residence was spread over two thousand square meters in the heart of Islamabad. The Margalla Mountains towered over the rear of the palatial home, and the backyard garden, at the foot of the Margallas, was beautifully appointed. The gathering was small, less than fifty people in all. Mark was led to the UAE ambassador by his protocol officer, who had met Mark at the gate. The ambassador greeted Mark in the traditional Arab fashion, by rubbing cheeks, and welcomed Mark to his "humble home." As soon as the protocol officer left, the ambassador told Mark that whenever he wanted he should inform his assistant, who would escort Mark to a room for private discussions with one of the guests. With that the ambassador moved forward to greet one of the other newly arrived guests.

Mark moved around the party and met many Pakistani businessmen and politicians. Some he already knew; others were eager to get to know him, and they were all interested in the inside track on what was going to happen in Pakistan in the future. Meeting American diplomats and picking up snippets of information made these people important in their own social circle, so Mark had been told. He had also been warned by his embassy that anything he said would likely appear in the media the next day, so he had to be very careful about what he said and whom he said it to.

Once dinner had been served, Mark made his way to where Sultan was in an animated discussion with a group of businessmen. As Mark approached, the group's attention turned to him, as did Sultan's. "Mark! It is indeed a pleasure to meet you again. I hope you are enjoying our country."

Mark smiled and politely said to the group, "May I have a few minutes with Mr. Sultan, please?" With that, he steered Sultan near the open French windows of the house. Before happening upon the group Sultan was engaged with, Mark had already whispered to the ambassador's assistant that he was going to need that room he had been promised.

As they walked toward the window, Mark said, "Mr. Sultan, I need a few moments alone with you."

"Have you heard of calling to make an appointment?" Sultan retorted, obviously not pleased at this intrusion.

"Sorry; this could not wait." This was deliberate; Mark wanted to put Sultan off balance and keep him on the defensive.

They were shown to a room overlooking the garden. Mark took out a small transistor radio and placed it on the table between him and Sultan, expecting the room to be bugged. Sultan eyed him suspiciously but didn't say anything.

"Mr. Sultan, I have been authorized to offer you my country's financial support in your party's bid for gaining power. But we are concerned about the political associations you have formed and would like you to reconsider those associations. In fact, let me be forthright. We would like you to realign your party, sever all ties with the Afghan leader who is funding your party and the religious cleric whose political party is organizing yours; we also want you to distance yourself from General Bhaya. You do that, and we will use all the means at our disposal to help you in your quest for power." Mark paused, waiting for Sultan's response.

A sarcastic smile spread across Sultan's face. He bowed his head in mock submission and said, "My Lord and Master, is that all?" Before Mark could react, Sultan exploded, "How dare you? How fucking dare you come here, in my own country, and tell me who I can work with and who I should take into my party. You imperialist dog! Your days are numbered; the time is soon coming when you will not be allowed to roam freely in this country, dictating to us, running our government, invading our country with your drones and mercenaries. The people of this country are sick and tired of you; your government only looks after the interests of Jews and Hindus, both our sworn enemies. I am not a prostitute like many generals and most politicians in this country are. I stand for change, and we will bring change." Sultan exhaled, his eyes on fire.

Mark quickly and calmly interjected, "Don't misunderstand me, Mr. Sultan, but every politician and power broker in this country knows that without our blessing, no one can lead this country. Zia, Benazir, Nawaz, Musharraf—they all had our blessing, and as long as they had our blessing they stayed in power. And when we wanted, we sent men as prime ministers straight out of New York and Washington to Pakistan. Need I remind you of Moeen Qureshi and Shaukat Aziz, bankers we sent to Pakistan as prime ministers? I am offering you help, but you must understand that for us to help, you too must be realistic. Having these people— the general, the Afghan, and the Maulana—is going to jeopardize your chances of success. What is more important to you? These people, or saving your country from the corruption and misgovernance that are destroying it? We are not your enemies; we see great potential in your country, but the change must come from within. Corruption is so deep in your society that it has destroyed the economy and the moral fiber of the society."

To Mark's surprise, Sultan abruptly got up, bowed his head slightly, and started to walk out. "Mr. Sultan, you cannot walk away from difficulties. You need to face them and resolve them. Think about our offer—we mean well."

Sultan looked at Mark with eyes that were sad and replied, "Let me save you time. I am not interested in any help from Americans. I would sooner give up politics or die than compromise on my beliefs." He walked out.

Shehzad's words echoed in Mark's ears. *This is a madman.*

Later, Mark placed a call to his boss. "Hey, Peter, I just finished my meeting with Sultan, and I think this man is seriously off balance. I don't think we are looking at someone like Ahmadinejad, but more like a hybrid of Ahmadinejad and Qadhafi of Libya. Both those men caused plenty of grief to the United States, and if we allow Sultan to get anywhere near power, than we may have a nuclear nation running amok with a madman as its leader," Mark said.

"Okay, tell me specifically what the man said that has convinced you to label him a madman," Peter said.

"Well, as you suggested, I laid it out for him. I told him he had to ditch his pals if he wanted to get anywhere close to real power, and if he did, that we would help him; we would make it happen. And that seemed to trigger a rage in him. I'm surprised and relieved this didn't come down to an exchange of blows," replied Mark.

"Well, I'm sure if it had come to blows, you would have held your own; your training as a US Marine would have come in handy," Peter said, joking. "Mark, is it possible that you have gotten off on the wrong foot with this guy? I am just saying, you know, these things happen."

"Look, Peter, I have been following this guy's political career for some time now, and I know him pretty well. If you go to back to the first report I ever filed on him, these were the concerns I voiced then. Right from the beginning, this guy has been consistent in one thing, and that is his hatred for the United States. But you are certainly welcome to try another approach," said Mark resignedly.

"Okay, Mark, I hear you. For now, you sit back and monitor the situation at your end, and I will take it from here." With that, Peter put the phone down. Mark figured "Plan B" would now be put into effect.

The next morning, Mark woke up and turned his TV to the local news channel. The ticker on the screen showed the key stock exchange index of the country. KSE 100 was in a free fall, and according to the news anchor, there were sellers but no buyers.

What a shitty way for the investors to start the week, Mark thought as he got into the shower.

As soon as Sultan had turned his "Market Monitor" on, he knew the trouble that was brewing. The Market Monitor was the equivalent of a Reuters screen that gave him a live feed about Pakistan's stock markets. Sultan's brother ran the business that Sultan had set up and left to concentrate on politics. Sultan had also invested a lot of the funds he had raised for the party's organization and operations into the stock market through his company, so this not only affected his personal wealth, but also his party's funds and financial position.

His brother Sam walked in while Sultan was mulling these developments. "Bro, the market is down 5 percent. There are sellers across the board, but no buyers. The market is technically trading, but there is no business happening. And this behavior has panicked investors—it looks like tomorrow will be the same," Sam said.

"Well, let us see what happens tomorrow," Sultan replied dismissively. One day's drop in the stock market was not something he wanted to start panicking about.

Two weeks and ten trading sessions later, his brother was back sitting in front of him, along with all the senior members of his team. Their faces exhibited fear and morbidity, like someone had died and they too faced imminent death.

"The market has fallen every day for the past ten sessions. Every day stocks have been offered at the lowest tradable price, and there have been no takers. Investors have a simple logic: if we had bought yesterday, today we would already be out of pocket by 5 percent of our investment, and tomorrow we will get everything 5 percent cheaper, so why should we buy or invest? We have run out of margin deposits from our clients, and our investors' shares are worth half of what they were a fortnight ago. The banks are demanding more security and margins, which we don't have; the only saving grace is that the banks can't sell our or our clients' shares, because there are no buyers. As of today we are broke, and if we don't get any fresh liquidity, we will not be able to open for business when the market does eventually start trading. The banks will carry out a 'fire sale' of all our liquid assets, and we will have no choice but to file for bankruptcy. And once we are down, everyone will start suing us for anything and everything," Sam said.

Sultan had already figured all this out, and like his brother, feared the worst. But for now, he put on a brave face. "Okay, listen, you all. We have seen market crises before; this is not the first time and will not be the last time. I am meeting investors later this week, and we will find enough support to see us through this. So I want you all to keep it together."

But he was worried. Apart from the sudden loss of personal wealth, the crisis, if not contained, would end his political career before it took off. This would not just be the loss of business or wealth, but his life. Sultan sat grimly looking out of his office window at the traffic passing on the road, and beyond at the scavengers who dove in to claim whatever little piece of garbage they could grab from the rubbish dumps that had appeared on the edge of the swamps visible from his window. His mind went back to his conversation with the American. He didn't think the Americans could be behind this; no, this was just some panicky fund manager in Hong Kong in dire need of liquidity that had started this crisis. But maybe he could talk to the Americans for some help.

While the idea was still half-baked in his own mind, Sultan laughed at the absurdity of it. It would be better that he let his business collapse than turn to the Americans for help, because then the Americans would own him, and he would be just another of their puppets. No, he had to find some other way out.

His reverie was broken when his phone started ringing. The caller ID revealed it to be one of the people from Sultan's old neighborhood. Sultan answered. "Hey, Zaf, how are you?"

Zafar replied, "You tell me: how are you doing? There are rumors about the health of your family's business. Is everything okay?" So vultures were circling, Sultan thought, but his delay in replying encouraged Zafar to go on. "Look, I have some friends who like you, and if you need any help, I can talk to them."

Sultan was well aware that the friends Zafar was referring to were a gang from the underworld of Karachi. They controlled gambling dens, the betting mafia, liquor smuggling, and many other illegal activities.

"Oh yeah, and what do they want in return? My kidneys?" Sultan retorted.

"No, for now they will just take your balls—the rest they will take in easy installments," replied Zafar with a laugh. "But other than your body parts, which are useless by the way, they want 10 percent profit on their money per month, and if and when they ask you for a favor, you cannot say no."

Sultan reflected on this, fully aware that he was between the devil and the deep blue sea. Sultan also realized he was out of time; he had been so engrossed in his political designs that he had allowed this problem to escalate, and now there was no time and really no options.

"Okay, Zaf, I will agree to both the conditions, but they can only ask for one favor; they cannot keep on coming back for more."

"Okay, let me arrange matters, and I will get back to you," Zafar replied. Sultan slowly placed the receiver back in the cradle.

Sultan felt very lonely; he wished there was someone he could talk to, so he could seek advice and unburden himself. But there was no one he could turn to; he had to carry his burden alone.

Mark had been monitoring the financial markets and figured his boss had really taken things seriously. Mark had learned from his contacts on the *Wall Street Journal* that the selling in the Pakistani stocks had been ordered by an Emerging Market fund manager. Apparently his exact instructions were, "Sell, sell, and sell at any price; just get out of the damn country. I don't want to see a single share of that country in my portfolio." Once sell orders had been unleashed, the word got around and became a self-fulfilling prophesy. Everyone wanted to sell and get out; such was the nature of the beast, thought Mark.

Mark had called one of his contacts on the Karachi Stock Exchange, a former chairman who loved to hear the sound of his own voice, and learned that Sultan's family business, which was run by his brother, was down in the dumps because of the crisis. The rumor was that it was merely a question of time before it went under.

This should teach Sultan and other novices a lesson, thought Mark. You cannot and must not challenge the power of the United States of America, but people forget. The Japs forgot, the Germans forgot, the Russians forgot, Saddam forgot, the Afghans forgot—and they all had paid dearly. This country was no different; Uncle Sam got what it wanted.

General Bhaya had been aware of the crisis unfolding in his country's stock market and had called in a few favors from his contacts in the Western embassies to get some idea of what was causing the panic. What he had learned was disconcerting to say the least: the fund that had unleashed massive selling and a meltdown was a front for CIA money. General Bhaya had confirmed this with a former banker also.

The general's informer within Sultan's business group had informed him of the dire situation Sultan's business was in, and that it could collapse any day.

Bhaya decided it was time to pay Sultan a visit.

Sultan's phone buzzed, and his secretary informed him that he had a visitor. Sultan was annoyed; his staff was well trained to make sure no unscheduled or unannounced visitors were welcomed, and yet he had been disturbed by some unknown visitor. Sultan walked to the meeting room and was surprised to find General Bhaya sitting there. Even more surprising was his attire. The general was dressed in a well-tailored dark business suit, something Sultan had rarely seen.

"Salam, General, this is indeed a pleasant surprise," Sultan said, not at all feeling pleasant or happy at this untimely intrusion right in the middle of the biggest crisis of his life.

General Bhaya shook Sultan's hand and sat down facing him. Before Sultan could say anything, the general asked, "How much time do you have, and how much money do you need?"

Sultan was taken aback at this direct, and what he considered improper, approach. He was on the verge of brushing the general off but didn't get a chance.

"The fund that has brought the stock market down is owned by a CIA front company. Now, this may be just a business decision on their part, but we have come too far to let our plans be jeopardized by the decision of a random fund manager. The gossip I hear is that the market will resume trading any day, and when it does, your family's business may face challenging times. So, my friend, time is of the essence."

"General, it is very sweet and considerate of you to come out here and extend your support, but I really have this thing under control," replied Sultan. This tone was even, but a vein in his temple was throbbing, which told the general everything he needed to know.

General Bhaya, concealing his anger, took a folded piece of paper from his pocket and gave it to Sultan. "Does this number accurately reflect the amount of funds your group needs to survive this catastrophe?" Sultan stared at the piece of paper in disbelief. The number was exactly what he had read off that morning from his company's confidential management information report.

"Now, I know the banks are not lending to anyone. I am also aware that your friends in the financial world are too busy with their own problems, and your wealthy in-laws would rather see you go down than lift a finger to help you. So tell me, how do you hope to raise the money to come out of this problem?"

Sultan was so shocked at the depth of information the general possessed, including the bit about his strained relations with his in-laws, that he blurted out, "There is an old friend of mine. He knows some people who have offered to loan me money at 10 percent per month."

"Who are these people? Because if you borrow money from the wrong people or do business with the wrong kind of people, then our plans and your career will not proceed as we planned. This is not a threat, but what your friends in the finance field may call 'risk assessment.'"

"I believe it is an underworld gang led by someone called Shoaib; I have never met him, though. Zaf—that's my friend—he is going to get back to me after confirming with them." Sultan felt dejected. He didn't like to be on the defensive, and the general had just turned the whole thing around and put Sultan in a tight corner.

"I know Shoaib and his gang. Don't go near them, and don't touch their money, even with a barge pole. I realize this is not completely kosher, but I suggest we use some of the money that our Afghan friend has loaned us for the party organization to bail your company out. Just make sure the money is replaced at the earliest possible time. No one else needs to know this."

But you know, thought Sultan grimly. The ultimate secret keeper will now have a hold on Sultan. But he had no choice; it was either the Afghan's money or the gang's money. At least with the Afghan's money he would only have the general to worry about. Sultan nodded. General Bhaya heaved a deep sigh of relief, realizing that had he delayed this meeting another day, then the problem would probably have gotten out of hand.

The Elections

The cool evening breeze was gently blowing along the coast of the Arabian Sea in Karachi. The night was young, the sky was lit with stars, and the moon was slowly rising in its full bloom on the city, its bright-orange glow giving it a mystic and exotic appeal, enthralling the viewers and giving much to the poets to talk about. The shore was dotted with beach huts; this part of the beach was known as Sands Pit, a reference to pits of sand in the shallow water, which make it dangerous for people to swim there, because more often than not the strong current pulls the swimmers in. There have been many instances when groups of young men have drowned trying to save friends and family members. It was a treacherous setting for a treacherous meeting that was about to take place on the beach.

Sultan arrived at the hut in a white Toyota Corolla, the model, make, and color all carefully chosen for their anonymity. There were thousands of these all over the city; they were easy to buy and easier to sell.

The security guard of the hut walked up to Sultan and greeted him. He was followed by two dark, burly Baluch boys. Sultan told him to set up a small fire in front of the hut, as close to the water as possible. He got four cheap radios from the car, gave these to the guard, and asked him to place one next to each chair. He was aware how easy and common it was to bug everything nowadays and had taken some rudimentary steps to minimize the damage as much as possible. As arranged, the table and chairs were laid with mineral water for each person and a pot of green tea with cups, and the radios were turned on low volume. With all set, the Baluch boys and the guard each received a crisp thousand-rupee note (about ten dollars) and left.

It was coming up to nine in the evening. The breeze had dropped, and there was stillness in the air. In the distance a dog could be heard barking. The sound was followed by the whirr of an engine. The noise came nearer and stopped outside the hut. A second white Corolla pulled up in the car park of the hut.

General Bhaya got out of the car and slowly walked toward the beach where the table and chairs were set, while his host started walking toward him in quick strides. The general's manner suggested he was in no hurry, a man completely at ease. He looked straight ahead, but his eyes took in every small detail of the landscape. He went over the security angles of the venue, weighing the security threats that might suddenly appear if this was a trap. There was always a trap; one couldn't be too careful in a country where the Americans had complete freedom to kill and kidnap anyone they wanted, and they did. The general knew he was on their hit list, but that didn't bother him.

The general embraced his host with genuine warmth, and they walked together back to the beach. "Sultan, before the others arrive, I need to discuss something with you. That is why I had asked for us to meet earlier than the others. Insha'Allah, in a few months we will be occupying the highest office in the country. I have started planning to put everything in place to bring Aafia back. We will use four separate teams and make sure none of them overlap, know each other, or share any information except what is passed through me, strictly on a need-to-know basis. I will identify the players for the third and fourth teams but will not approach them till the final stage.

"The first team will carry out all the research necessary for the project: where she is kept, when she is moved, what visits she is allowed, what her rights and privileges are, every location she is allowed to visit. We want detailed maps of every building she is taken to, along with the map of the alternate routes, and a complete profile of each person involved in her security and movement.

"The second team will carry out the surveillance when we give the go-ahead and will document everything. Both the first and the second teams will be handpicked from my retired colleagues.

79

"The third team, the snatch team, will consist entirely of for-eigners; they will just be given the assignment, for a fee, to snatch and deliver her to us, and then they can disappear. This team would be hired through one of the Afghan warlords or reneged Taliban groups, so we can divert American attention toward them and perhaps get some of them 'droned.'" This was a reference to CIA drone attacks, which regularly killed suspected terrorists in-side Pakistan.

"The fourth team will be the export team. This team's job will be to transport her out of the United States and deliver her to us at a mutually agreed location, from which we will bring her to Afghanistan or maybe even to Pakistan," concluded the general.

"General, you are sure of this?" Sultan asked. "You know my commitment to restoring this nation's dignity, sovereignty, and in-dependence is total, but I want to be sure that we don't push the Americans too far too early in the game."

"The Americans will never own up to losing Aafia, and besides, I have a plan that will let them save face. There will be no proof linking us to Aafia's freedom. As I explained, we will use proxies like the Taliban to take the blame—or credit—so any American wrath should be directed there," replied General Bhaya. He knew, though, and he had guessed Dr. Q knew too, that the Americans would come after them with everything. That was why they needed the nuclear device, but the general didn't want to "burden" Sultan with over analysis. He was, after all, a budding politician, and poli-ticians liked things simple.

Sultan didn't buy the general's argument about the Americans, but at this late stage, he had no other option but to let Bhaya plan the plan. When the time came to execute, he would decide.

They chatted about everything under the sun for the next fif-teen minutes until the next car arrived. This one was a Toyota Land Cruiser and had an armed escort. The Maulana emerged from the back of the Jeep; the Jeep and the escort vehicle quickly reversed and drove back to the road, where they were to set security outposts at five hundred meters in opposite directions. They were to keep watch on everything.

The Maulana was warmly greeted by the host and the general. They all embraced each other in turns and started back for the table and chairs. The Maulana sat down and immediately reached for the mineral water. Making sure the seal was intact, he opened it and quickly downed two glasses. Unable to suppress it, he burped loudly, uttering something in Arabic, and then took over the meeting.

The others didn't mind or object; they knew the Maulana liked to feel important and in control, so they let him enjoy the moment. "So, Sultan, tell us, where are we?"

"Maulana saheb, we have achieved several milestones since our last meeting. Let me briefly update you: we have registered a new political party and have enrolled over two million workers all over the country with the help of your party cadre and the retired soldiers' association. I am proud to report that we have the largest network of workers and offices throughout the country, and this is even before the official launch of our party. We have established ourselves on Facebook and Twitter, and have a technology and communications team from all over the country. The workers all are in their late teens or early twenties. We have a mailing list of every countryman who is on any list anywhere in the world. In fact, the total number of people on all our lists far exceeds the total population of the country, but that is to be expected given the duplication of names. We have regular podcasts, webcasts, newsletters, video briefings, and presence on tens of thousands of blogs. Our 'angels,' as I like to think of them, are spreading the word and receiving positive feedback about the arrival of a new leadership and launch of a new party to rid the country of the slavery of the Americans. Under the leadership of the general, we have a team of hackers who check and validate all the data and spy on everyone to make sure we are on top of things. Let me assure you our organizational network will make MQM—the most effective and organized party in the country—look like a bunch of amateurs. We have also recruited teams of defense experts, economists, political scientists, jurists, environmentalists, and human-rights activists to study and prepare recommendations for our election manifesto."

This brought the Maulana back to attention. "What do we need these people for? I thought we already had an agenda agreed upon. We want the Americans *out.*"

"You are right, Maulana, we do, but that agenda has to be translated into a 'product' we can sell to the people of this country, the voters, to achieve power. Without that it's all a pipe dream. We also need to learn from the Americans and plan for every eventuality by doing scenario building. We have given dozens of scenarios to these 'think tanks.' Some of these are unthinkable, at least for them, but they have just been told that we must study even the unthinkable and its effects on the country. Thus, we are preparing the groundwork and doing the homework for the ultimate goal— to rid the country of the Americans and restore the dignity and the freedom of our people."

The stillness of the night was disrupted by the noise of car engines, and the mobile phones of the Maulana and the general both flashed with incoming messages, announcing the arrival of the fourth and the last participant in tonight's meeting. The medium-height, slightly built Afghan in traditional Afghan shalwar, shirt, and turban, with a flowing white beard, stepped out of his car with a rosary in one hand and a Kalashnikov in the other. The gentleman had plainly refused to come unarmed, but then he was an Afghan warlord wanted by the Americans and Afghans alike. His guards left and took up positions at agreed-upon points.

Sultan quickly walked to receive the Afghan guest. They shook hands and slowly walked back to where the Maulana and the general were standing to receive the Afghan. The Afghan embraced the Maulana and the general, and they all sat down. The Afghan was quick off the mark, shooting a question at the host. "So, Mr. Sultan, tell me: what have you done with my money?"

Afghans, thought Sultan: no subtlety, and money always comes first for them. Still, he needed someone to bankroll his dream, and there weren't many takers for radicalism in this day and age, so he had to make do with what he could get. The Afghan was it.

"Khan saheb, I have prepared a summary of money spent and placed it in a folder that has been put in your car, so you can study it and have it checked by your accountants. You will find it is all in order and as discussed. I don't want to bore our friends here with minor details." Sultan then repeated the briefing he had already given the general and the Maulana, so everyone was on the same page.

"We are now entering the launch phase of our plan. 23 March, later this month, the day the resolution to create a separate Muslim country for Indian Muslims was passed, will be the day our party will officially announce its intention to take part in the forthcoming elections. We have, with your help and consultation, already put in place the initial central committee. We have also set up party offices in one hundred countries of the world; this will be the largest international political organization. The international offices have been tasked to prepare recommendations for improving business ties with their respective countries and to 'recruit' media persons to give us positive coverage. Each of our two million workers has been given the target of paying one hundred rupees a month as a party membership fee. This means we have earnings of two hundred million rupees a month already; this money is invested in the stock market through my friends, in safe investments, and is nicely increasing. Each of our workers has been given the target of recruiting ten sympathizers or volunteers, and a donation target of one thousand rupees per month. This should bring in an additional two billion rupees a month in income. We have promised a 10 percent reward to each worker for achieving target and a 20 percent reward to those exceeding target. We have started acquiring newspapers, magazines, radio and TV stations, and advertising and public relations companies. We have built the biggest media empire in the country, even before we get into the government. The new jobs we have created have all gone to our registered workers, strictly on a merit basis, of course.

"In the next phase we will hire journalists, drama writers, songwriters, and singers. All of these people will be given new scripts for preparing the nation for social change, for a bloodless revolution. We will have our ideas projected through TV dramas, and we will have songs and tunes that will be on every mobile phone in the country. Our election symbol will be a mobile phone, and we will have a party flag that will be green with a red circle in the middle, and a party anthem in every regional and national language. We will form a shadow government three months before the elections. This shadow government, with the help of our think tanks, will tear apart the policies of the present government and start presenting viable solutions, alternate ideas for better government. After the announcement of the election date, we will announce our manifesto, but we will only announce our 'reforms package' three days before the elections, so as not to give time to our opponents to thwart our bid for power."

"What about throwing the Americans out? When are you going to do that?" the Maulana asked eagerly.

"Maulana saheb, if the Americans get the slightest whiff that we have any intention to block them and force them out of Pakistan, then they will come after us, will not allow us to proceed, and will do everything in their power to postpone the election, even impose martial law. You know how eager our friends in Rawalpindi are to step in."

"Sultan is right, Maulana saheb," General Bhaya said. "The current government is making a complete mess. Things are so bad that the people in Rawalpindi talk about intervening every day. If the economy wasn't so bad, they would have taken over in the blink of an eye, but they know that the kitty is empty and the American economy is going through a rough patch, so there is going to be nothing from Uncle Sam except promises. We know that to be true because the Americans have not paid a dime under the Kerry-Lugar Bill; they have not set up a single project in the tribal areas or elsewhere. They are not even paying the money they owe us under the logistics and support program—they owe Pakistan two billion dollars. And we have to borrow this money at exorbitant rates from the IMF, which is dictating ever-harsher terms. Friends of Pakistan in the five years since its establishment have given absolutely nothing. They all have excuses, but no money, and every time we go back to them, they rub our noses in the ground about corruption and transparency. This is why I have agreed to this plan. There is simply no other way, and it is now or never."

Sultan now turned to the Afghan. "Khan saheb, we need your help in setting up and managing 'thunder squads.' We expect a considerable amount of violence against our political workers, and we want to be able to retaliate and send a message that we will fight back and it will be an eye for an eye, nothing less."

The Afghan replied, "Just tell me when and where, and my people will take care of it."

"Well, gentlemen, we are on schedule, so we will meet as a group after the elections are announced to review our strategy."

Three Days before the Elections
General Bhaya's car turned off the Super Highway, which connected Karachi to Deh Taseer, a new suburb that sprang up a decade
ago. As the car headed toward the complex, as the general liked
to think of it, he marveled at the lush green farms, golf club, and
new housing colonies his car was passing through. It was amaz-
ing, General Bhaya thought, how the city had spread and was
continuing to spread, defying all odds. The car drove up to the
main gate of the complex; his driver had a remote control for the
iron gate, which opened electronically as they approached. The
general's office was on the ground floor. As he walked toward his
office, he surveyed with some satisfaction the party's headquarters, which were spread on twenty-two acres of land donated by a
party supporter. The sprawling complex had accommodation for
five hundred people, an auditorium with the seating capacity for
a thousand people, offices for various departments of the party,
and a training center. It was totally self-contained; it generated its
own electricity and drew water from a well. The auditorium had
been equipped with video conferencing facilities, and today it was
connected to twelve major cities across the country. The rest of
the country was covered through the electronic media and TV
channels' coverage. Having made a brief stop at his own office, the
general headed to the auditorium. As he entered he smiled with
satisfaction. It was filled to capacity with the analysts who worked
for the party, the technocrats who developed policies, candidates
for upcoming elections, party office bearers, and sponsors.

This is going to be the pinnacle of the election campaign, the
general thought. It was 7:00 p.m. on a hot and humid evening, still
two hours before the speech. But then the general watched in horror as one of the screens in front of him was splattered with red.
The vein running on the right side of his temple started throbbing, and his fists clenched at the sight. Some troublemakers had
opened fire at one of the party's rallies in Karachi. The attackers

had positioned themselves on both sides of M. A. Jinnah road, where the rally was passing on the way to Nishtar Park, the venue for the party gathering. The general assumed that the attackers must be from the local ethnic party, trying to scare his party's supporters, and it was timed to divert media attention from Sultan's speech. General Bhaya had no idea how many were killed or injured, but he was sure the numbers would be high. The attackers, riding a motorbike, had opened fire from both sides and within minutes had fled the scene. The party workers and the local police had no time to react.

General Bhaya's phone rang. He saw the name of the caller and answered. "General, this is not good: the whole country will now focus on this tragedy. What do you suggest?" It was Sultan's agitated voice on the other end.

"We move according to plan. Too much work and preparation have gone into this, and if we abort, then our opponents will have won. Their killing of our workers and supporters will have profited them," replied the general, who had seen too much death during his career.

"Okay, we will stay the course, but let us mobilize our workers to ensure that every injured person receives the fastest and best medical care. All their medical expenses will be covered by the party, and every dead person's family should be looked after. The party workers should attend to the families of dead and injured workers, and provide total moral and financial support. Our legal team should register a report with the police and name those who have been making threats against us as the suspects. We shall not let this pass. The blood of our people shall not go to waste," concluded Sultan.

"Do you want to have some thunder squads respond in kind to our opponents?" General Bhaya asked Sultan.

"It would be good for the morale of our workers, but it would trigger a running gun battle that we can neither win nor afford at

87

this stage in the game, because the elections may be postponed if violence escalates, and all our work will go to waste. This may actually open a door for the army to step in and take over. No, we shall not retaliate—not yet—but I swear we will avenge life for life once the elections are over," replied Sultan, almost choking on his last words.

General Bhaya left the complex and headed to the scene of the tragedy. In twenty minutes the general was there. Twelve people had been killed on the spot, and over forty were injured, some critically. Blood was everywhere, and the dead and injured were still being loaded into the ambulances. The general helped in loading one of the dead bodies into the mortuary van—that of a young man no more than twenty-one years old. Tears rolled down his cheeks at this unnecessary loss of life. After consoling and reassuring the party workers, the general headed back to the complex. He tuned into live TV on his laptop, and watched in horror as a stampede broke out at one of the party rallies in the major city of Punjab, where some opposition goons had tossed a few snakes into the crowd.

Sultan's car, escorted by almost one hundred other vehicles, drove through the masses at a snail's pace, arriving just in time for the speech. Sultan hated to be late. He was escorted to the preparation room, where he changed into a fresh white shalwar kameez and sat down for some last-minute touch-ups that the TV crew insisted on. While the makeup artist brushed foundation on Sultan's cheeks, his thoughts returned to that first meeting over three years ago. He thought about all the obstacles, insults, and threats he'd had to deal with, but he had stayed the course. He had learned one thing in his career: that until you make the rules, you had to play the game, so Sultan had played the game. His kids were out of the country, and for most of the last year, he had asked his wife to stay with his kids too, because he didn't want her in any danger. Pakistani politics could be lethal, as was seen in tonight's attacks on his rallies. But this was all for a greater cause—for the good of two hundred million people who were suffering because of corruption and incompetence of the country's establishment: the conglomerate of the military generals, the clergy, the corrupt politicians, and the ever-more-corrupt bureaucracy. This was his destiny; this is what he had come back to his country for. His time was coming. The wait was almost over.

At 9:00 p.m. on the dot, Sultan appeared in front of millions of people all over the country, on TV and radio stations simultaneously.

As cameras focused on Sultan's face, he lowered his eyes, tears running down his cheeks, and recited verses from the Holy Quran. Millions of people across the country, seeing the emotions in play and hearing the verses of Holy Quran, fell silent. Sultan had decided that the only way to avert a public relations disaster was to become part of the tragedy that had just struck his party, so he had decided to alter his speech. There was eerie silence across the country, as if the whole country was suddenly mourning the tragedy that had just occurred; the media commentators were speaking in hushed tones so as not to offend the audience. Sultan finished reciting the verses from the Holy Quran and then raised his hands skyward in a gesture of prayer, speaking to God Almighty. "Oh God, give a place in heaven to all those who have been martyred today, and by your powers, heal all those who are injured. Oh God, I seek justice from you because only you can give justice for all the blood that has been shed today by our opponents. Aamin."

Sultan then turned to the cameras and pointed to the people, screaming his question in anguish, "You know who did this. Don't you?"

"Yes, yes," chanted the crowd, in many different places across the country.

Sultan continued, "And you also know"—he paused, his voice grave and serious—"these criminals have been killing innocent people for years, but the police, the legal system, and the old-school politicians have done nothing to stop it. In fact, they get these killers freed from police custody so they can kill again."

Sultan raised his voice in another cry full of anguish and fire. "I ask you how long, how long will we let innocent people die? How long will we let the police free the killers? How long will we allow corrupt politicians to continue supporting the killers?"

The crowd chanted, "No, no," and Sultan responded, "No more! The killing ends with these elections. Every one of us must vote against the status quo; we must vote against the killers; we must vote for those who have been martyred today; we must vote to keep our children and grandchildren safe. Tell me, are you ready to vote against the killers?"

The crowd chanted, "Yes, yes!"

"Are you ready to vote against the corrupt police?" Sultan asked.

"Yes, yes," came back the chorus from the crowd.

"Are you prepared to vote against the corrupt politicians who are allowing and supporting these killers?" Sultan drove the point home.

"Yes, yes!" the crowd chanted back.

The tragedy had gotten tens of millions of people who otherwise would have missed the speech to tune in, and as they watched in their homes, in their shops and in cafes, they too chanted, "Yes, yes!"

Sultan had turned the tragedy into the biggest public-relations coup imaginable.

"But these corrupt politicians are not the only ones we need to rid ourselves of," Sultan went on. "We must rid the country of those forces that have allowed the corrupt politicians to oversee the murder of our people and the rape of our economy. And that force is America; do you agree?"

"Yes, yes, down with America! Down with America!" chanted the crowd.

"These politicians and corrupt generals allowed Americans to kidnap our daughter, the daughter of this nation, Dr. Aafia Siddiqui. Do you want your sons and daughters kidnapped by the Americans?"

"No, no!" came the crowd's reply.

"These politicians and generals allowed a CIA agent, Raymond Devis, to kill Pakistani citizens like dogs on Lahore roads, and then allowed him to leave the country safely. They allowed an American consulate vehicle to run over Pakistan's citizens in Lahore, and no action was taken. They allow Americans to kill innocent women and children by drones that fly from within Pakistan, and also from Afghanistan. Do you want your women, children, sisters, brothers, mothers, fathers killed by Americans on Pakistan's roads, or while they are sleeping in their homes in their villages?"

"No, never, no!" screamed the crowd in a frenzy, and they continued chanting, "Americans, go home! Down with America!" It seemed like the crowd was out of control and gripped in a frenzy.

Sultan raised both his hands in a gesture for people to calm down, and the party workers shooed the rest of the crowd into silence. "I promise you, we will end America's enslavement of Pakistan. I promise you, we will end the slavery of the people at the hands of the corrupt politicians and generals. I promise you, we will bring every Pakistani who is illegally imprisoned abroad back home with dignity, including Dr. Aafia.

"I promise you, we will take the wealth from the rich by making sure they pay taxes, and give it to the poor. We will spend your money, the money that has been stolen from you, on building schools, hospitals, and roads. Do you want schools? Do you want hospitals? Do you want roads? Do you want the rich to pay more taxes?" Sultan fired up the questions in quick succession.

"Yes, yes, yes!" chanted the crowd.

"You want change? You want revolution? You want freedom?" Sultan went on.

"Yes, yes, yes!" echoed the crowd.

"Then vote for us!" said Sultan, not just to those present at the rallies, but also to those watching from home. He stared into the camera, into the eyes of everyone watching on TV.

The crowd was clapping, jumping up and down, dancing, and waving their fists in the air, all chanting at the same time. "Yes, yes, yes!"

Back at the party headquarters, everyone was giving a standing ovation to their leader. Mohammad, who had risen to the post of the party's general secretary and was one of the candidates in the forthcoming elections, asked the general, "What do you think, sir?"

General Bhaya patted him on the back. "He has become a great politician, and what makes him effective is that he truly believes in what he is saying. That makes all the difference."

"But that's what I think; let us turn to the box and see what others are saying." With that, General Bhaya took Mohammad along to their media monitoring room, where the analysts were watching and tracking the news coverage.

Shehzad, who had become head of the media-analysis team, approached them and shook their hands vigorously, saying, "That was a superb performance, General, a truly superb performance."

"My boy, that was no performance; he means every word he said," replied the general.

"Sir, you don't really mean we can realistically throw the Americans out. They will never go, and in the process, we will destroy our country," Shehzad replied, concern rising in his voice.

"Well, the Americans will do what they will do, and we must do what we must do," said the general, brushing aside Shehzad's concerns. "Now, tell us what the national media is saying about tonight's rally and the speech."

"Well, sir, we had live coverage from almost all the TV channels," said Shehzad. "So that was good, but on three major networks, they had a strong presence from our opponents. The media pundits, who are all pro status quo and believe that change is only possible through continuation of the electoral process—through stability, they say, and not through any revolution. They argue that revolution will only turn Pakistan into another Iran, which is completely isolated in the international community and has been suffering under American sanctions for over a decade. They argue that our nation is not as strong as Iran, and any revolutionary policies will backfire. That's pretty much a summary of what they are saying, in different words from different mouths." Shehzad's mind was still trying to absorb what the general had told him, because so far he had taken it for granted that fanning anti-Americanism was just a ploy to get votes.

"Well, that is their opinion, and they are entitled to it, for now at least," replied General Bhaya with a smile.

This comment made Shehzad even more jittery.

Was the general implying that the people would not be allowed to air their opinions in future?

The question was still hanging in midair for Shehzad when the general fired another question. "What is the international media saying?"

"Nothing so far. They have given some coverage to the shooting in Karachi, but have ignored the politics almost completely," replied Shehzad in a monotone.

"And what is the media assessing as our electoral success chances after this rally and speech?" General Bhaya went on.

"Well, sir, the shooting is certainly going to swing some undecided voters in our party's favor. It also attracted a lot of neutral voters to tune in to the speech, and that should be positive, but the national media is still skeptical. However, the numbers on the major newspaper and TV channels' online surveys are picking up in our favor," concluded Shehzad, this time with a heavy heart.

"Okay. Keep us posted, Shehzad, and get some rest. You look exhausted." The general left the room with Mohammad in tow.

As General Bhaya entered his office, he speed-dialed his contact in ISI. "I want you to monitor someone; I think he is working for foreigners," the general said.

"Okay, sir, tell me his name, and we will take it from here," replied the voice at the other end. General Bhaya gave him Shehzad's name and mobile number.

The general didn't know for sure that Shehzad was working for foreigners, but something in Shehzad's manner had triggered alarm bells in the general's head. General Bhaya had been in espionage and counterespionage all his life. It was second nature to him to smell a rat before anyone else did, and something about Shehzad wasn't right. Who better to flush him out than the ISI? If Shehzad had any foreign connections, the ISI would find out in no time.

The ISI officer, Khushnood, had been a student of the general, so for him, the general's word was enough. He called up people in the wireless intelligence wing of the agency and asked them to start tracking all communications from Shehzad to the outside world.

Mark Bloomberg had watched the speech and the attack on the rally in real time, sitting in Langley. Ever since he had come back to the States, he had kept tabs on Sultan and his party's work. Mark had found out that his ouster from Pakistan soon after his second meeting with Sultan was but a coincidence. He was a victim of the tensions between the CIA and the ISI, Pakistan's premier intelligence agency. ISI was quite peeved at what they considered excessive interference by the CIA and its contractors on its turf and wanted to send a message. A story about Mark's identity as CIA station head had been planted by local agencies through their "sources" in the media.

Mark had left the second meeting with an uneasy feeling and had decided to keep an eye on things from Langley. His source, Shehzad, had kept him up to date on the party's progress.

Mark's phone rang. It was a call redirected from his Hong Kong number, and nowadays the only person using that number was Shehzad. Mark picked up the phone and asked, "Hey buddy, 'sup?"

"Charlie, I will send you a detailed report late tonight, but I just wanted to tell you, I just spoke to the general, and these people are damn serious. They definitely want the Americans out; it is not just an election slogan. Charlie, please do me a favor: please get me American visas. I want to get out of here. I will do any job, anything, please..."

Shehzad would have gone on pleading, but Mark stopped him. "Hey, my friend, don't worry. I will get something going here for you, but remember it will take six months to a year for anything to happen. But I promise, I will set wheels in motion, okay? Now calm down and tell me why you are so worried."

"Charlie, the national media is mocking Sultan and his party, but you know the national media is dominated by the establishment-controlled people who support the status quo. But I have a lot of friends at the town and small-city level working in the media, and I am hearing the same thing from all of them: that Sultan and his party have really shaken the people out of their apathy, and they have a very good chance of winning. If they win, there will be a confrontation with the Americans." Shehzad finished stuttering his last words out, the knuckles on the hand holding the phone had turned white, and he was getting constant hiccups, which he always did when he was anxious.

"Okay, Shehzad, that's very good information. I will definitely write a report on this for the newspaper and tell them you have done a great job. You keep at it, buddy, and get me some more solid information, and I will oil the wheels here to get you your visa for America. You take care now, buddy." Mark ended the connection.

⚔ ⚔

In Islamabad, an ISI sergeant listening in on the conversation called Khushnood and told him a copy of the conversation was on its way. The sergeant also informed Khushnood that though the call was made to a number in Hong Kong, it terminated in Langley, Virginia, United States, where the person receiving the call was located.

Khushnood was jubilant. The general had been bang on target, as always. He called General Bhaya, shared the information with him, and promised to courier him the tape of the conversation immediately.

General Bhaya placed a call to the party's secretariat office and got Shehzad on the line. Now that the general knew Shehzad was working for the CIA, he didn't want to use Shehzad's cell number because he no longer wanted any evidence of any direct communication between him and Shehzad.

"Shehzad, my dear boy, how are you?" asked the general affably.

"I am fine, sir, what can I do for you, sir?" asked Shehzad nervously. The general always made Shehzad nervous. Shehzad didn't know why that was, because the general was always polite and formal, and had never spoken a harsh word to Shehzad. Yet having him at the other end of the phone completely creped him out.

"Shehzad, you know Sultan is in a tough competition. You are close to his constituency; I want you to spend some time in our election office there and also take a tour of the area, get a feel for the situation, and update me with suggestions on what we can do to help improve Sultan's election chances. I suggest you use your journalist credentials while touring the streets, so as not to put you in harm's way. Report to me if you find anything of interest," the general concluded.

"Certainly, General. I will head there in couple of hours and will report back to you." As General Bhaya disconnected, Shehzad gave a sigh of relief. He should have thought of this himself. The general was right—this was the most important contest for the party, and Shehzad, as head of political research and analysis, needed to be on top of it.

After putting the phone down, the general called the cell number of another one of his old students, who was now based in Karachi and had infiltrated the ranks of a local ethnic party. When the general's former student answered the phone, General Bhaya told him he was sending him a picture of the subject, for his usual services. The general sent Shehzad's picture to his student's cell phone and put Shehzad out of his mind. Shehzad wasn't his problem anymore.

When Shehzad arrived in the Kharadar area of the constituency where Sultan was contesting elections from, he parked his motorcycle across from Taj Café, which was hustling and bustling even at this time of night. It was past ten o'clock, but evidently the night was still young in these parts. The evening was clammy, and the area was surrounded on all sides by tall, square, badly designed buildings. Most of the apartment balconies were laden with laundry, the roads were narrow, and cars were parked on both sides of the street. Many people were sitting outside closed shops, either sipping tea and chatting, or playing some kind of board game or cards.

Shehzad walked into Taj Café and ordered a tea. He said hello to a guy sitting at the next table and, motioning to the TV, casually asked, "Who do you think is winning in this area?"

The guy looked at the TV and replied, "If there is any chance that a candidate from any other party but MQM is winning, then there will be no elections. There will be so much shooting that people will simply not come out to vote."

Another man, who looked like a dockworker, chimed in. "What do we care who is going to win? It's not like our life is going to change."

"Don't you think Sultan and his party will change things?" Shehzad asked.

The dockworker replied, "I was teenager when Ali Bhutto was elected and promised bread, clothes, and housing. Thirty years and four times Bhutto's party has been in power. Bread is scarce, clothing is unaffordable, and housing we can only dream of. Benazir Bhutto was married in this neighborhood. She had great promise, she was prime minister twice, but our lives didn't change. She used to come here many times when she was the prime minister. See that mausoleum across the road? She came here to offer prayers. She is dead now; the mausoleum didn't do anything for her, and our lives are, if anything, worse than before."

Shehzad smiled, paid his bill, and left. He next stopped by a tobacco shop that sold cigarettes and *paan* (betel nuts wrapped in betel leaves packed with some other assorted ingredients). There were a couple of young men standing around talking.

A young man in a blue shirt said to another one who was wearing thick spectacles, "This is our chance. Let us this time vote for Sultan and rid our country of all these politicians who are for sale."

"Yeah, sure, but we need to get other people out too. But I am really worried about these other parties. They tell us not to bother and stamp our ballot papers themselves," the bespectacled guy replied.

While Shehzad was getting his paan, a motorcycle stopped by, and the riders told anyone within hearing range, "Be ready tomorrow—we will come and pick you up to vote." The riders were carrying MQM's flag; the blue shirt and his friend, along with others, meekly nodded their heads.

Shehzad gave a deep sigh and moved on. He was passing through a narrow lane, with shops on both sides that were closed at this time of night. The street was not well lit; rival parties' flags and banners were spread all over the street, blocking what little light there was and creating shadows. As he moved deeper into the street, he heard a motorbike approaching. He quickly moved aside, well aware that underage drivers roamed these streets, and it was quite normal for them to hit passersby. But the motorcycle stopped in front of him, and the guy riding behind the driver asked, "Shehzad?"

Shehzad looked at the guy who had said his name. His face was long, somewhat angular, eyes sunken, with a narrow forehead, long hair, and a small, well-trimmed mustache. But what held Shehzad's attention was the eyes; it was as if he was staring into the abyss. Shehzad nodded and replied, "Yes," trying to place their faces. What happened next seemed to be in slow motion.

A gun appeared as if by magic in Shehzad's face. Shehzad's mouth opened, registering surprise, shock, and disbelief, in that order. The bullet hit Shehzad just above his left eye, knocking him backward. As Shehzad fell back and was losing consciousness, two more bullets were pumped into him; the second bullet pierced his heart, and the third lodged in his stomach. Shehzad died before his brain could process the reality. As he lay in the pool of his own blood, the motorcycle sped away. People quickly gathered around, gawking at the dead man.

Mark made a summary of his discussion with the source, Shehzad, and his own input, and sent it to the deputy director of operations, CIA. Much to Mark's surprise, he got a call from the DDO and was asked to come to the DDO's office.

Fifteen minutes later Mark was back in his cubicle, somewhat dazed. The DDO was on his way to a meeting with the president, so he briefly told Mark that he should do whatever needed to be done to derail Sultan's election. "Look, the way I see it, Sultan and a few of his key people are the problem, so let us do what we can to make sure these three or four people don't win their seats in the general election. The rest of them we can do business with, so get on with it. Talk to our cousins in London. I have already spoken to Tim; his people will help you. We don't want to interfere with the whole election—just a few of these Chavez-Ahmadinejad kind" was how the DDO had put it before dashing off to the White House.

Shit, Mark muttered to himself. His zeal had landed him in this soup, and now he had to fix an election in less than three days. For a while Mark just sat there, chewing his lower lip, trying to figure things out, but it was like he was suffering from writer's block. He just could not get his head around to the problem, so he decided to get out of the office and clear his head.

Mark headed to the gym, and after an intense work out of ninety minutes followed by fifteen minutes in the sauna, he felt rejuvenated.

Back in the office, Mark wrote down two names on his writing pad: Sultan and General Bhaya. Everything he had seen and read about the new Pakistani party pointed to these two main characters. Sultan was the charismatic one, and the general was the strategist, so perhaps the DDO was right: cut off the head of the snake and the snake will die. There was one good thing Mark found on further digging. Whereas most leading politicians in Pakistan contested elections on more than one seat of the parliament, Sultan and the general had both confined themselves to contesting elections for just one seat, hedging their bets to make sure they won from at least one place. So Mark's problem was reduced to just two election constituencies in Pakistan.

Sultan was contesting from a constituency that had been a stronghold of an ethnic party, whose leader was a British citizen and an honored guest of Her Majesty's government, so there was some wiggle room there. But the general was a different story. He was contesting from a constituency that was full of ex-military men who seemed to love the general. Furthermore, in the past three decades, no one political party had secured this seat. In fact, on more than one occasion, the seat had gone to an independent candidate without the support of any major political party, and all indications, looking at an assortment of media reports, were that the general had the election sealed in his favor. Therein lay the dilemma for Mark. If Sultan lost and the general won, then the general would take over the party and become the prime minister. Looking at the general's dossier, which consisted of several volumes covering forty years, Mark didn't think that was going to be a good idea.

It was past midnight, but Mark decided to check the Pakistani news channel before turning in for the night. The local Pakistani TV channel was flashing a picture of someone. The face looked familiar. Mark read the caption below. "Political party worker killed in target killing in Karachi, rival party suspected." Mark concentrated on the face and realized he was looking at Shehzad's picture. Mark's heart sank, and he felt sick.

Mark had never met Shehzad in person, but he had been Mark's asset for several years now, and Mark had grown to like the young man. Mark's mind went back to their last phone conversation and the desperation he had heard in Shehzad's voice.

For the next hour, Mark browsed through every available news site to scrounge details of Shehzad's murder.

Unable to sleep, Mark called the CIA's station head in Karachi. "Hey, Bernie, this is Mark from Langley. Can you tell me what you know about the death of Shehzad, the guy who was shot this morning?" asked Mark, without much preamble.

"Hey, Mark, what is our interest? These guys are killing each other every day, man. This is no different than gang wars in Los Angeles or Miami," replied Bernie.

"This guy was working for us; I have been his handler for a few years now. I need to know if he was killed because of his work for us," replied Mark reluctantly. Now that Shehzad was dead, there was no risk of information about his link to CIA leaking.

Bernie exploded. "What the fuck, man; I am head of the station in this jungle, or hadn't you heard? Why wasn't I told? Why didn't you hand him over to me?"

"Bernie, he was just sending us information—some research on the local political scene. He wasn't important enough to waste your time or resources. Besides, he didn't know he was working for the CIA. He thought he was providing information to a newspaper," Mark explained.

"Well, then, why do you think he may have been found out? What are you not telling me, Mark?"

"He called me with a report yesterday. He was in a total panic about Sultan's party's plans vis-à-vis the United States, so much so that he wanted me to get him visas to get out of the country. And within twenty-four hours he is dead. That is too much of a coincidence," said Mark.

Having established his authority, Bernie decided to be more cooperative. "I will find out more and get back to you, Mark, but you know we're in the middle of an election here, so give me some time."

Mark had slept for four hours when his phone rang. It was Bernie. "Mark, Shehzad was visiting his boss's political constituency when two guys on a motorcycle stopped him and shot him three times before fleeing. They definitely belonged to the rival party, but here is the interesting part: I talked to that party's local leadership, and they swear they didn't order the hit. They are also swearing on oath that the hit had not been ordered by their London office either, where the party's leader resides. They think it was a paid hit carried out by their guys, who frequently freelance to make some pocket money."

"Bernie, this is solid gold; thanks. I need another favor. I know you are up to your neck with this election, but can you please find out who ordered the hit? We need to know if Sultan and his people had anything to do with it."

"Okay, Mark, I'll see what I can find out, but don't hold your breath." Bernie disconnected and put the problem out of his mind.

Mark decided he didn't want to exclusively rely on his colleague in Karachi, so he called another friend in MI5 and told him what he needed to know. The British friend agreed to see what he could learn.

Later in the afternoon, Mark got a call from his friend, who had gone directly to the head of the Karachi party in London and reported that the hit had not been ordered by their party. But this is where the trail went cold. No one seemed to know who had ordered the hit.

The picture emerging about Sultan's party was very disturbing, thought Mark. They didn't tolerate dissent and were murderously ruthless and rabidly anti-American. This was the Revolutionary Guards of Iran all over again, Mark thought.

Election Day

It was half past midnight, or half an hour into the new day, election day. Sultan was sitting in his office looking at the TV.

The scene on TV was of the constituency in Karachi, from where Sultan was contesting the election. Tires and debris had been set ablaze, and black smoke was rising from the fire. It was as if Sultan's office was filling with the black smoke from the TV screen. Rapid gunfire could be heard coming from AK-47 assault rifles, which were carried by duos riding motorcycles all around Sultan's election constituency. According to the media reports, gun-toting motorcyclists were roaming the streets and terrorizing neighborhoods. Police and security forces had disappeared.

The reporter covering the streets was saying, "We don't think elections in this constituency are possible today; in fact, I am sure elections will be postponed because of the adverse law-and-order situation in this constituency, which has in the past been a safe seat for the ethnic party. This time Sultan, the leader of the new Revolutionary Party, was to contest from this constituency. It looks like Sultan made a bad choice, and now he may not get into the parliament. Over to you, Jibran Bhai in the studio."

The camera shifted to the studio of the most widely followed TV channel in the country, where Jibran was hosting a live show.

"I will now take Anjum Bethi on the line; he is a senior political analyst. Anjum, can you hear me?"

"Yes, Jibran, I can hear you," replied Anjum at the other end.

"Anjum, tell us, what do you think of these developments, and what do they mean?" Jibran asked.

"Jibran, the scenes we are seeing on the TV leave little doubt that under these circumstances, elections in this constituency of Karachi cannot be held," replied Anjum.

"Anjum, if that happens, then who will lead the Revolutionary Party in the parliament?" questioned Jibran.

"Well, the most senior person in that party is General Bhaya, and let me tell you, he is all set to win the election from his constituency. So if Sultan doesn't win his seat, we may be looking at the general as the next leader, and that will be a game changer," replied Anjum.

Sultan gave a deep sigh: so near and yet so far.

Sultan picked up the phone and dialed an international number, using his scrambled satellite phone.

The phone was answered on the fifth ring. The voice at the other end sounded as if it were laced with a lot of alcohol. Sultan looked at his wristwatch and calculated the time at the other end. It must be around eight thirty in the evening. But then, alcoholics never drink by the clock, he thought.

The hello was followed by a coughing fit that lasted for a good thirty seconds. Finally, the person on the other end spoke in his singsong fashion. "So, Sultan Bhai, you have finally decided to remember us. It is so sad what is happening in your election constituency. But you know, the boys are very angry. They don't want outsiders hijacking their election and representing them in the parliament. I can understand their anger, can't you?"

It was the leader of the ethnic party, known as Bhai or sometimes as Pir Saheb (Mr. Saint). He didn't contest any elections; he just controlled the party like a mafia boss and extorted the money.

"Bhai, I need you to call off your people. Tell them to go back to their homes and party offices. Let there be elections, fair elections. That's all we ask; that's all we want," said Sultan.

"I, too, want something," the lyrical Bhai said. "I want the beautiful maidens promised to us in paradise before I die. But I cannot have that, because I have to die to go to paradise. So you see, we all want something, but it is not always possible." There was silence. Sultan didn't know it, but Bhai, under the influence of alcohol, had dozed off.

Sultan patiently waited for a full minute, and then spoke. "What will it cost me?"

Bhai was nudged back to wakefulness by his secretary, who told him the question Sultan had just posed.

"Ten million British pounds in my account in the next hour, and you will have a peaceful election." With that, the line went dead.

Sultan calculated. The vein in his temple above his left eye was throbbing. This was almost US$16 million—an exorbitant price—but without that there would be no election, and everything Sultan had worked for would go down the drain.

Under different circumstances Sultan would have consulted his party's Central Executive Committee (CEC), but there was no time. Besides, he didn't think the CEC would have agreed. He would have at least consulted the general, but in this case, if Sultan didn't win, the general was the winner, so there was really no point in consulting the general either. Sultan felt very alone.

It wasn't just the money, though this was a huge amount by any standards, but a configuration of so many moral dilemmas all thrown into one that tore Sultan apart.

He didn't like to be blackmailed, and yet this was precisely what was happening. He didn't want to indulge in corruption; the money belonged to the party, and if he diverted it for his own election victory, then he would be just another corrupt politician. By paying, he would compromise every principal and belief he had founded his party on, and yet by not paying, he might be surrendering everything he believed in. The clock chimed. Sultan looked up and was surprised to see that he had been lost in his reverie for almost two hours. It was 3:00 a.m.

Sultan rose, performed ablutions, and knelt in prayer. At 5:30 a.m. Sultan rose from prayer, typed a short fax to the office of the chief election commissioner, and sent it from his personal fax machine.

The general arrived at his election constituency at 8:00 a.m. He had lots of his supporters in tow, some beating drums, others dancing. It was not the arrival of a voter but the march of a victor. Some party supporters put a few garlands of flowers around the general's neck and shook his hand. General Bhaya smiled all around, waved to his supporters, and headed for the ballot box. The election office where votes were to be cast was in a girls' school. General Bhaya walked into the building. The paint on the walls was chipping off, the ceiling showed signs of water leakage, some of the windows were broken, and as he passed a lavatory he had to hold his breath to stop the nauseating stench. The scene pretty much described the state of education in the country, thought the general with some dismay.

As General Bhaya approached the ballot box, his thoughts returned to the events he had seen on the national TV network last night. There had been a lot of trouble in Sultan's constituency, and there were rumors that elections in that constituency may be postponed. If that happened then he, General Bhaya, would be put in a position to lead the party in parliament. And given that the party CEC had already planned a rapid takeover of power in the event of a victory, there would be no time for Sultan to enter the fray, leaving the door wide open for the general. Hmmm, thought General Bhaya, who can fight destiny? He had been denied the post of the army chief, which was his right. Maybe this was to be his reward.

After sending the fax, Sultan took an hour-long nap. As he got out of the shower and changed into fresh clothes, the clock chimed 7:30 a.m.

Sultan left the complex where his office was (and where he had spent the night) and headed for the Jeep that was to take him around.

Sultan's Jeep was part of a convoy of four identical Jeeps, and as a security precaution, the Jeeps kept changing position from front to middle to back. Thus, any observer would not know which car Sultan was riding in.

As the convoy entered the Super Highway, it split into two groups. One group took the route through the northern bypass, a road that skirted the northern boundaries of the city and ended in the port area, which was very close to Sultan's constituency.

Another convoy headed back into Karachi on the Super Highway, passing through the Central District and heart of Karachi. All of this area was a stronghold of the ethnic party.

A motorcyclist concealed behind a tree near the complex gate had made a phone call to his controller, giving information about Sultan's four-Jeep convoy. At the entrance of the Super Highway, another motorcyclist conveyed the information to his controller that the convoy had split in two. Neither motorcyclist had followed the convoy; at every major intersection on the route Sultan was to take, a motorcyclist had been posted to convey the information.

The two-car convoy heading through Central District approached the Karimabad bridge. The bridge had been built some fifteen years ago but was already in need of repairs, and it ran over a railway crossing. On both sides of the bridge were small and large buildings.

As the Jeeps climbed the bridge, the mobile phone on a rooftop across from the bridge rang. "ETA one minute" was all the caller said.

On the rooftop, a young man in his early twenties straightened himself, stabilizing a rocket launcher on his shoulder and looking through the crosshairs.

As he sighted the target, he pressed the trigger. The force of the launcher made him stagger back. As he got his feet firmly planted, he saw the rocket descend like a bird landing on a lake. And *boom*, the rocket hit the first Jeep, completely destroying it.

The second Jeep was hit by the shrapnel and flying debris from the rocket and the first Jeep. The driver of the second Jeep tried to swerve away from the carnage, hit the barrier of the bridge, and went over, plunging some thirty feet below.

The smoldering Jeep on the bridge was surrounded by several young men, all belonging to the ethnic party, carrying concealed firearms. Having made sure there were no survivors, they took off, informing their controller of the success of the attack. A second team of party workers did the inspection below the bridge and found one security guard with minor bruises and another with serious injuries. Both were shot dead.

As part of the security protocol, no one was ever informed who would be traveling in which car. That decision was always made on the spur of the moment by Sultan himself. Similarly, no one decided beforehand which car would travel which route. That too was decided by Sultan himself.

This morning, Sultan had gotten into the fourth vehicle. Once reaching the Super Highway, Sultan had told his driver to take the northern bypass road to go to his constituency. The other two cars, which had fallen behind, had automatically taken the fatal route that led through the Central District of Karachi.

TV and Internet reception on this route was not good, so the driver was instructed to keep the radio on. Sultan watched the barren hills on both sides of the road. On the other side of the hills lay the province of Baluchistan. The car was traveling at 110 kilometers an hour heading toward the Hub area, a new industrial zone, which they would pass on their way to the constituency. The radio crackled, and a breathless voice of a news reporter came online. "Breaking news, we have breaking news that a two-car convoy has been hit by a rocket launcher on the Super Highway in the Central District near Karimabad. Our sources tell us that the car belonged to Mr. Sultan and his party. It is believed Mr. Sultan was in the car, but we have no confirmation of that. We can, however, confirm there were no survivors."

Sultan felt his heartbeat racing. Emotions welled up inside and rose to his eyes, ready to burst with tears at the loss of life of his close associates, who had embraced death in his place. Tears silently rolled down his cheeks. He loudly recited a few verses from Holy Quran, blessing the victims of the rocket attack on his second convoy. Then he picked up the phone and called two of the biggest TV networks simultaneously.

The calls were put through to the respective news channel studios, which were reporting the attack. Sultan spoke into his phone. "As you have heard, there was an attack on our party's vehicles carrying my security staff. Eight persons belonging to our party are martyred in that attack. *Ina lillahe w ina illahe rajeoon.* We are all from Allah, and we all have to return to Allah. But by the grace of Almighty God, I am not hurt, and I want to assure the nation that these cowardly acts by a dying party and a dying system will not stop me from my mission. I ask the nation to pray for all those innocent people who have been martyred today, and not to be intimidated. Show the cowards that we are not afraid by coming out to vote and by defeating them. Vote for change; vote to honor those who have been killed, *Allaho akbar.* God is great." The anchors in the studio disconnected the call and went on with reporting. Now that it was known that Sultan had survived, the sensation had considerably diminished, and the news was slowly pushed back.

As Sultan entered the outskirts of his constituency in Kharadar, he saw deserted streets. There was almost no traffic on the roads or in the streets. It was like everyone had decided to stay at home and not venture out. It took Sultan thirty minutes to travel through various parts of his constituency, a journey that on a normal business day would have taken two hours because of traffic and congestion.

Sultan headed to his party's constituency office, which was tucked away across the railway tracks in an old warehouse.

As he entered the office, his party's workers and supporters started applauding and cheering, obviously relieved to see their leader in the flesh and safe.

Sultan walked up to the podium, which had been set up at one end of the room. "Brothers and sisters, you know some of our workers have been killed this morning in a cowardly terrorist attack by our rivals. Let us say a prayer for them."

Sultan went on after a collective prayer. "We have a more immediate problem to deal with, and that is to bring the voters out of their homes to vote. I have some good news. In the early hours of this morning, I spoke to the chief election commissioner, and on our party's petition the commissioner has decided to extend the voting time till 10:00 p.m. tonight. So we will have five more hours to bring the people out. I have looked at the record of strikes and shutdowns in the city over the past thirty years, and every time it is the same: after 2:00 p.m. people start coming out, and after 5:00 p.m. the whole city is back to normal. So let us prepare to mobilize voters after 2:00 p.m. We will not give in to terrorism, and we will not be scared out of the political arena. The best revenge will be to defeat these people today. Democracy is the best revenge. So let us use this time to gather our forces, our energy, and our resolve—and emerge stronger. I am staying here till it's over. We are going to do this together, and when the voting is over, we are going to march victorious." Sultan stepped down amid thunderous applause, cheering, and chanting of slogans. The depression had been lifted, and his party workers were charged up to take on the fight.

After talking to the ethnic party's leader early this morning, Sultan had decided to fight on rather than trying to buy his way to an election victory. The attack, no doubt planned well in advance, was a reaction to Sultan not taking the offer and fighting on. If he had taken the offer, there would have been no attack. Sultan felt sad that eight of his people had died, but according to his belief, those eight persons' time had come, and they would have died today, at the same time and the same place, no matter what. That is the inevitability of death and fate.

After morning prayers, Sultan had spoken to the election commissioner and then sent in a petition by fax requesting the time extension. Before Sultan left the complex, the petition approval had been received from the election commissioner's office. Sultan had also requested the election commissioner to deploy some army troops and rangers in his constituency. Around 1:00 p.m. the rangers and army troops started moving in and around many polling stations in his constituency, taking positions to ensure peaceful voting.

It was now up to his party machinery, and of course, the voters.

The news of Sultan's likely death in the attack on his convoy had angered not only the party supporters, but also those who otherwise chose not to vote. The subsequent revelation that Sultan had survived the attack (most people didn't focus on the fact that Sultan was not in the convoy) convinced a lot of the undecided voters that God was watching over Sultan, and they felt motivated to vote for him.

Slowly traffic on the roads started picking up after 2:00 p.m. Seeing the army and rangers deployed visibly, all around, the people started coming out, and by 5:00 p.m. the voting was in full swing. The ethnic party's workers and supporters had planned on just stuffing the ballot boxes after the official time was over at 5:00 p.m. They were caught off guard by the extension in time and the large presence of the army and rangers.

The voting continued without any further incidents till 10:00 p.m. The ethnic party filed a petition with the election commission for cancelling the election, on the grounds that the extension was unfair and was given without due consideration and without giving them a chance to put forward their view. Their petition was put away by the election commission for hearing in due course.

At midnight, a polling agent of Sultan's party called from the Okhai school polling station in Kharadar. The first count had gone in favor of Sultan. However, five more polling stations after that, from Burns Road and adjoining areas, reported voting in favor of the ethnic party's candidate. Till 2:00 a.m., Sultan was trailing behind his opponent, and then results from areas dominated by the business community started coming in slowly. Sultan was gaining ground, and by 5:00 a.m. Sultan had emerged a clear winner with a small lead. The ethnic party immediately filed another petition to stay the results, alleging rigging and voter intimidation by Sultan's party, as well as a partisan approach from the election commissioner.

⟛ ⟛

Mark received a call from Bernie, CIA station chief in Karachi, who informed him of the unofficial result declaring Sultan the winner.

Mark gave a sigh of relief. After mulling over the decision of the deputy director, Mark had done some research and presented the results of his research in an executive summary to DDO. He recommended staying out of the election process on the premise that even if they succeeded in influencing the result, which in Mark's opinion was not likely, they would end up with General Bhaya as the new leader. In Mark's assessment, the general was a much nastier customer than Sultan. The DDO had accepted his recommendation. Mark had tuned into the elections, constantly monitoring everything in the past twenty-four hours. Mark wondered if his boss knew of the attack on Sultan before it happened, but decided not to speculate about it; Mark knew this would be highly unprofitable speculation.

The Day after the Elections

Ironically, the first seat to be captured by the Revolutionary Party was NA 1 from Peshawar. This had traditionally been a stronghold of the Pakistan People's Party, but their candidate was defeated by a huge margin. The other popular party in Peshwar, Awami National Party, only mustered a few thousand votes; thus, the die was cast. Result after result confirmed the verdict of the people: the Revolutionary Party was winning. By the early hours of the morning after the elections, history was made. The Revolutionary Party had won majority seats in the National Assembly. Sultan was elected from Kharadar Karachi, General Bhaya had been elected from his hometown in Attock, and Sultan's right-hand man, Mohammad Abdullah, a.k.a. Mohammad Bin Abdullah, was the winner of a seat from the northwest of Karachi city.

Day One in the Assembly—Election of the Speaker

Sultan's motorcade drove the short distance from Chak Shahzad, a suburb of Islamabad where Sultan had stayed the night at a friend's farmhouse, toward the parliament. Seated next to Sultan was General Bhaya, who was thinking about how close he had come to becoming the leader of the party. Once again, fate had denied him, just as all those years ago he was denied the chance to become the army chief. None of this showed on the general's face. He sat impassively as the car drove toward the parliament.

Sultan stared ahead, thinking about all those people who had lost their lives during the elections, and said a silent prayer. The car went past the lustrous greens of the Islamabad Golf Club, stopped at a traffic light across from the best hotel in town, and, when the light turned green, entered Constitutional Avenue facing the beautiful Margalla Hills. About a kilometer down the road, they turned into the gates of the National Assembly of Pakistan.

As Sultan got out of his car, he was cheered on by his party members, who all thronged around him. Sultan walked toward the entrance of the square-shaped building that was the National Assembly. The white building was devoid of any architectural appeal or beauty.

He entered the Assembly Hall and was led to the seat designated for him as the party leader, which was in the front row. General Bhaya followed him and took the seat on his right. Mohammad bin Abdullah took a seat immediately behind Sultan.

The first order of business was election of the speaker. This would be the first real test for Sultan's party. A candidate from Sultan's party had filled out the paperwork and was one of the three contesting for the post; the two other candidates were from PPP and PMLN. The voting was to be done by a secret ballot, but Sultan had done a head count and was confident that his party would get the speaker's slot, because PPP and PMLN, though combined having a greater number of votes, had been at loggerheads for decades, and their animosity had taken a turn for the worse in the past year. It was unlikely they would vote with each other.

The former speaker, who was chairing the session, announced that he had just received a letter from the PPP candidate for speakership, withdrawing his name from the contest.

The assembly was electrified by this unexpected development. There had been no indication that a deal had been reached between the two archrivals, and yet here they were cooperating.

The media covering the event went into frenzy, speculating that this co-operation might evolve into a broader coalition between the two parties, and they might field a joint nominee for the post of the prime minister. This was a big setback for the Revolutionary Party, and for Sultan, who was aspiring to be PM.

The voting for the speaker's position started and continued for almost three hours. It took another two hours for the assembly staff to count the votes and compile the results.

As the former speaker walked back to his chair, presiding over the session, his eyes searched for Sultan and settled on him. As their eyes met, there was a smug look on the former speaker's face. Sultan more or less guessed what the result was.

The name of Makhdoom from PMLN was announced as the speaker. Sultan's party candidate was defeated by a small margin.

After the oath taking, the new speaker said to the members, "I now propose to call for the election of the leader of the House. Does anyone have an objection?"

Sultan rose from his seat. "Mr. Speaker, let me congratulate you on behalf of my party, and indeed every member of this august house, on your election as speaker of the House." The members cheered and clapped. Once the clapping died down, Sultan went on. "I would make a request on behalf of my party. The time is now approaching for the evening prayers, so I ask that we take a break and postpone the election of the leader of the house till tomorrow."

As Sultan sat down, the former prime minister rose from his seat. "Mr. Speaker, my party opposes any delay in electing the leader of the House. We insist that after a break for evening prayers, we reconvene to complete the democratic process of elections and transfer of power." He was followed by the leader of PMLN, who also insisted on the immediate election of the PM.

"Having heard all sides, I order the election of the leader of the House today, after a two-hour break for prayers." The speaker banged his gavel and left his chair.

The house broke out in a sudden chorus of voices from all sides. Sultan quietly rose and was followed by his party members to the chambers that had been temporarily arranged for them. Sultan called the Maulana on his mobile phone. The Maulana was quite close to PMLN and would know what was going on. "Maulana, you of course know that one of your old students, Makhdoom of PMLN, has become the speaker. He was supported by PPP. Tell me, what's going on?"

"Sultan, this is a gesture of goodwill by the PPP chairman to the PMLN chief. PPP has been asking PMLN to form a coalition, but PMLN, after the previous elections experience, will have none of it. There is no deal yet, but maybe Makhdoom's election will swing it. I doubt it, though, because Makhdoom would sooner make a deal with the devil than PPP. So I think Makhdoom would rather make a deal with you." Maulana chuckled at his own joke. Sultan disconnected the phone and turned to General Bhaya, who was also finishing a phone call with someone within PPP. He had the same information. There was no deal so far, but they were talking.

Sultan and his party men entered the assembly hall to find that the other two parties had jointly asked for one hour's further delay in starting the session.

Sultan's phone started vibrating. The caller ID showed the Maulana calling. Sultan pressed the answer button and put the phone next to his ear. "I am sorry, Sultan, but my information is that both PMLN and PPP have reached a deal. The worst of it is PPP has supported PMLN without any preconditions, just to keep you and us out of the government."

What the Maulana didn't tell Sultan was that he had also agreed to support PMLN, as long as he got chairmanship of the Kashmir Committee and two ministries for his chosen people.

Sultan conferred with General Bhaya about this latest development, and they decided they only had one move left.

Sultan called the chairman of PPP and offered him and his cronies complete immunity from any accountability for their corruption and wrongdoings, as long as PPP didn't support PMLN. The PPP chairman's reply shocked Sultan. "I don't need immunity, Sultan; I have already been guaranteed that by the Americans and the army, and they have told me that under no circumstances is my party to support you. I am sorry, but this is how it is." And with that, the phone line and Sultan's dreams were dead.

Meanwhile, the ISI chief visited PMLN's leadership at the Punjab house where they had camped and were gearing up to head to the National Assembly to claim the prize of creating the government.

There were three people from PMLN present: the PM hopeful, his brother, and their chosen candidate for the Finance Ministry. After formal greetings, the ISI chief bluntly laid out the army's terms for allowing PMLN to take power. "Congratulations, gents, on reaching the deal with the PPP. Here are the conditions you must agree to in writing. These conditions have been discussed with our friends in Saudi Arabia and Washington, DC, and they have guaranteed your acceptance. First, the army chief will continue in office for the next three years, and should he decide for any reason to step down, then I will succeed him as the army chief; second, only the army high command will negotiate with NATO, the United States, and the Taliban (both local and Afghan), the political leadership will not interfere. Third, there will be no direct peace talks with India; these will only happen based on the army's guidelines and discussions previously concluded between Pakistan and India when General Musharraf was president of the country. Last but not the least, the defense budget will not be reduced; in fact, the government will make sure that the defense budget is increased at least at the rate of inflation.

"Now, I have all this typed up for all three of you to sign, so we can move on." The ISI chief laid down a piece of paper in front of the three men.

The PMLN prime minister hopeful's face had drained of color; he was not angry, just dejected. After fourteen years of struggle, during which he had abided by every condition thrust on him, he was back where he had started: conditional power, or rather the appearance of power without any real power.

His brother had been aware of what was coming, but he had been warned not to let his brother know lest he change his mind in panic. The idea was to present the future PM with a fait accompli, but his face betrayed none of this. He just stared at his shoes, waiting for his older brother to comply with the conditions of the real masters of this country's destiny. The arrangement they were being offered was simple: they could continue to run the largest province of Pakistan like a family fiefdom and could even enjoy the trappings of the prime minister's position, but no more.

The would-be finance minister, knowing something like this might happen and fearing that the future PM might react irrationally, leaned forward and whispered in his ear. The PMLN chief nodded lamely. "General Kaka, we are very grateful for this wonderful opportunity, but we need till tomorrow morning to confer with our senior party members."

The ISI chief rose. "Well, don't take too long. It is not like we are short of candidates for premiership." And he left without further ado.

＝≒+ +≒＝

Sultan didn't want the tension he was feeling to show, so he took out his personal copy of the Holy Quran and started studying it.

The clock chimed, and the senior leaders of both parties, PPP and PMLN, walked into the assembly. Their faces were passive, not giving any indication of what had transpired.

The speaker entered the House from his chambers, and called the House to order. Much to Sultan's surprise and pleasure, the speaker announced, "I have considered the request of the honorable member from Kharadar Karachi and have decided to postpone the assembly session till tomorrow at 2:00 p.m."

Early next morning, Sultan's lawyers filed a petition in the Supreme Court alleging rigging in the elections and therefore denial of fundamental rights to the people, asking the Supreme Court to stay the elections of at least forty candidates from PMLN and PPP.

The chief justice too had heard from his sources that the army and the Americans were maneuvering to take the party with the largest number of seats out of the process of forming the government, and decided to stay the elections of forty assembly seats.

Thus, when the assembly reconvened at 2:00 p.m., PMLN and PPP were short forty seats, and had little prospect of forming a government.

The PPP chairman was woken up from sleep at midday and informed of this development; he cursed at the judiciary and the PMLN chief for failing to form the government the previous evening. He quickly reviewed his options and called Sultan. "I have reconsidered your offer, and I have convinced my party leadership to not support PMLN's candidacy for the premiership in the parliament. My secretary and legal adviser are on the way to you with the necessary paperwork of the deal we discussed."

Sultan wanted to scream at him and tell him to go to hell but realized that even with forty elected candidates of the opposition parties temporarily disqualified, he still needed this man's support. He grudgingly said, "Of course, and thank you, Mr. Chairman, for your and your party's support."

But the PPP chairman really wanted to rub salt in his wounds. "Let us be very clear, Sultan, we have agreed to not support the PMLN, but we will not vote for you either." The phone was disconnected.

At 2:00 p.m. the parliament convened, and the speaker read out the names of three candidates for the election of the leader of the House. Sultan's name was third. Everyone waited with bated breath, wondering if the PPP or PMLN candidate would withdraw at the last minute, but no announcement came. The speaker continued to read the procedure for election of the leader of the House.

The election of the leader of the House proceeded, and the results were announced long after midnight. Sultan had won the election and was to be the new prime minister of the country.

General Bhaya, who was sitting next to him, got up and gave him a warm embrace, whispering, "Get some rest, Chief; we have busy days ahead." Sultan didn't see the general after that.

Younger members of the party had lifted Sultan off his feet and were carrying him on their shoulders, chanting, "Long live Sultan; long live Pakistan," and "Revolution, revolution, revolution is here! Revolution has won."

Speech to the Nation

Sultan sat in his chamber in the parliament, the chamber of the leader of the House. As he looked around, his heart sank at the waste that could be seen everywhere. It depressed him thinking about millions of people who had no shelter, while the elected representatives of the people indulged in opulence. But for now, he had to concentrate on his speech to the nation.

He looked at the text of the speech, which had been written and rewritten many times in the past twenty-four hours. The crew from the media team worked around him, applying some powder to take the shine off his forehead and nose. Sultan waved them off and rose, walking toward the assembly hall to deliver his maiden speech as leader of the House.

"Mr. Speaker, members of the House, Your Excellencies"—turning toward the gallery where the diplomats were seated—"ladies and gentlemen of the media, and my dear countrymen. I thank Almighty Allah for giving me this honor, and I thank all the people for giving me this opportunity to serve the country as prime minister. As I sat in my office and looked around at all the money wasted in its furnishings, my heart went out to tens of millions of people who have no shelter, no roof over their head. As I drank tea in my chamber in the porcelain cups, I shivered thinking about all those people who have not eaten today. I shivered because after today I am responsible for the affairs of this country; Allah will hold me accountable if people go hungry during my time in office, if people have no shelter. This is a heavy burden, and God willing, I will prove worthy of it.

"My dear countrymen, it is no secret that I believe that Americans have interfered in our country for too long, and it is their support of our corrupt politicians and generals that has caused this mess. So I am putting the Americans on notice today. From today, there will be no more expansion of America's embassy and consulates in this country, there will be no more use of our air bases, there will be no more drone attacks, and there will be no more kidnapping and imprisoning of Pakistani people in American prisons. We don't want their money, we don't want their aid, and we don't want their promises." Sultan's party men started thumping desks and chanting slogans. Sultan waved at them to calm down and went on.

"But the Americans are not alone in trying to enslave us. They are aided and abetted by their cousins, the Brits. The British have given asylum to everyone who is working against Pakistan. Terrorist attacks are ordered out of London headquarters of parties that have strongholds in our cities. These parties collect extortion money from our cities and send it to foreign accounts. This is indirect taxation of our businesses and people, and we will not allow this to continue. Our Foreign Office is drafting a letter to the British government to pack up their embassy and consulates and leave our country. Let the message be clear: we shall not be enslaved any more, we will not tolerate interference anymore, and we will not allow you to patronize those who are destabilizing our country while sitting in your country." Sultan's party men cheered, but the rest of the assembly members were very quiet, as were the press and diplomatic galleries.

Sultan went on. "From now on, foreign embassies and their staffs will be strictly monitored. Visas of all American and British defense contractors and security companies are canceled, and they have been told to leave the country within seven days.

"But freedom has a price. For too long, the poor have paid the price, and the poor have sacrificed. Now the rich will pay; now the rich will sacrifice. We are documenting everyone's income and wealth in the country and will soon increase the number of taxpayers many times over. The money we get from taxes will help us reduce dependence on foreign money; we will spend that money on building our country, on freeing the poor from the yoke of poverty.

"The nation has seen how my election campaign was attacked, how my security team was murdered in an attempt that was meant to kill me. In the same fashion, the foreigners, through their puppets in this country, will do anything to stop us, to stop our march to a better future, to stop our journey to a better life. They will spread rumors, they will spread terror, they will try to destabilize the government, and they will attack our economy. They will try everything, but we must remain steadfast. Our forefathers sacrificed everything for liberation from the British Empire, and now once again we must be prepared to face the empire that is trying to make us slaves, trying to take our liberty away.

"Soon we will speak from a position of strength, and we will bring our brothers and sisters back from foreign jails to Pakistan."

The majority of the assembly members rose in a standing ovation to the newly elected leader. The diplomatic and media galleries emptied very fast; reports had to be made and stories filed.

In Washington, Mark had heard the speech live. None of it was unexpected; most of it was the rhetoric Sultan and his party had been playing throughout the election campaign.

But the notice to the Brits, as Sultan called them, was a shocker. Before jumping to any conclusions, Mark wanted to verify if the Brits had indeed been given their marching orders, and if so, what they proposed to do about it.

While he waited for confirmation from the Brits, his mind turned back to his last conversation with Shehzad, the slain journalist from Pakistan. His panic and desperation were etched in Mark's mind.

At this moment Mark wanted to be sitting in the CIA's operations center, guiding a drone to take out Shehzad's killers, who were now threatening the United States.

Prime Minister Sultan left the assembly hall and headed for his office, the prime minister's secretariat—another monstrosity that every prime minister had occupied for the past twenty years, another monument to the rich and the powerful, another reminder to the poor of how their money was squandered away. The drive from the assembly to the secretariat was less than a minute. This could have been a nice walk, but another time, perhaps. Right now there was too much to do.

As he walked into his office, which was a vulgar display of a complete waste of money, he was followed by his principal secretary, Altaf.

"Mr. Prime Minister, your speech has caused a great deal of tension, and ambassadors from every major country in the capital have phoned to see you. The American ambassador's secretary has called and said the ambassador is on his way over as we speak," said Altaf breathlessly.

"Altaf, tell all the ambassadors to talk to General Bhaya, who is our new foreign minister, with the additional portfolio of defense."

"But sir, what about the American ambassador?"

The prime minister turned and looked at the secretary. Something sent shivers up the secretary's spine. This was a different man than the one the people had elected.

This was no affable national leader; instead, he had transformed into a cold, calculating, and ruthless individual. There was a fury in his eyes that seemed to be coming from the depth of his soul. This frightened the secretary.

Sultan also saw the look on the secretary's face and could almost taste his fear. He decided that the secretary would have to be monitored very closely, but that was not a problem. The general's people had already set up extensive surveillance of every member of the government. Clandestinely, the prime minister had hired a shadow intelligence chief whose job was to watch the general, the Maulana, and the Afghan.

"Mr. Altaf, when the American ambassador arrives, you ask him if he has made an appointment, which of course he hasn't, and tell him and all the other diplomats that they have to go through the Foreign Office and the foreign minister to see the prime minister. Make sure you meet them in the grand Blue Room."

Before Sultan finished the sentence, another secretary knocked gently and entered. "Sir, the American ambassador has arrived." The principal secretary quickly left to deal with the American ambassador. The prime minister decided it was time he had a talk with his staff. This kind of behavior and lack of protocol had to be stopped.

Principal Secretary Altaf quickly rushed to receive the ambassador, who was sitting in one of the waiting rooms, and then stopped in his tracks, recalling the PM's instructions to meet them in the Blue Room. He told the assistant secretary to bring the Americans into the Blue Room and went to the men's room. By the time Altaf got back, the ambassador was sitting down with other senior members of his team. Altaf greeted them affably and sat down; however, the grave look on his face warned the Americans that the meeting wasn't going to go as planned.

"Mr. Ambassador, may I ask if you have a prior appointment with the prime minister?" The omission of the proper title and Altaf's tone and body language were speaking volumes.

The ambassador decided to go on the offensive. "Mr. Principal Secretary, you damn well know we don't have an appointment and that we don't need one. We want to see the prime minister, and we want to see him now." The ambassador's voice had risen a couple of decibels, taking Altaf by surprise.

"Mr. Prime Minister, umm, sorry—Mr. Ambassador—the protocol requires that you contact the foreign minister through the Foreign Office for arranging an appointment. You know the PM is extremely busy and cannot just meet anyone who walks in," Altaf replied, flustered. It actually felt good telling the American ambassador off, and he started regaining his composure.

"Mr. Principal Secretary, who do you think you are talking to? I am not the Ambassador of Bangladesh or Sri Lanka, I am the representative of the government of the United States of America. I am sure you and your prime minister have not forgotten that."

Altaf decided to have some fun. "How can we forget, Mr. Ambassador? Your drones intrude into our air space every day and kill our citizens at a whim. The murder of innocent civilians is a pastime of your soldiers, and they are just collateral damage to your country." This felt good. Altaf himself didn't realize where these words were coming from; he was, in fact, as surprised as the Americans were. Unbeknownst to all the people in the room, their conversation was video recorded and watched live by the prime minister in his office. The video feed was also watched live by the foreign minister, the general, in his own office.

"Mr. Principal Secretary, let me refresh your memory with a little bit of history. Thirty-five years ago, there was a prime minister in this country—I am of course referring to the meeting between our late prime minister Ali Bhutto and the then–secretary of state Henry Kissinger—who told the American secretary of state, 'Who do you think you are talking to? I am the prime minister of the country; my seat is powerful.' He too was drunk on power and refused to listen to reason. Within one year that man was removed by your own army and within three years hanged. You just remember this and make sure you relate this to your boss, too." With that, the American ambassador stalked out the door.

Altaf heaved a sigh of relief at the end of the ordeal. His palms were sweaty; it was just as well the Americans had not stopped to shake hands. He felt completely off balance. Alarm bells were ringing in his head. He knew that he was caught in the wrong kind of situation, the kind of situation that destroys careers and lives. Now that the adrenaline in his body had run its course, his training as a bureaucrat returned, and he started thinking of ways to hedge himself. He didn't know quite how, but he knew he had to.

He walked back to his office, stopping again at the men's room to release the tension built up during the meeting.

When he arrived back at his office, he found that a red light, the "do not disturb" sign, was on above the PM's office door. This was surprising, because he knew of no scheduled meeting.

In fact, this is what had caught him off guard when the PM had refused to meet the ambassador, because he knew that the PM had no meetings scheduled at that time. He reflected that the Americans probably knew that too (as they had spies everywhere) and felt like a fool for not seeing this before.

He was being used as a pawn in the big game and didn't even know it.

He asked the assistant secretary sharply, "Who is inside?"

"The foreign minister came in a few minutes ago," replied the flustered assistant secretary. Altaf recalled that the prime minister had ordered that all his cabinet members (there were ten of them) sit on the same floor within walking distance of each other, so this is how the foreign secretary had gotten here so fast.

Inside the room, Sultan and the general looked at each other. Sultan spoke first. "We will release this video of the American ambassador to the media at an appropriate time. You summon the ambassador to your office within the next few hours for the next phase, and let's see if he again acts as we expect him to. This was far too easy. They are so arrogant; what a shame. We will follow this up tonight with another piece of bitter legislation, to make sure that the people are not too bothered and remain focused on the diplomatic row with the Americans. Let us meet later as planned to discuss other things." The general nodded, rose, and left the room. He knew that the room was swept every hour, but still, the less said the better. After all, they didn't have to impress anyone.

The American Embassy

Mark looked at those present in the meeting at the embassy in Islamabad. He was in Langley and had joined the video conference. The DDO, CIA, had requested that the State Department loop Mark into any meetings regarding the regime change in Pakistan. The request had been granted, and the ambassador had been informed. Mark had accessed the ambassador's file before the meeting.

The ambassador, at fifty-three, had served the State Department for almost thirty years. This was his second stint in this country, and he was halfway through his three-year posting. His previous posting had been in Karachi, seven years ago, as the consulate general there. Those were the days when General Musharraf was in power and did pretty much whatever the Americans wanted.

The meeting was attended by four people: the men from the Pentagon and the CIA and a woman from the State Department. The ambassador was the fourth. The ambassador briefed all those present on the meeting that hadn't taken place and the attitude of the Pakistani government. "People, the floor is now open. Let's hear your take on the developments. Let us first talk about the attitude of the PM's office and then examine the speech."

The ambassador turned to the CIA man, Tom, and asked him to start with his own briefing. Tom said, "Henry, I don't have a good feeling about this. The prime minister and his team have been planning this for four years, so they obviously have a head start. I am also hearing that every move has been planned and 'gamed' through a series of think tanks, which have been at work for at least two years. So in my opinion, this is no random knee-jerk reaction of someone on a power high. There is a bigger game afoot. Langley has been monitoring this, and Mark, who is with us on the video conference, has been the focal point within the agency."

Mark decided to interject. "Mr. Ambassador, so far the new PM has put the Brits on notice and not confronted us directly. I know from my contact, who had checked the PM's diary, that the PM had no other meeting planned and was sitting in his office throughout the time your meeting took place. I also received a text message from my source that immediately after you left, the PM met with the foreign minister. I think we need to start preparing for the worst-case scenario."

The ambassador replied, "Mark, what is your assessment of the worst-case scenario?"

"Let's go back to the speech. We have been told to not expand our missions here. Our contractors have been told to leave, their visas cancelled. A list of five hundred people who are supposedly working for us has been released, cooperation in Afghanistan has been terminated, and there is the usual noise about drone attacks. But what is different is instructions to the air force to shoot down any drones we fly—and I have confirmed that written orders have been issued to this effect—our aid has been rejected, and the British have already been told to get out of the country, which in my opinion is to tell us they mean business. I interpret this as a declaration of hostilities, and we should start dealing with it in the same way."

The ambassador thought Mark was being an alarmist, but he wanted to hear the others. So he turned to Lyn, who was from the State Department "Lyn, give us your take on the situation."

"Henry, I have seen this before. This man has a heavy agenda, and like a good magician, he is distracting his people from the bitter medicine they are being administered. I am sure the story will be leaked to the media as to how tough they are being with the Americans, and so on and so forth, with a lot of juicy details. We have to watch to see what 'bitter medicine' they are administering, but I don't think we have to read too much into this." Lyn stopped, obviously having concluded her analysis.

The intercom in the room buzzed. The ambassador picked up, listened, and replied, "Okay, bring it in." The door to the secure room opened, and a secretary brought in an envelope, which had been opened and logged as per the protocol. The ambassador took the envelope and thanked the secretary. He opened the envelope and took out a sheaf of papers on the Pakistan government's letterhead from the Foreign Office, officially conveying to them the relevant portions of the prime minister's speech, telling the ambassador to carry out the instructions of the government. This was already getting worse. It looked like the worst-case scenario described by Mark was at their doorstep. There was nothing new in the papers, so the ambassador decided to conclude the meeting.

As the ambassador settled back in his office, his secretary came dashing in. "Mr. Ambassador, the foreign minister's office has called and requested you to call on him at his office. They have suggested a meeting in four hours' time, if it is convenient." The ambassador looked at the clock on the wall. It was three o'clock in the afternoon, and at seven he was due to have dinner with the British ambassador and his wife. "Call the British ambassador and request a postponement of tonight's dinner. Don't suggest a new date. Then tell my wife I am going to be busy and will be late, and confirm to the Pakistani Foreign Office I will be arriving at 7:00 p.m. to meet the foreign minister."

Washington, DC
As the screen went dead, Mark got off the chair in the conference room and headed to his desk. He prepared a report on developments in Pakistan and the meeting the US ambassador had attempted to have, which was declined. Mark was convinced that the State Department was misreading the situation; his analysis, based on many years of experience, convinced him that the worst was yet to come. Mark sent the report to the DDO, and from there it found its way to the White House in the next morning's briefing by the CIA director.

The president of the United States read the report that he received from the CIA, put it down, and picked up the report from the State Department. Both had different conclusions. The State Department was convinced this was posturing by the Pakistanis. The CIA, on the other hand, was convinced this was not just posturing, but the shape of things to come, and it would get much worse. Ordinarily, the president would not have bothered with a small, developing country on the other side of the world. But Pakistan was different.

Pakistan possessed over a hundred nuclear bombs and was on the way to developing tactical nuclear weapons. Soon they would have a bigger nuclear arsenal than Britain, thought the president Besides, this was a country with a history of three wars and many "to the brink of war" situations in the past two decades, more than any other country in the world. As if that was not enough, Pakistan had become a hotbed of Taliban resistance and a launch pad of attacks on American troops in Afghanistan. Add to that the fact that most of the top al-Qaeda leadership had been either captured or killed inside Pakistan. Then there was China constantly trying to gain access to Central Asia through Pakistan, and trying to build bases in the Arabian Sea with Pakistan's support. This one country had taken more of his time in the past year than the continents of Australia and Africa combined, thought the president. Pakistan was not just a headache, but a head-splitting migraine.

President told the CIA director to continue monitoring the situation through his sources and told his secretary to have the secretary of state come in for a discussion on the State Department's report.

Islamabad: The Prime Minister's Office
Principal Secretary Altaf entered and announced the arrival of
the Afghan for an appointment that had been arranged previously. This time, the Afghan had been stripped of his trademark
Kalashnikov before being ushered into the PM's office. This was
a private meeting, so no cameras, no press coverage, and no assistants were present. Sultan walked from behind his desk and met
the Afghan as he entered the room; the Afghan was all warmth
and charm.

Sultan escorted him to the plush sofas on one side of the room,
and they sat down.

The Afghan started. "Sultan saheb, when you came to see me
the first time, I didn't believe in you, but now I see that you are a
man of your word and a man of vision. I salute you and am happy
to tell you that the gift I gave you need not be returned."

"Dalbadin, I thank you from the bottom of my heart for supporting our cause, and the people of Pakistan will be forever thankful
for your quiet but very powerful behind-the-scenes role in making
our dreams come true. However, as you mentioned, I am a man
of my word, and a deal is a deal." With that, Sultan reached for a
folder that was sitting on the coffee table, opened it, and took out
a check for Pakistani rupees equivalent to US$10 million. This he
handed to the Afghan, who hesitated a little before accepting it.

This was not what the Afghan had expected. He had believed
that the prime minister would happily keep the US$10 million gift.
The Afghan, from his sources, knew that through four years of
planning and campaigning, Sultan's party had collected billions of
rupees in donations and party subscriptions. His sources also told
him that there was bookkeeping for every rupee spent, which gave
the Afghan some comfort. It's a shame, he thought, that Sultan
went into politics. Otherwise, the Afghan would have hired him for
his own multibillion-dollar business empire. With these thoughts
passing through his mind, he stretched out his hand and accepted

the check, which was drawn on the party's main bank account, made out in favor of one of the Afghan's companies, which had officially loaned the money.

Sultan took out a second, larger envelope. "This is the second part of our agreement. A company has been formed, all legal requirements are dealt with, and the company has permission to work as an oil marketing company as promised. This folder contains all the details, which have been translated into your language for convenience. This brings us to the third part of our agreement: ouster of the Americans and their allies from Afghanistan. As you have seen, we have set in motion the chain of events that will ensure that the third part of our agreement to get you in power in Afghanistan is achieved successfully. The general is already working on that and will liaise with you. Last, and the final part, the general is going to meet you tonight to discuss the matter of the daughter of the Muslim Ummah who has been wronged by the Americans. With your help we will remedy that situation, and our deal will be complete."

The Afghan was impressed. Not only did this man have balls, but he was honorable and knew how to deliver on his promises. Maybe he was really an Afghan, thought the Afghan with a silent inward chuckle. His host rose, bringing the meeting to a conclusion. As they shook hands, the prime minister held his hand in a firm grip, looked into the dark eyes of the Afghan, and said, "Dalbadin, do you remember in our second meeting, you threatened to kill my family if things went wrong? Well, my friend, remember never to make a threat like that again toward my family. Ever since that meeting, each and every member of your family has been carefully watched by my people, who would have slit their throats at one signal from me—including your young mistress whom you keep hidden in a bungalow in the Defence area of Karachi, not far from where your wife lives. All of my people have been called back today, and you can check with your household how many servants and handymen have suddenly left them. My friend, learn to know your friends and your enemies." The prime minister opened the door, and the Afghan walked out. The Afghan felt like he had been hit by a truck. He was a hard man. He had buried many relatives who had died violently; he had killed many men with his own hands; but he had never been so off balance. Here was an accountant who had outsmarted him and could have completely destroyed his family without him having any inkling it was coming. He was angry at his own lapse, but he also felt new respect for this man and swore to never again underestimate him.

But he had one more port of call here and was guided to the office of the foreign minister, General Bhaya. The general was expecting him. The Afghan's meeting with the prime minister had lasted exactly thirty minutes. This was already factored into the general's planning, so he was ready.

"Dalbadin, how good of you to come. How did your meeting with the boss go?" asked Bhaya.

"He is a piece of work, your boss, he is. He keeps on surprising me, and I am not easy to surprise. He had put watchers on all my family members, did you know? Just because I had tried to put the fear of God in him lest he tried to con me out of my money."

"I know, Dalbadin. They were my men, every one of them, and they would have done their jobs—you know how our trade is. After thirty years I have found a man who can do the job we have been trying to get done—to start the collapse of the American empire, to have the guts to take the Americans on and stand up against them. He is intelligent, charismatic, and has some vision; people like him don't come around every day. So I have decided to back him. You know that when I back someone I go all the way. I did the same for you, but you came under pressure from your fellow warlords and compromised; otherwise, the Americans would never have had the chance to destroy Afghanistan as they have. But anyway, the time is coming for them to pay the price and you, my friend, need to play your role."

The Afghan relaxed. He knew that the bigger game was afoot, and he also knew instinctively he was going to be asked to pay a price that was never negotiated. This too was not unexpected. To be fair, he had never expected to see a dime of his US$10 million or to walk away with an oil-marketing company. So he waited patiently for the general to lay the trap. He would decide how to play the game.

General Bhaya went on. "We need your help in sending one of your people to meet Alex Karimovo. He is a Chechen and operates out of Miami, and we have a job for him."

The Afghan said, "Are you sure we should be talking here?"

"Yes, this is the most secure room in all of the country. Millions of dollars have been spent on making this room impossible to penetrate or bug; it is even more secure then the PM's office or GHQ."

The Afghan quietly took out a small tape recorder and placed it on the table, pushing the "play" button. The tape played a conversation of the general's that had taken place in that same office on the previous day, with one of his trusted lieutenants. General Bhaya was in a shock. This was totally unexpected; he realized that among the team of foreign contractors he had used to make the room secure, one must have been paid off by the Afghan to place a device that was otherwise undetectable. His shock turned to fury. This was a loss of face he could not tolerate, but there was nothing he could do presently. The Afghan enjoyed the general's discomfort, giving him a little satisfaction for what the general had done by putting his men around his family. He figured they were about even now; this would put the general back in his place, down from his high horse.

The general recovered. "Okay, Dalbadin, we will meet at another time, later tonight. I will set up the meeting, and I thank you for opening my eyes."

"No, General, I will set up the meeting, and will let you know the time and the place." The Afghan rose and left without any farewell.

This was a setback; the Afghan had seized control of the situation and was in the driving seat now. This was not what was planned. Bhaya needed to consult the prime minister. He picked up the direct line with the PM, who picked up the phone and just said, "Yes."

"I need to see you," the general said.

"Okay, come in fifteen minutes" was the brief reply.

The general entered the PM's room. Sultan said, "General, you look worried. When you look worried, there is bad news, so let us have it."

"Our security has been compromised. I had the Afghan in my room a while back, and he gave me a tape recording of a conversation that had taken place in my room in the past twenty-four hours," replied the general.

"Okay, tell me: what conversations have you had that could hurt us?" Sultan asked.

"Well, there is nothing of great significance, I am sure, but I thought you should know," replied the general.

Sultan wasn't too happy with this reply, not when it was coming from the most senior member of his team, who had spent his life in the intelligence business. This was not a very intelligent reply, and when he spoke again, his tone reflected this. It was subtly altered and hardened, which was not lost on the general. "General, I suggest you go back to your office and take two hours off, and jot down every conversation you have had since you occupied that office. You have your appointment diary; that will help you. And I know you have a superb memory. We will meet back here in two hours and decide on what action to take."

Sultan rose, indicating that the meeting was over. "And, General, no more conversations in that room until we figure things out, okay?" This was obviously an insult to put the general in his place. The general let it pass; he decided he had it coming.

Meanwhile, the Afghan had had second thoughts; he decided his latest move of exposing his hand to the general had put him in imminent danger. The Afghan had not survived the Soviets and the Americans by being careless or reckless. He had no intention of meeting the general later in the day or anytime soon; in fact, he was already speed-dialing his son to arrange for his immediate departure from Pakistan. While he talked on the phone, his driver took him to Chaklala Airport in Islamabad, where a private plane was waiting for him. It was a small plane but enough for the job, and it had been hired for the trip. The plane would take the Afghan to Quetta; from there he would travel by road to Iran and take some time off to rethink his own plans.

After two hours the general walked back to the PM's office, having jotted down every conversation he'd had in the past two days. He had been right: there was nothing that was significant. Fortunately, everything he had talked about in the past few days had come to pass and was covered by the world media already. All the planning and execution for recent actions had been done long before they had gotten into the PM's secretariat. The only breach was the name of the American gangster, Alex, and the meeting in Miami, but there too he had been fortunate that the Afghan had stopped him just in time.

He entered the prime minister's office. Sultan had been waiting for him, and he quickly briefed his boss about all his conversations.

"Okay, so that leaves only the issue of the gangster in Miami and the reference to the United States. All right, this is manageable. Cancel the gangster off the list; don't talk to him or use him now or in future. Move to the second choice on the list. As for the Afghan, you need not worry about meeting him. Our friend has taken off for Quetta and will head to Iran from there. My guess is, he is going to lie low and figure things out for now, but if he does not come back with complete cooperation and submission, then we will have to assume the worst and take remedial action. But for now, we wait and watch."

The general did not believe in waiting and watching. "I think we should move now, while he is still within our reach, and have his plane shot down by one of our friends in the Baluch National Army. Better to cut our losses now."

"No, General, let us not. The Afghan has nowhere to run. He does not have enough information to be useful to the Americans, and the Afghan government would sooner have his head on a platter. Our friend does not have many options; he will either stay out of circulation or come back to us. Get some of your friends to keep an eye on him while he is sojourning in Iran."

Sultan rose and walked the general to the door. "Let us meet for a game of golf later in the evening," he offered. The general knew that this was for their off-site meeting and discussions about the project that needed to be launched immediately.

The White House—The Oval Office

Mark was surprised when he got a call from his boss to come up to the director's office. As soon as he arrived, the director emerged and asked Mark to follow him. In the elevator the director said, "Mark, the president wants a briefing on Pakistan. I want you to come along. In the meeting, sit behind me, and I will ask you if I need any information. Otherwise, pretend you do not exist. Got that?"

"Yes, sir," replied Mark.

They got in the director's car and headed to the White House.

Mark and the director arrived at the West Wing and entered the cabinet room adjoining the Oval Office. Mark looked around the room and noticed the national security advisor, David Balham, the defense secretary, Matt Clapton, and the secretary of state, Thelma Louise, had already taken seats. His boss took a seat next to David Balham, and Mark sat behind him, pretending not to exist. Shortly afterward, the president of the United States walked into the room. This was a double first for Mark; he had never before been in the White House, and never before in the presence of the president.

The CIA director started the briefing and brought the team up to speed on developments in Pakistan in the past twenty-four hours—a country that had gone from being a close ally to possibly becoming the biggest terrorist threat to the United States. When he had finished briefing the president, including all the details of the experience the ambassador and his team had shared, the president spoke.

His question was directed at the secretary of state. "Thelma, give us your take on the situation."

"Mr. President, I agree with our team's analysis. We are fast moving toward an Iran-like situation, and we must take measures to contain it."

The secretary of defense decided he could no longer contain himself. "Mr. President, if these people, the Pakis, go through—"

He was interrupted by the president. "Let us not get down to name calling, okay, Matt?"

Thus rebuked and chastised, the SecDef continued, "I am sorry, Mr. President, but we have given these people more than twelve billion dollars in the past decade, and we have committed another fifteen billion in the next ten years. And all we get is some jackass threatening to cut off our supply lines to our forces in Afghanistan. I have discussed this with the service chiefs, and they concur that we should be ready to show some serious muscle to the Pakistanis if they try to carry out their so-called reforms against us. We simply cannot let them cut off our supply lines and allow them to dictate to us, and we must not allow them to encroach on our global strategic interests." The SecDef paused, picked up a tissue, and wiped away the sweat that had appeared on his forehead.

The president understood his emotions; there were tens of thousands of American and allied soldiers at risk here, not to mention the long-term strategic and geopolitical interests of his country.

But the president was not about to start another war, not with an economy that had defied all measures to revive it, and at a time when his own government had faced shutdown because of lack of agreement between Democrats and Republicans on various budget issues. "I agree the situation is very delicate, and therefore we will be monitoring it very closely. If anything develops, I want to know immediately. In the meantime, our first step is going to be to send our ambassador to see the foreign minister and let him know in plain English that we will not be held to ransom. I also want a contingency plan prepared with all options on the table, within the next twenty-four hours. Thelma, would you please take charge of that?"

"Yes, Mr. President" replied the secretary of state.

The president got up, bringing the meeting to an end.

So this is it, thought Mark: this is how the great United States of America is being run! Feeling a bit let down, Mark followed his boss out.

Islamabad—Foreign Minister's Office

The American ambassador arrived at exactly 7:00 p.m. and, much to his relief, was escorted to the foreign minister's office without much ado. General Bhaya was waiting behind his desk but did not come around to shake hands or show any kind of warmth or politeness. Almost as soon as the ambassador's trouser seat made contact with the chair, the general fired away.

"Mr. Ambassador, I have called you here to discuss the incident earlier today when you barged in demanding to see the prime minister, and in the course of the meeting made threats and were rude and obnoxious to senior members of our government. This is unbecoming of a diplomat, and I would like to remind you, sir, this is an independent country, and you are our honored guest here. We will not tolerate behavior as if you were our masters. And as for meeting the prime minister, that is out of the question for now. We are putting together a schedule for the prime minister, but let me advise you, shaking hands with diplomats and having pictures taken with them is somewhere close to the bottom of the PM's list, so don't hold your breath. If you have any issues you need to discuss with the government of Pakistan, then please take them up with the foreign secretary. And, Mr. Ambassador, do make an appointment to see him; don't just barge in. We are not your colony."

"Mr. Foreign Minister," the ambassador started, barely able to contain his anger, "our countries have enjoyed a mutually beneficial relationship for six decades. We see Pakistan as an important ally; we are your biggest donor country and trading partner. Our relationship transcends governments and individuals. We would like to understand, first hand, by meeting the prime minister, what concerns and thoughts are behind his recent statements and the speech he made. We fully understand that as a new prime minister he needs to win public support, so playing to the galleries is quite acceptable, but we would like to be assured that Pakistan's commitment to our friendship and cooperation in the war on terror remains unwavering."

"Mr. Ambassador," the general said, "let me remind you of a foreign policy maxim of your government, one which we have been at the receiving end of many times: 'There are no permanent friends, only permanent interests.' We are carrying out a review of all our policies, especially our foreign policy, and our Foreign Office will keep you informed of our position. Thank you, Mr. Ambassador, for coming on such a short notice." The door to the minister's office opened, and his secretary walked in, a clear indication for the ambassador to leave.

The ambassador rose slowly. "And, Mr. Ambassador, the speech the prime minister made and the statements that have been issued are neither rhetoric nor playing to the galleries. These are well-thought-out pointers of the policies we are going to follow. Have a good evening, sir."

As the ambassador got into his car, he dialed the cell number of the chief of Pakistan's army, simply known as the chief, but the number was giving a busy tone, so he dialed the chief's home number. The chief's secretary answered the phone on the first ring and greeted the ambassador. "Good evening, Mr. Ambassador."

"Good evening, I would like to speak to the chief, please."

"Mr. Ambassador, we have received instructions from the chief's office to direct all calls from outside the military, including those from diplomats, through ISPR, Inter-Services Public Relations." Without bothering to reply, the ambassador ended the call. It seemed like things were changing at a very rapid pace, and his people had been caught napping again.

The ambassador asked the driver to take him to the embassy; this was going to be a long evening. When he arrived at the embassy, his secretary was ready and waiting. He asked her to fix him a double scotch on the rocks and moved to his desk to send an update to Washington. He signed a detailed dispatch and sent it to the State Department.

He knew that sooner or later he would get a call from the State Department, so there was no point in going home. He rose from his desk and settled on the plush sofa across the room, turning on CNN. His secretary came in and, without asking or being told, moved behind him, loosened his tie, and started giving him a shoulder and neck massage. Soon the ambassador started feeling relaxed from the combined effect of alcohol and massage, and before he realized it, he was snoozing. The secretary quietly left the room and went back to her desk.

The White House—The Oval Office

"Mr. President, the secretary of state is here," announced his chief of staff.

"Show her in," replied the president.

"Mr. President, we have just received another cable from our ambassador in Pakistan, after he met the foreign minister there."

"Sit down, Thelma; catch your breath and let me see the cable." This was unusual, but the secretary of state understood. The president wanted to feel the emotions in the ambassador's dispatch and wanted to develop his own assessment. This was part of his training as a lawyer, and the team working with him was used to it by now. She handed him the cable from Pakistan. The president read it very fast but did not take his eyes off the cable. He was analyzing it, every word and syllable. "Okay, Thelma, tell me what you make of it."

"Mr. President, the fact that the army chief didn't take our ambassador's call and our ambassador was given the message by a telephone operator clearly indicates that the ground situation in Pakistan has significantly changed. We are fast running out of friends in that country."

The president said nothing. Instead, he pressed the button on the intercom to call his secretary and told her to ask the CIA chief, the SecDef, and the NSA to join him in the White House ASAP. While Thelma waited, the president continued with another meeting.

Within the hour, the others arrived. As soon as they were all seated, the secretary of state briefed them on the latest developments, which were no news to any of them. They all had heard from their own sources what had happened in Pakistan and were up to speed on it.

The president walked in and took the seat at the head of the table. "Now, tell me your assessment and recommendations. Thelma, you first," he said.

"Mr. President, this reaffirms what we concluded this morning. Our view remains that Pakistan is fast moving toward a situation like Iran in 1979, and we must be prepared for all eventualities."

The others nodded their heads in agreement, thus making it redundant for the president to ask anyone else. "It seems like you all are in agreement," he said. "Okay, do you have any initial recommendations?"

"Yes, sir," the secretary of state answered. "We should delay shipment of spare parts for the fighter jets, which are due any day now, hold the disbursement of any further funds under various aid programs, and tell IMF, World Bank, ADB, Japan, Saudi Arabia, and the Islamic Bank to delay any and all disbursements to Pakistan and not to roll over any loans. We will do the same with all the commercial banks who have lent money to Pakistan or Pakistani corporations. We will get credit rating agencies to start downgrading Pakistan's ratings and tell our friends in multinational companies as well as in the mutual fund industry to start pulling their investments out, to freeze existing investments, and to spread the good word. Next, we will get the Department of Trade to speak to key people in the industry to delay payments for exports, cancel all pending orders, and freeze all future orders. We will follow up the same measures through Europe and other friendly nations."

The secretary of state paused for breath, ending her narrative of measures. She knew that all these were pretty standard prescriptions and usually took about forty-eight hours to put into effect. She had already called a meeting in her department to deal with it as soon as this meeting was over.

"Okay, Thelma, let's start increasing the pressure. We are not going to sit idly by and watch them make a mockery of us," replied the president.

Next, the president turned to CIA director John Deskovanci. "John, what do you have for us?"

"Well, Mr. President, we can launch a project in India that will preoccupy the Pakistanis for a while," replied the CIA director. He knew that the president would not want to know the details, nor could he be allowed to. The project would be to carry out a terrorist strike inside New Delhi, the Indian capital, targeting the ruling family, who were like royalty in India. A group of Pakistani Taliban would be used for this purpose. All evidence would lead to the planning having been done inside the tribal area of Pakistan, and the people carrying out the attacks would be Pakistanis who had fought in Kashmir against India, or those fighting American forces inside Afghanistan. They would be on a mission that they would believe was sanctioned and organized by their own umbrella organization, TTP (Tehrik-e-Taliban Pakistan), and al-Qaeda. The end result would be increasing tensions between the two countries, and if need be, they would escalate these tensions into a limited war between the two archrivals.

"Okay, John, prepare for it, but do not launch anything until we have crossed a red line. I will tell you when that red line is crossed."

It was now the turn of SecDef Matt Clapton; the president merely nodded to him. "Mr. President, we are working on the assumption that our supply lines will be compromised, and are coming up with scenarios on how to minimize the damage. We propose that the State Department accelerates the pace of dialogue with the Taliban inside Afghanistan, so we can move quickly toward reducing hostility there and minimize our risks. We also suggest we engage Iran by lessening pressure and sanctions on them, as quid pro quo to shift our logistics through that country."

"Thelma, what is the State Department's position on reducing pressure on Iran?" The president turned to the secretary of state.

"Mr. President, despite our sanctions and other harsh measures, we have not succeeded in checking Iran's progress on their nuclear program, though it is very slow. Therefore, it makes sense to go with SecDef's recommendation to minimize the risk and danger to our forces in Afghanistan—which may be caused by the logistics crisis created by Pakistan—by giving some concessions to Iran."

The president nodded. "Okay, people, let's do it. We will go with all the recommendations we have discussed in this meeting, and I want to be informed if anything—and I mean anything—further develops. Thank you all."

A Golf Course in Margalla Hills, Outside Islamabad

General Bhaya was waiting for Sultan at the golf course. The temperature was coming down from the one hundred degrees it had been during the afternoon. It was nicer in the hills, which were thick with the pine trees. The golf course had been developed by one of the former presidents, who was also a military general with great love for golf. It had lights so the elite could enjoy a round even after dark, while the majority of the country had no electricity. However, tonight's meeting was not about golf. The lights had not been turned on, except those in the clubhouse and along the paths. This area was only accessible to senior military officers and the elite in the civilian government; it was one of the places where foreigners were not encouraged. Thus, if there was any eavesdropping, then it would be done by their fellow countrymen. However, the general had taken precautions; because he knew what they would discuss tonight could never be allowed to come out.

Sultan arrived, escorted by just two vehicles—one in front and one at the back. This was a great departure from the security previous heads of the government had enjoyed and demanded. They had usually traveled in convoys of a hundred vehicles, blocking traffic for hours at a time. Most Pakistani politicians thrived on protocol; give them no power but all the protocol, and they were happy. But this man was different. He did not want elaborate protocol, but simply to serve his country. This is why the general had committed himself completely to making his mission a success, and he knew he had risked everything.

Sultan disembarked from his car. They shook hands and walked down the path that led into the golf course. They walked for five minutes, till they got to a part of the golf course that the general had made sure was swept clean of listening devices.

Sultan began, "General, what happened today with the Afghan was an unmitigated disaster. If that old man panics, he can do serious harm to our plans. We must be ready to give him a warm send-off like the late Ahmad Shah Masood, the lion of Panjsher, if it becomes necessary."

The general remembered how Masood, a veteran Russian-Afghan war commander, had been blown to pieces by a suicide bomber pretending to be a press cameraman. The general just nodded; it was enough.

Sultan continued, "Move to the number-two guy on your list for the snatch, and use one of other Afghan groups to set it up. And use Russians, not Chechens or any other Muslim group. On June 5, Dr. Aafia is going to be brought to the court for her appeal hearing. This is when we have to execute the plan. You have everything planned to the last detail; you just need some mercenaries to carry out the task, so let's get to it. From now on you handle all the details. I will be eagerly watching CNN to learn of success of our mission."

The Great Escape
General Bhaya's Office
After finishing the meeting with the Sultan, General Bhaya drove back to his office inside the PM's secretariat. This was a departure from the past, when the foreign minister sat in his own office inside the Foreign Ministry. But Sultan had decided that all his cabinet ministers should be available within walking distance, so each minister had been given an office inside the secretariat with some staff.

General Bhaya opened his safe and took out the file marked Teams, which consisted of three folders. This contained complete details of three different teams the general had identified and investigated over the past twelve months. The first choice, the Chechen team, was no longer an option because of the unpredictable behavior of the Afghan and the possible breach of security. So the general put the Chechen gang's file through the paper shredder.

There were two more folders. One was of a Russian gang that was active in the New York area, and the other was that of a Puerto Rican gang operating in Miami. The Russian gang leader was a former KGB officer who had fallen on hard times after the breakup of the Soviet Union, and after trying the honest and straight path for a few years, eventually had decided to make his way to the United States and start his own criminal gang. Some of the gang members were from Russia's elite commando services and had, like their gang leader, drifted into the gang over the years.

The general picked up the phone and called Amir. While the phone rang and the general waited, his thoughts returned to events that had transpired some six years ago.

━✦ ✦━

General Bhaya and recently retired Major Amir, along with their respective wives, had traveled to Mecca for pilgrimage, or Umra.

Amir had called his daughters after the pilgrimage to the holy mosque, and his younger daughter burst out in sobs. At first Amir thought that the daughters were missing him, but his older daughter immediately took the phone from her sister and told Amir not to worry, that the head cleric had told them everything would be fine. She asked him to pray for them and quickly got off the phone.

Amir had lived a tough life. He had killed Russians with his bare hands during the Russia-Afghan war; he had taken part in numerous military campaigns and had never been afraid; his wife knew that. But now, as he put the phone down, his hand was shaking, and the color was drained from his face. He checked the time. It was close to midnight in Pakistan, so he could not call anyone there at this late hour. The general saw Amir's face and instinctively knew something was wrong.

After morning prayers they found a Pakistani restaurant and got the owner to turn on the TV. It was the morning of the ninth of July. The seminary where his daughters were studying was surrounded by commandos of the Pakistani army. In total panic, Amir rushed out of the restaurant, forgetting his wife and the general's family. His wife dashed after him; she too was in total panic. Amir stopped a cab and asked to be taken to his hotel, still oblivious to his wife, who managed to jump into the cab. It took less than five minutes for the cab to drop them at their hotel. Amir asked the cab driver to wait and negotiated with him to take them to Jeddah Airport. Amir, followed by his distraught and tearful wife, ran upstairs, picked up his bag, and quickly packed. His wife did the same. Within a few minutes, they went to the checkout counter and settled their bill. Amir still had not said a word to his wife.

The general knew that Amir's daughters were studying at the seminary and, sensing the gravity of the situation, he too followed Amir in a separate cab to the hotel. The general called the hotel and asked them to pack his bags and check them out. His next call was to a Saudi prince who owed the general more than one favor. The prince agreed to the general's request and called Jeddah airport to give instructions. By the time the general and his wife got to the hotel, Amir and his wife had just gotten back into the cab and rushed off. The general and his wife followed Amir and his wife in another taxi, and arrived at the airport a few minutes behind them.

General Bhaya paid ten Saudi riyals to a porter to run after Amir and bring him over. The porter grabbed Amir by his sleeve and pointed him in the general's direction. Amir stopped for the general to catch up to him. "Amir, I have arranged transport to Pakistan; come with me."

Amir followed the general without a word. As they approached an NAS Airlines counter, a man in a Saudi military uniform was waiting at the counter. He saluted when he saw General Bhaya. The general returned the salute and extended his hand in greeting. "General, I am Major Saud, and I will escort you to your transport, sir."

General Bhaya nodded and followed the major, with Amir and his wife in tow. Once on the plane, the general spoke. "Amir, I have spoken to Shaujaat, and he assures me that there will be no military operation against the seminary. The preparations are to show the militants that the military is serious, and General Musharraf wants to portray an image of strength. Shaujaat has promised me that he will get some people to try to look for your daughters and bring them, as well as all the other children, out peacefully. I have talked to some friends in the army, too, and they are saying the same thing."

As soon as the plane landed at Islamabad Airport, Amir ran through the airport, through immigration and customs, waving his old army credentials. He tossed his passport to an immigration officer. "Do your entry; I will get the passport later." The officer knew Amir, so he waved him through.

Amir grabbed hold of the first taxi, gave the driver a thousand-rupee note, approximately twelve US dollars, which was four times the normal fare, and screamed, "Take me to Red Mosque."

Once in the cab, Amir asked the driver, "What news of Red Mosque?"

"Shaujaat and the others are going in for another round of talks. That is what the TV reported two hours ago," the driver replied.

At another time, Amir would have marveled at the beautiful lush green Margalla Mountains surrounding Islamabad. But today the scenery didn't exist for him; it was like he was traveling through a dark tunnel. The cab ride from the airport to the Blue Zone in Islamabad took twenty minutes. As they arrived at the barricade, which was set a kilometer before the Red Mosque, they were stopped by army soldiers.

Amir sprinted toward the mosque. As he approached, the army started shelling the mosque with phosphorus bombs; "Operation Sunrise" had started.

Amir arrived at the second barrier and was grabbed by two powerfully built soldiers. "Oye, you can't go in there! Are you blind?" said one of the soldiers sharply. "Can you not see the terrorists are in there, and the army is going in?"

Without thinking Amir kicked the soldier in the groin, broke free, and punched another soldier in the face. A third soldier lifted his rifle butt and smashed it into Amir's head. Amir was unconscious before he hit the ground.

By the time the general got there, the soldiers were dragging Amir's unconscious body to the side of the road. The general screamed profanities at the soldiers. By now, the captain in charge of the barricade had arrived and recognized General Bhaya. "Sir, who is this man? Do you know him?" the captain asked.

"He is with me, God damn you, and his daughters are in the seminary," the general replied, tears running down his cheeks.

The captain ordered the soldiers to lift Amir up and put him in an ambulance on the other side of the first barricade. Then he took the general gently by the shoulder and guided him toward the ambulance.

As General Bhaya reached the ambulance and turned around, he could see that the whole seminary was on fire. He knew no one could survive that. He didn't know what he was going to tell Amir, but he got in the ambulance and was driven to PIMS—Pakistan Institute of Medical Sciences.

Amir was unconscious for twelve hours, and when he came to the general was at his side. Amir could barely speak, but he managed to ask, "Sir, my daughters?"

Before the general could answer, Amir heard a sob from the other side of the bed. It was his brother-in-law, quietly weeping. His wife wasn't there. Confused, Amir looked back at the general, who was choking back his own tears. The general said, "Amir, your daughters are with God now. Please forgive me; I could not save them."

A shriek, as if a thousand animals were having their limbs torn apart and screaming in unison, rose from Amir's guts through his lips and echoed across the hospital. The nurses in the operating theater dropped their instruments at the sound, not knowing what it was. It didn't sound human. Amir felt as if knives had been driven into every part of his body; he felt like his heart was exploding with pain and his mind was in an agony that had no words to describe it. He kept on screaming and screaming until a doctor summoned up the courage to give him a heavy dose of sedation and quickly left the room.

Amir's wife, on hearing the news of both daughters' deaths, had lost her mind. She was taken back to her parents' village.

Amir got out of the hospital after a week, his head still bandaged. He was taken from there to the general's home. As he entered the house, General Bhaya was waiting for him. "Amir, nothing can replace the loss you have suffered, but this was an operation approved by the American lackey General Musharraf. Even though his own ministers were against it, Musharraf wanted to show the Americans that he is their strong man in Pakistan, and they must help him to stay in power. He sacrificed thousands of lives; we are told that as many as 2,300 people died in that operation. We must all work together to make sure this tragedy is never repeated."

"General, I am going to leave this afternoon. I need to be on my own." Amir walked away. His luggage from Saudi Arabia was still packed and sitting in the guest room, which was set up for him. He took out a few things, put them in a small backpack, and left from a back door that was used by the domestic staff.

That was six years ago. But now Amir was in New York waiting for the general's call.

Three days before the elections, Amir was told to proceed to the United States and await further instructions.

Amir had taken up residence in the Jamaica district near JFK International Airport in New York. He had an old school friend, Riaz, who worked for the airport cleaning service and had helped Amir in finding the accommodation and settling down. Amir had told him that he had received his green card, and his family was soon to join him. This was, of course, his cover story—and far from the truth.

It was three o'clock in the afternoon. Amir was in his apartment, lying on the bed, reading a book he had picked up from the library on Riaz's card. The book was about the life story of Che Guevara.

Amir's Blackberry flashed, showing an incoming call. The number was not showing, meaning that the caller was scrambling the call and the ID had been blocked. Well aware that the call would be monitored by a host of international agencies, Amir pressed the "receive" key and put the phone to his ear.

"*Salam walaikum, Moaalim,*" said Amir.

"How are you, *bacha?*" asked General Bhaya.

"Ready and waiting, sir," replied Amir.

"Okay, your wait is over. I have sent you the file for recruitment of staff for the new company. Proceed. Time is of the essence. Call me back with your progress."

Amir left his home and walked ten minutes to Jamaica station, where he got on the train headed for downtown. He got off at Times Square and made his way to a public library, which he had identified well in advance as one of the places where he could use the Internet. He went to an empty desk with Internet and logged on to his email account. This account was especially set up for this purpose, and was only to be used once. After today's use he would delete the account and all the information on it. No doubt the information would remain hidden somewhere in cyberspace, but it would make the process of recovery and discovery a little bit slower. His account had one new email. He opened it and printed the Word file attached to the email. As soon as printing was complete, he deleted the email and the email account, collected his printout and walked toward the port area, where he sat on a bench watching seagulls flying around in search of food and opened the papers he had just printed.

He went through the printout, which was a biography of the person he was supposed to hire for the assignment. The general had said this was code "RED," which meant immediate implementation. The biography included a contact number. Amir took out his disposable cell phone and dialed the number. A man answered. Amir could not place the accent, but it was neither American nor

Hispanic, so he figured it was probably some sort of European accent, probably Russian.

The man on the other end of the phone asked him to call back after a short while. Amir waited for thirty minutes and called back. The man, who had not volunteered a name, simply said to call again and ended the call. This happened three times. On the fourth call, Amir was given an address and the call ended.

Amir headed to Long Island, where the Russian was based. It took him over an hour and half to get there; he had to be sure he was not followed, so he had to double back a few times on the subway to make sure he had not grown any tails. As far as he could judge, he had no tails, so he proceeded to the nightclub where the Russian was at this time of day. The working day was ending, and people were heading to bars to get a drink before heading home. The nightclubs were still deserted, even though some of them offered "happy hours." Amir arrived at the nightclub and went straight in the front door. He was dressed like any ordinary American, wearing jeans, a T-shirt, Converse shoes, and a backpack. He had burned the printout and thrown the ashes in the water after memorizing all the details.

Amir went to the bartender and offered him a hundred-dollar bill. The man started to pocket it, but stopped when Amir said, "I want to meet Yuri." Instead, he put the note on the table and simply asked, "What's your drink?"

Amir replied, "Give me an orange juice."

The bartender poured an orange juice and returned the change from the hundred dollars without another word. Amir knew how the game was played, so he took his orange juice to a table in the far corner, making sure his table was against the wall. The bar was out of his clear line of sight on his right, but that was not a problem; there were enough mirrors in this place for anyone to get a 360-degree view. Thus seated, Amir waited.

After five minutes or so, two men, obviously bodyguards, entered the club from a side door and approached his table. "Come with us," said one of the muscle men in gruff, heavily accented English. Amir rose and walked quietly between the two of them. They headed to the same door where they had come from. Once through the door, they grabbed Amir and thoroughly frisked him, making sure he had no weapons and was not wearing a wire.

They led him downstairs to the basement and through a tunnel into another basement. After exiting the second basement, they came to a lift and entered it. The doors slid shut. There were no buttons; one of the escorts took an ID card out of his pocket and flashed it in front of a black pad. The cards were programmed to give access only to certain designated areas. The lift was equipped with a secret chamber that could release lethal gas and kill a person in a few minutes, or completely disable him, depending on the need of the hour. It was possible to get into the lift by pressing a button from outside, but no way to get out of it.

The lift doors opened. Amir had no clue what floor they were on—not that it mattered, because if his hosts decided that he was not to leave here, then that would be that and pretty much the end of the road for Amir. They entered a room that was furnished like an executive office: a big mahogany desk set against the wall with a chair behind it, two visitors' chairs, a sofa set, and a coffee table on one side. One wall was covered by a bookshelf. The curtains were open, and Amir could see he was on the first floor of a house. The office was located at the back of the house, so the view he got was of the backyard. It was decorated like a Victorian lawyer's office in London, but the man occupying the chair behind the table was no Victorian lawyer in London—he was the gangster Yuri, and was reputed to have killed dozens of men. No one had crossed Yuri and lived to tell about it. On each side of Yuri was a heavyset man, both clearly carrying weapons under their suit jackets.

"I am going to take an envelope and put it on the table," Amir announced. The hands of all four bodyguards, two on each side of Yuri and the two who had escorted Amir, reached for their guns. Amir slowly opened his jacket, and very slowly and deliberately took out an envelope. Keeping it in full view of the armed men, he opened the envelope and took out ten thousand dollars, which he placed on the table in front of Yuri. The tension in the room eased, but no one said anything or made any move.

"Mr. Yuri, my name is Zareen Khan, and I have a business proposition for you. My people will pay you one million dollars for a job."

"And what is this fantastic job you bring for me?" asked Yuri.

"We want a prisoner freed from the Americans' custody," said Amir. "May I use your computer?"

Yuri gave a slight nod. Amir moved to the desk, and the bodyguards tensed, their hands twitching around their guns. He pulled the laptop toward him, took a flash drive from his trouser pocket, and inserted it in the computer's USB port. He had noticed that the laptop had a cable that connected it to an overhead projector; he found the remote for the projector on the desk, picked it up, and turned it on. He asked one of the guards to close the curtains. On Yuri's nod, the guard closed them and quickly resumed his defensive position.

The computer was turned on, and Amir opened the files on the USB. The first thing to appear on the screen was a picture of a woman—Dr. Aafia Siddiqui, in her robes when she had received her degree from MIT. Amir pressed on. "This is the woman we want to free from the Americans' custody." He paused and waited for the Russian gang leader to say something, but the Russian didn't say anything, didn't even move a muscle. So Amir continued, "In seven days she will be brought to a court in New York. This is where we want you to snatch her from and deliver her to our men."

Finally the Russian spoke. "And what makes you think that, even if I agreed, this job could be pulled off in one week?"

The fish was nibbling at the bait—always a good sign, thought Amir, but he didn't show any emotions lest he offend the Russian. "We have every aspect of the escape planned. We need you to provide us with the team to carry it out."

"And who is this 'we' you speak of? Or perhaps you think of yourself as 'we,'" the Russian said with some scorn.

Amir let the insult pass. "Mr. Yuri, I am from Afghanistan, and I represent Mohammad Dayaf, who is a commander of the faithful based in the Herat province of Afghanistan."

This was, of course, a lie, though Commander Dayaf existed, and he did operate from Herat province. But the Russian had no way of verifying if Amir did indeed represent Dayaf. Amir had read the Russian's dossier and knew that in his young days at the KGB, the Russian had served in Kabul, so he knew some basics about Afghan commanders, but just basics. This was the cover story the general had told him to use.

"Why don't you just hire anyone from the streets in Harlem? There are thousands of boys who will do this job for thousands of dollars. Why are you offering a million dollars?" the Russian asked.

"Mr. Yuri, we want a professional team. Most important, we want you to lead the team. That is what the million dollars is for."

The Russian was facing a bit of financial crunch. He had expanded into new territories and was incurring losses; he needed cash to buy more product and to move it faster. Without that he was as good as dead, so this could be the chance that propelled him to his goal of getting a much bigger share of the local market. But a million dollars was simply not enough.

"Mr. Khan—and I know this is not your real name—if I agree to this job then the fee will be ten million dollars, nothing less. I suppose you now have to run back to your bosses and get a reply?"

Amir knew he had the fish hooked; he just had to be careful to reel it in. One wrong shake of the hand and the fish can break free, so he let this insult also pass. He had not been given any budget; he knew whatever he decided, the general would back him, and this was no time to show weakness or lack of authority. "Mr. Yuri, our final offer—and it is not negotiable—is five million dollars."

This was pretty close to what the Russian had in mind, but he didn't show it. "I want 50 percent payment in advance," said Yuri.

"Mr. Yuri, we will pay you one million dollars before and four million dollars after the job is done."

"Nothing doing, Mr. Khan. It's 50 percent before and 50 percent after the job is done."

"Mr. Yuri, the best I can offer is one million dollars now, one and half million dollars before the job starts, and 50 percent after the job is done, when you hand over the package."

"Okay, Mr. Khan, you have yourself a deal." They shook hands, and Amir turned to leave. "Where do you think you are going, Mr. Khan?"

Amir tensed and paused, then turned back and faced the Russian. "I thought we had made the deal," said Amir, a bit off guard.

"Yes, we have made a deal, Mr. Khan, and you promised to pay one million dollars now. So now is here, and I am waiting for my million dollars."

Amir stared back, looking into the dead eyes of the Russian, fully aware that any wrong move would end his life. He calmly said, "Give me your account number; I will have the money transferred right now."

The Russian handed Amir a card on which a seventeen-digit account number was written, with the name of the bank and the SWIFT code. Amir took out his cell phone and dialed the general's number. It was quite late in Islamabad, but he really had no choice.

Much to Amir's surprise, the general answered on the first ring, and even further surprising him, asked straight away for the account number, which Amir gave. The general said the money would be transferred within the next hour, and much to Amir's astonishment, the Russian received the confirmation within the hour that the money had been received. This considerably warmed the Russian toward Amir, who received a bear hug from his new-found friend.

Amir and Yuri sat down together, and Amir took the Russian through all the details of the plan. Yuri interjected with questions from time to time and made suggestions. Amir could see he was dealing with a true professional who didn't miss any tricks. Amir gave Yuri the list of equipment and things needed. The Russian scanned the list and stopped when he came to a certain item. He looked up and met Amir's eyes.

"You know this is a very difficult item to get hold of," the Russian said.

"Yes, Yuri; this is why we have chosen you, because we know that you have had access to these materials in the past and surely have some put away for just such a deal," replied Amir. The Russian just smiled.

They agreed that they would meet in three days to finalize the plans. Amir was given a phone number he was to call in three days' time for the location of the meeting.

It was almost 9:00 p.m., and Amir decided it was time to catch a flight to Houston, where his next meeting was to be. Besides, Amir did not want to go back to his apartment, knowing full well that the Russians would be following him. He headed to JFK and bought a ticket with cash. The flight was due in two hours, so he decided to get something to eat. As he was walking toward the restaurants, he saw two Russians wearing well-tailored suits approaching the ticket counter where he had purchased his ticket. Well, let them know—Amir knew they would not follow him outside New

York; it was too risky for them. Their turf was local, and they didn't yet have a network to put a tail on him in Houston.

Amir approached a Subway counter, ordered himself a veggie sandwich, and sat down to consume it. After finishing the sandwich, he went to a phone and called a number that had just been activated in the Pakistan Consulate in New York.

Amir told the duty officer, "The Ramadan moon has been sighted."

This was the code for Amir to let the general know that the snatch team had been successfully recruited.

The duty officer had instructions to pass on any message that came on this special line instantly to his counterpart in Islamabad, which he faithfully and immediately did.

That done, Amir went through security to the flight departure gate, and sat down to wait for his flight's boarding call.

Houston
Amir arrived at the George Bush Intercontinental Airport at 2:30 a.m. local time, and decided to check into a local motel, because he wasn't likely to make contact with his party till afternoon. Amir took a taxi from the airport to a nearby Days Inn motel, where he produced his fake American driver's license and got a room for one day, paying cash in advance.

He settled down in his room and decided to sleep for a few hours, but before that he said his *fajr* (early morning) prayers on a traveling mat he always carried in his backpack, using the compass built into his watch to determine the direction of Mecca.

When he woke up, it was noon. He rose, quickly showered, and decided to offer his afternoon and evening prayers combined (a practice that traveling Muslims are allowed) so as not to miss them. He then checked out of the hotel and took a taxi to an address that was in the south of the city. The taxi dropped him on a street that had a few garages and some other shops. This was the run-down part of the city, and mostly populated by Hispanics of one kind or another. The area was considered very dangerous for outsiders and a no-go area after dark, though none of that worried Amir. He had survived the Russians and the Americans in Afghanistan; he had survived in Chechnya, and he had survived the militants in his own native town in Swat Pakistan. Death didn't frighten him— capture did, and he had vowed never to be captured alive.

He recognized the garage he was looking for, tucked away in the darker, dingier part of the street. He slowly walked toward it, mindful of unseen eyes watching him and shadows in the dark recesses around him, ready to pounce, like some creatures of the dark. But they were just kids, Hispanic kids, very dangerous kids who were paid by gangs to keep watch.

Amir's host knew as soon as Amir had disembarked from the taxi; the taxi driver was only too happy to drop him and rush out of this area, knowing full well the dark reputation of this neighborhood. Once Amir entered the garage, he looked for the office. While his eyes were still searching, he caught sight of a kid in his late teens wearing mechanic's overalls, who raised his eyebrows and tilted his head upward. Amir realized he had to find stairs and head up, which he did. As he climbed the iron stairs, he came upon an office. In the reception area of the office, there was a water cooler, a clock machine that could stamp the time on workers' cards, a rundown PC that didn't look like it had been used in a while, and no receptionist.

Amir cautiously walked through and knocked on the inside door. After the third knock, he tried the door handle, which turned. The door opened on the inside, and he found himself standing in the doorway of another office. Behind the desk sat a balding Hispanic man with an overgrown moustache, wearing just a vest and baggy trousers. Amir decided he had wandered into a mechanic's shop, and these were not the kind of people he was looking for. The man behind the desk was clearly some overweight, undereducated bookkeeper. While he was still toying with the idea of walking out, he heard, "So, what business brings you to this neighborhood? Are you part of the same Afghan gang that has been making enquiries about my business? Either way, you must have a very good reason to be here—that is, if you have any wish of leaving alive."

The voice that had addressed Amir was quite well educated and cultured, with only a slight touch of foreign accent. Apart from the culture in the tone, Amir also detected a note that convinced him that the man in front of him, apart from being very deceptive in his appearance, could prove to be very dangerous. Amir, having initially misjudged the situation, was fully on guard now.

"My name is Aafreen Khan, and I am looking for Carlos," said Amir.

"And what business do you have with Carlos?" the Mexican asked.

"That I can only tell Carlos," Amir replied with a poker face, but deep inside he was not so confident.

"So tell Carlos," the Mexican said, and just looked at Amir.

Once again Amir was caught off guard. This man in shabby clothes with the appearance of a bookkeeper fallen on hard times appeared to be Carlos, the man who was one of the fastest-rising stars in the world of human smuggling. His name had been dug up by General Bhaya's contacts in Pakistan's human-smuggling underworld. The general had been told that there was no better and more daring man than Carlos in the business.

Carlos, too, was judging the visitor, well aware that this man was not Aafreen Khan. He was probably a Khan by race, but certainly not Aafreen. But that was to be expected, because Carlos wasn't his real name either. In fact, at times he had difficulty recalling his own real name. Carlos had started in street gangs in Mexico and diligently worked his way up, eventually arriving, illegally, in San Antonio, Texas. He found that crime wasn't flourishing there enough for him to make a name for himself, so he had moved to Houston. Now, in this city, the only thing flourishing was crime, and with that, Carlos. But even after all the risks he had taken, which had earned him his daredevil reputation, he was still a small fish because he had no powerful patrons and he had no capital. Carlos had been around long enough to realize that money attracts friends like honey attracts flies, but so far he had not hit a big score to get to the next level. Maybe this Pakistani/Afghani fellow would bring him some luck.

"Mr. Carlos," Amir began, addressing him. There was a puzzled look on Carlos's face that made Amir stop.

Carlos was looking around, and then asked Amir, "Are you talking to me?" For a minute, Amir thought Carlos was doing an amateur imitation of Robert De Niro's famous lines in the movie *Taxi*, but immediately realized Carlos was neither imitating nor joking. "If you are talking to me, then drop this 'Mr.' shit. I am just Carlos to friends and enemies—just Carlos."

Amir started again and had a wicked thought to start by addressing Carlos as "just Carlos" but decided to abandon humor, realizing it would be lost on "just Carlos." He continued, "Okay, Carlos, I have an offer for you. We want you to deliver a package to us in Turkey."

"And what is this package, Khan?"

"A woman who would be delivered to you in Houston, from where you have to take her to Turkey," Amir replied.

"And what are you prepared to pay for this service you ask for?" asked Carlos.

"You will be well compensated," Amir replied cautiously, not wishing to tip his hand.

Carlos had grown up in the toughest neighborhood in the slums of Mexico City, so he knew when he was on to a good thing, and this man smelled of real money. "Tell me more about this package, and who else will be chasing the package?" asked Carlos.

Amir decided that if the job was to be done well, then it was best to level with Carlos. "Feds, Homeland Security, and everyone else you can think of will be after this package, no holds barred," replied Amir.

Carlos appreciated the honesty. He also enjoyed a challenge, and this certainly seemed like one. "Tell me more" is all he said.

"She is a prisoner, and she is going to be freed by our people, who will deliver her to you, and you have to deliver her to us in Turkey." Amir paused, and then decided to go further. "The most important part of the project is that it has to happen next week."

Carlos burst into laughter. "You had me completely fooled. I thought you were for real. My friend, what you ask for is impossible in a month, and you are asking for collection and delivery in a week. I can perform miracles, but suicide missions are a specialty of your people, not mine." Carlos was rising from his seat.

"We will pay you one million dollars." Amir decided it was time to make the deal sweet. "Besides, we have everything planned. We need your contacts and network to make things happen. This would be the quickest million dollars you ever earned. Deals like this only come once in a lifetime."

Carlos also realized this and knew from experience that a lot of blood and sweat has to be spilled before a few hundred thousand dollars are made. A million was, after all, a million, but he decided to not give in so easily. After all, if this man had traveled across the world to meet him and was prepared to offer him a million dollars so easily, than he was worth a lot more. Carlos did not pause for one moment to think about the legal implications and fallout of what he was being offered. He had no illusions; he operated on the wrong side of the law, always had, and until he made serious money, he would have to continue doing it, so it was not really a matter of choice.

"I will do it for five million dollars," Carlos offered.

"No, Carlos, my final offer is two million dollars, no more," Amir countered.

Carlos decided it was time for his final bluff. "Three million dollars and not a dime less." He looked at Amir, who had not moved a muscle. His face was expressionless. Carlos, for all his experience, could not judge what he was thinking, so he started rising again, indicating an end to the meeting and negotiation. Amir still did not make any move; Carlos rose and walked toward the door, wondering if he had blown his chance of two million dollars for three. Amir decided it was time to close the deal. He stretched his hand out and said, "Deal."

Carlos's face broke into a wide grin, and he took Amir's hand in his iron-like grip. "I want half now and half on delivery."

"You get one million dollars now—that is, within the next twenty-four hours—another half a million when you collect the package, and the balance of 50 percent on delivery of the package in Turkey."

Carlos handed him a crumpled piece of paper on which were the details of an account in a Mexican bank. The company, by the name, appeared to be a fertilizer exporter. Bullshit, thought Amir, and smiled at his own humor. They agreed to meet in one week's time.

Amir checked his watch. It was 4:00 p.m., and the date was May 30, 2012. It was a little late to inform the general, but he sensed that these days the old man wasn't sleeping much, so he decided to call anyway. Once again Amir's call was received by the duty officer in the Pakistani consulate, and Amir simply said, "*Roza mubarik*" (or congratulations on the fasting, a greeting usually exchanged on the first day of fasting in the Muslim holy month of Ramadan) and hung up. General Bhaya received the message on his bedside phone and went back to sleep with a satisfied smile, content that things were progressing as planned.

Department of Homeland Security (DHS), Washington

Andrew Ridley was an analyst; his job was to study different research reports from various agencies, analyze them together, and try to detect patterns that otherwise might not be obvious to someone accessing just one of the reports. He was one of the four analysts covering Pakistan and Afghanistan, from where a large amount of data came. Most of it was useless chatter, but once in a while some rare nuggets were found, and it was Andrew's job to sift through and find the nuggets.

When the Pakistan embassy in Washington had asked a local phone company for a new phone line, as a matter of routine the information was passed on to DHS, where the information was filed for future reference. One of the other agencies had placed a tap on the phone; again, this was a very routine practice, more so in the case of Pakistan, because so many terrorists seemed to favor that country as their destination of choice. Also, the al-Qaeda leadership was supposed to be hiding over there—plenty of reasons to monitor them, in Andrew's opinion.

A report had crossed Andrew's desk today, saying that the phone line had been used, apparently for the first time. The call to the Pakistani consulate's new number had originated from JFK airport, one of the public phones. The call had been brief, hardly lasting thirty seconds. What intrigued Andrew was the message, "The Ramadan moon has been sighted." Andrew had checked the Muslim calendar and knew that Ramadan was not due to start for at least another six or seven weeks, so the only obvious explanation was that this was a coded message.

Andrew took the elevator to the office of Deputy Director Simmons. Simmons was busy in a meeting but asked him to wait while he wound it up. Within a few minutes, he was shown into Simmons's office. Andrew briefed Simmons about the report, and was told to await further instructions.

Simmons included the phone call report in his briefing papers for the joint intelligence briefing, where chiefs of all the intelligence agencies shared information. The CIA chief suggested to Simmons's boss to involve Mark Bloomberg in the investigation dealing with the Pakistani phone call. It was agreed that Mark would be seconded to DHS.

Mark arrived at his new office at DHS and put together a team of four people, whose job it was to run Operation Waterloo. Mark had picked the name because it was at Waterloo that the British had defeated Napoleon's forces and turned the tide in favor of Great Britain. Mark hoped that this operation would also prove to be Waterloo for the Pakistanis, Al-Qaeda, and the Taliban. The first thing Mark did was to call Leslie Gill in the National Security Agency, which was entrusted with the tapping of phones, including that of the Pakistani embassy. He quickly outlined what he needed; he was assured that as soon as any activity was reported, he would be informed.

The "W" team had three other members. Each one of them had multiple talents; they had all done active service in the military and had either served in Iraq or Afghanistan. The second member of the team was Junior; his real name was Augustine Michael Boota, an African-American who had grown up in Harlem and had worked his way up from there to college. He'd joined the army and was now working for DHS, having attended night school for four years. Junior was six feet four inches tall and was a genius with computers. The third member of the team was Mario Barcini, an Italian-American who was born and raised on Long Island, and had joined the army to get away from the family business. His father owned a restaurant and wanted him to follow in his footsteps. Mario hated anything to do with cooking, so the last thing he wanted was to run a restaurant. In the military he had enjoyed the rush he got when confronted with danger; he realized he thought better under fire and in difficult circumstances. He could just cut to the chase and get to the heart of the matter. This was a quality that had endeared him to Deputy Director Simmons, who had come across him in an Afghan prison interrogating an al-Qaeda suspect. This was not a routine job for Mario, but he had been asked to fill in for another colleague. Mario had shown a natural talent for putting strangers at ease and extracting information from them. Mario had also picked up both the Pashtun and Persian languages, which made him invaluable. Once his tour was complete, Deputy Director Simmons had him invited to DHS and recruited. The fourth member of the team, Garcia Rodriguez, an American born to Mexican parents, had grown up in the poorer part of Houston. He was a gifted mathematician, and had gone to Pakistan as part of one of the defense contractor teams to provide complex logistics solutions for moving cargoes in and out of Afghanistan. After returning to the United States, he had gone to college to continue his studies, from where he was recruited by the CIA but somehow ended up in DHS. What Garcia didn't know was that his superiors had decided that he was too much of a geek for the CIA and better suited to some other agency, so when an opportunity presented itself, they passed him to DHS as a big favor.

The W team was assembled in the afternoon, and Mark gave them a complete briefing of what they knew, which was precious little—just one phone call, the contents of which were highly suspicious. "Guys, I want you to start tracking the caller—for now we will call him Abdul. I want you to start tracking everyone Abdul has spoken to and met. Also try and see if you can track his movements before he arrived at JFK—that could be a real breakthrough. We want to become this guy's shadow. I want to find him, and I want to know everything he is doing. Junior, why don't you start tracking Abdul down, and start from the JFK security camera footage. Garcia, why don't you work your magic with mathematical formulas that only you understand, and build yourself some models to develop various scenarios about where Abdul may have gone. Mario, would you mind looking through all the reports that have been coming out of Pakistan and Afghanistan in the past two months, because there has been a change of government there recently and I am guessing, given that the call was to the Pakistan embassy and then to their capital city of Islamabad, that we may have some government people involved in this. I am going to get in touch with the NSA and set up electronic surveillance of everyone we all come up with, starting with Abdul and his contact in Pakistan. How does that sound to everyone?" All three nodded in agreement.

Junior started going through the video recording of the pay phone at JFK, from where the call to the Pakistani embassy had originated. The video recorded by the security camera showed a man wearing a baseball cap, glasses with shaded lenses, baggy clothes, and a long raincoat. The man also had a beard covering his face. Junior realized that the caller was a professional and had taken all the basic precautions to avoid identification.

Next, Junior logged on to the airport security database and started viewing film from other cameras. After four hours of searching, he did find the same man heading for the toilets, but after that there was no sign of him. Maybe he was still hiding in the toilets, thought Junior, but decided that was unlikely. It was coming up to nine in the evening, so Junior decided to call it a day.

In the meantime, Garcia had written a short program to collect and analyze the data of all the flights taking off from JFK starting from the time the phone call was made, till the end of the evening when the flights stopped. He then inserted a filter into the program to identify passengers who had either a Muslim or a Spanish surname. He had included Spanish because many Pakistanis looked like Latinos, and of late had started taking advantage of that. This narrowed down the list to some four hundred possible suspects. Next Garcia put in another filter to exclude all females and all males below eighteen and above sixty, and those traveling as a family. This brought the total down to eighty suspects. Garcia divided this list into Muslim and Spanish. The Muslim name search yielded thirty people. He decided to concentrate on these thirty.

Garcia started accessing the databases of various airlines and by midnight had phone numbers for all the thirty persons of interest.

—◁+ +▷—

Mario went through all the reports but failed to turn up anything of significance, so he called Mark and checked with him. Mark hadn't had any luck with tracking anyone down in Pakistan, so Mark asked Mario to see if he could work that angle. Mario called up the agency man, Tom, in Islamabad and asked him to find out who received the call in Pakistan and who the message was forwarded to. On hearing the request, Tom gave a hearty laugh. "Listen, Mario, right now we are enemy number one in this country, and our sources are shut tighter than a duck's ass, so don't hold your breath. Besides, I am sure you know their foreign minister is a retired general and former head of the top spy agency in this country. There is your link. Quite how it fits in, I don't know—we need to connect the dots. I will see if I can get some real intel."

Mario quickly responded, "I appreciate what you are telling me, Tom, but could you find out all the phone numbers that are installed at the general's house and office?" Mario had decided he had to give something specific to the agency man, and he had no time to lose.

"Sure, I think we can get that information. I will call you when I have it."

Next Mario called Mark and asked him to get the list of calls made from the phone number in the Pakistani Foreign Office that had received the call from the JFK airport pay phone.

Garcia arrived at the office at 7:00 a.m. and went through all the reports that had come during the night. There was nothing new and of immediate interest. Having taken care of his emails and routine memos, he sent the suspect list he had developed to the other members of W team on the local area network. The list would not go into any external network or emails to ensure security of the information. However, the recipient would be notified that there was a classified file waiting on their internal network.

Garcia had divided the list into four parts. Each member was to follow up and try to run down all the possible suspects. This was the best way to cut down on the time required to track down the suspect.

Garcia started with his own list. There were ten people on it, and he called each and every one on their given contact number, telling them that he was calling from airport security at JFK and that on the flight they had traveled on, a briefcase with money and some valuables was found. He was trying to track down the owner. Garcia had posted the same cover story to the other W team members, to ensure they all followed the same pattern.

After three hours Garcia had talked to everyone on the list and they all checked out. They were regular folks who just happened to travel on the same night as their suspect may have. Precious little to go on, thought Garcia, but that's how all investigations started, and then the breaks came and the jigsaw pieces started falling in place. This one would be no different. Garcia was confident.

Junior had eight people on his list, and when he came in at 7:45, he immediately got on the phone and started talking to all the people on his list. By 10:30 Junior was through his list but had no suspects to report. He was disappointed; he had hoped that he would find the suspect, or at least a lead.

Mark arrived at eighty thirty. He got himself some coffee from the machine in the pantry and started going through his mail, having made sure there was nothing else that was urgent. He too started down Garcia's list, and like Junior and Garcia, by eleven o'clock, having gone through the list, had nothing to show for progress. Everyone on the list was a bona fide traveler.

After going through the whole list, only one passenger was untraceable: number thirty, whose cell number was not responding. Mark decided this called for follow-up. He called Junior and gave him the number and told him to track down the purchase of the cell and its registered owner.

After two hours Junior reported that the cell number had been purchased using a false ID; however, he had managed to get a record of calls made from that phone. Interestingly, there were four calls to the same number, all within a span of an hour and a half.

Junior called the number and found another blind alley. This number too was disconnected. Junior's enquiries confirmed what he had suspected: this phone had also been purchased with a false ID.

Junior decided to get more technical help and got Garcia to access the locations from where the calls were made and received. That narrowed it down to the nearest radio tower from where signals were received.

The calls were made from near the port area in Manhattan, received by a tower in Long Island. Garcia came up with the most likely location of the caller in downtown New York, and they accessed recordings of street cameras for that time of the day; however, given that they didn't have any description and almost everyone was talking on their cell, it was impossible to make an ID.

They were luckier on Long Island. The call had been made from outside a bank, and the street camera outside the bank showed a tall Caucasian talking on the phone, but not much else could be identified. However, the call recipient had walked up to the ATM to withdraw some cash. Bingo, thought Garcia. Junior smiled broadly, exposing an array of beautiful white teeth.

Garcia called up the bank's security and told them that one of their customers was a suspect in a terrorism investigation. DHS needed all the data on him pronto. The mention of terrorism and Homeland Security in the same sentence usually worked miracles. The security supervisor promised to call back as soon as possible and gave them a name, phone number, and address of the account holder from whose account the money was withdrawn.

Junior called Mark and gave him a quick update. He told him to bring Garcia and Mario along and join him in the elevator. They were going traveling.

"Okay, guys, we are heading to New York. We have a plane ready at Reagan to take us there. I have asked the local FBI team to pick up the suspect and bring him to their office for questioning. The suspect is William Mathias. He is thirty-three years old and works for a local Starbucks. He is single and lives alone. He has no criminal or immigration record. That's all we know for now; I have people in DHS digging up more information on this guy."

New York Starbucks in Brooklyn

Given it was the lunch hour and it was highly likely that the place would be crowded; it had been decided not to go in with the SWAT team.

Agents Hutch and Johnson went in from the front, and agents Cynthia and Platt went in through the back entrance, which was for service and deliveries and opened in the back alley.

Hutch and Johnson approached William Mathias, who was wearing a name tag on his shirt and asked him if they could talk to him. Mathias followed them to a table, but he was gently escorted out by the agents. Outside, Hutch spoke into his miniature walkie-talkie and let the other agents know that they had captured the bird. Before Mathias could protest, he was shoved into the waiting black SUV, and the vehicle was moving even before everyone had got in.

By now Mathias was in a complete panic. He had realized that these were the Feds and he was in some serious shit, but he had no clue what it was. He tried to talk to his captors, but they asked him to be quiet, so Mathias did just that.

FBI Offices in New York

Mathias was placed in the interrogation room. After what seemed like an endless wait, the door to the room opened and Mark walked in, roughly dragged over a chair, threw the pen and paper he was carrying casually down, and sat across from him.

"Mr. Mathias, tell me who you were talking to on the phone here" he slammed down a picture of a man talking on the phone and using an ATM at the same time.

"That's not me," said Mathias, stuttering.

"We have checked with the bank. It was your ATM card that was used at the exact same time this call was made, from the exact same location. So it was you. Why don't you make it easier on yourself by telling me the truth and we can all go home."

Mathias began to realize he was in some kind of a gigantic mix-up. "Listen, Mister, I don't know what you are talking about, but I don't have an account with that bank. I have never gone near that bank, and that is not me in the picture. In fact, at the time of this ATM activity I was working. You can check with my boss and my time record at the coffee shop."

Mark felt his investigation falling apart. He had been so confident they had gotten a solid lead and were on the verge of a breakthrough that, in his optimism, he had omitted the error factor that was present in every investigation. He rose without another word and left the room. Mathias gave a deep sigh of relief.

Mark asked Hutch to check with the coffee shop owner about Mathias's alibi. Hutch and Johnson left for Starbucks. Mark asked Garcia and Junior to get the bank statements of this account and track down every activity. He and Mario left for the bank to interview the staff there.

The account had been opened and maintained at the LB (Lend and Borrow) Bank's branch on Surf Avenue. The manager was the soul of cooperation after he had verified the credentials of Mark and Mario. He took them to the records room, where on a computer they were able to access the signature card and copies of all the other documents that had been given at the time of account opening. The driving license was in fact that of the real William Mathias, as were all the details, including the address.

Mark wondered how the ATM card had been received by Mathias, or whoever was pretending to be Mathias, and where the bank statements had been sent. The ATM card had been delivered to Mathias's home address. Mario tracked down the courier company and got a copy of the receipt that had been signed by Mathias, or the impostor. The signature card from the bank and the courier receipt were sent to the FBI lab for top-priority analysis.

As Mark was leaving the bank, he got a call from Hutch, who told him Mathias's alibi checked out and he was indeed at the coffee shop at the time of the ATM transaction. This had been verified by Hutch and Johnson from the security cameras at the coffee shop for that day.

Mark called Garcia and told him to let Mathias go, and to warn him not to leave town. He also asked Garcia to liaison with the special agent in charge at the FBI office, and to place Mathias under surveillance.

Meanwhile, a clerk at the LB Bank, Surf Avenue Branch, called a cell number she had been given by the person who had opened the account in Mathias's name. The clerk had instructions to relay any unusual activity related to that account. The clerk had just learned that the FBI and DHS had put the account under complete surveillance. The Russian answered and listened without interruption, until the clerk had finished relaying all the information.

"Okay, you take your vacation. You will get your package." The clerk quickly filled out a vacation leave application form and submitted it to the HR department. The clerk, Madhu, smiled with satisfaction. She knew her package would include a cash payment large enough to pay for her vacation to the Maldives.

Garcia called back and informed Mark that small deposits had been made into the account over a period of time, always in cash and always from a remote ATM. In the same fashion, cash was taken out of the account, and the current balance was US$3,000. None of the money could be traced, so it was a dead end.

Mark decided to follow his hunch. He drove toward Brooklyn and the address where Mathias was living. If the ATM card had been delivered to Mathias's apartment, then maybe their suspect was someone who lived in the same building.

The apartment was located on the third floor of a building that must have been constructed in the 1950s and was in bad need of a paint job. He looked for the building supervisor, and having found him snoozing in his room, quickly got his attention by flashing his badge.

He asked for the names of all the tenants who were living in the building, and those who had come and gone in the past twelve months. There were only three apartments that had been turned over in that time, and one of those was across the hall from Mathias's apartment. The apartment had been rented for three months by a Russian gentleman. According to the supervisor, the Russian was there for a short period and had gone back to wherever he had come from. The description the supervisor gave—six feet tall, slender, white male with no distinguishing features, was of no help, as it fitted a couple of hundred thousand people at any given time in New York. The payment had been made in cash, and the supervisor had taken a copy of his driving license but could not find it.

Mark was almost certain that the Russian had somehow stolen Mathias's driving license, who too was a white male around six feet tall, used it to open a bank account, and intercepted the mail to receive the ATM card. This was a bit too long and complex for an ordinary criminal, thought Mark; this had the hallmark of terrorism planning written all over it. It was also likely that the Russian had sneaked into the supervisor's office and removed the copy of his own driving license, which in all probability was also a fake.

Out of desperation Mark decided to try another lead. He got Junior to track down the courier who had delivered the ATM card. Luck was on his side: the courier was still working for the same company and on the same beat. He also happened to be in the same area. Mark called Hutch and asked him to pick up the courier and bring him to Mathias's building.

Hutch and Johnson arrived within the hour, with a middle-aged man sandwiched between them. "Hi, Mark, this is Clifford. He is the guy who delivered the ATM card to Mathias."

"Mr. Clifford, did you deliver the ATM card to Mr. Mathias in his apartment?" Mark was sure that the Russian had intercepted the card outside the apartment.

"No, no, he was in too much of a hurry. That man, Mathias, he stopped me on the stairs and insisted that I deliver it to him there. He did show me his driver's license to prove he was who he said he was, so I gave him the envelope and got his signature."

"Mr. Clifford, do you have any recollection of the person who collected the envelope from you? Could you by any chance identify him?" asked Mark tentatively, but without much hope.

Clifford was an amateur sketch artist and was bestowed with a wonderful memory for faces, so he said, "I can draw you a sketch of the man who received the package."

Mark was suddenly very optimistic; this was the break he had been looking for. "Mr. Clifford, it would be very helpful if you could do that. Hutch will escort you to the FBI offices, where our sketch artist can help you in drawing a sketch of this man."

Hutch, taking the cue, gently steered Clifford toward their waiting car to drive him to the FBI offices. Mark and Mario followed in their own car. Mark checked the time—it was eight o'clock in the evening, and he was suddenly starving. They had not eaten anything since they arrived in New York. He called Garcia and Junior

189

to join them outside the FBI offices, and they all went to a little Chinese place Mark frequented when he was in New York.

By the time they got back from dinner, the sketch of the Russian was ready. They had no name, but this was a start. The results of the handwriting analysis on the signature card and the courier receipt had also come back from the FBI lab, and it was confirmed that these had been signed by the same person. That person was not Mathias, whose signature sample had been obtained from driver's license records.

Mark put in a request to the FBI, CIA, DHS, and all the other agencies, including the police and customs, to search their computers for a match of the sketch of the Russian.

Mark got to the FBI office in New York, where his team had decided to camp for the duration of their current investigations. He had a restless night and was up at six in the morning. By 7:30 he was in the office. Much to his surprise, Junior was already there.

Junior brought him up to speed; the computers had been at work all night, and they had a dozen possible matches. Mark and Junior divided the results equally and started studying the profiles. Within half an hour, Garcia arrived, took some files from Junior, and got to work without much ado. Around 9:00 a.m. Mario arrived. He looked like he had not slept all night; he headed straight for the coffee machine and, after getting a full mug, returned to join the team. Mark handed him two files to study. He had gone through two and had two left for himself. By 10:00 a.m. the team had gone through the profiles of all the twelve suspects, and each member started tracking down the suspects they had on their own little list.

Junior found that two of his suspects had left the country in the past few days. The third was still in the United States; in fact, his last known address was in New York and in an area Junior knew rather well. Junior briefed his colleagues and decided to take a trip up to his old neighborhood. Though he was born in Harlem,

190

Junior's family had moved to the Bronx when he was ten, and he had spent most of his life there.

Junior arrived at Pelham Parkway in a cab, paid the fare, and got out. The area was dominated by six- and seven-story buildings. Junior walked down toward Christopher Columbus School. The address he was looking for was just around the corner from the school. Of late, Russians had moved into this area, and this is where they had taken up residence.

Junior reached the address. It was a Tudor-style apartment building, reasonably well maintained, and had an entry phone at the door. Junior quickened his pace when he saw an elderly couple approaching the building door. He quickly got in behind them and took the stairs to the second floor. He knocked at the apartment at the corner of the floor and waited patiently. The door was opened by an old lady who didn't speak any English. She only spoke Russian, which Junior had no knowledge of. Junior decided to show her the sketch of the Russian and ask her about it. He was not looking for an answer, just a reaction.

Junior took out the sketch and showed it to her, pointing a finger at it and then at the apartment, trying to make the old lady understand he was asking if the man lived there or not. The old lady's reaction was too quick; she took one look and immediately shook her head in an empathic no. More or less shoving Junior away, she closed the door.

Junior decided he had come to the right address, and the person of interest to DHS was indeed living there. He left the building and called Mark for backup while he kept watch.

The old woman, after closing the door, went to the phone and quickly called her son. In Russian, she told him about the black man looking for him. The son thought it was probably a local hoodlum, but the mother was adamant that the man was with some secret service and instructed her son not to return home for a few days. Nikolai knew there was no arguing with his mother, and that there was no way he could return home unless his mother agreed. His mother had been an officer in the Russian army and had had her share of grief, violence, and tragedy; she was a woman of iron will and one who was not easily defied. But Nikolai was intrigued. Who was this black man, and what did he want with Nikolai?

Nikolai called Felix. Felix was a Cuban kid, around fifteen years old, who lived in the neighborhood. Nikolai had done him some favors and passed bits of work his way, so Felix was always happy to return the favor. Nikolai called Felix and told him what to do. His instructions were explicit: just observe and report.

Felix got on his bicycle and circled Nikolai's apartment. Almost immediately, he spotted Junior. Felix could tell that this guy was not from around here, not now anyway. His confidence told Felix two things: one was that the man had grown up either in these parts or in a similar neighborhood elsewhere, and the other was that he had left his origins a long way behind and had moved up in the world. The man didn't look like a policeman to Felix, and he didn't look like Fed, so this was a bit of a mystery. Felix took a picture of Junior and sent it to Nikolai.

Nikolai was pleased. He was happy he had invested in Felix, and the boy was paying rich dividends. Nikolai passed the picture to a friend who had a friend in the police department, to run an ID check. Within half an hour Nikolai received a call from his friend who had heard from his friend in the police. "What shit are you into, Niki?" asked Andi, whose real name was Andropov.

"Why? What happened, Andi?"

"The guy you sent me the picture of works for the Department of Homeland Security. He is ex-army, and was born in these parts," replied Andi, slamming the phone down.

Niki sat down. This was happening too fast. Why was DHS on him? He started to call Felix, but before he could, Felix called him. "Boss, there is some serious shit going down. There are Feds here, and they have just taken a position in front of your apartment."

"Okay, Felix, thanks. You have done a great job. Now get out of there and stay away," Nikolai said. Felix had already mounted his bike and was on his way out of there real fast.

God bless his mother, Nikolai thought. The old woman could smell danger miles away.

After debating his options, Nikolai decided he had done nothing he knew of to attract this kind of attention. So he called a lawyer he had used from time to time and told the lawyer what was going on. The lawyer told him to sit tight. Fred Summers had almost never had a situation where a client had called him without committing some felony, so this was a surprise and a departure from his routine.

Fred called the local FBI office and asked to speak to the agent in charge. He knew the last thing he would get was the agent in charge, but he would get someone's attention. A woman came on the line—a secretary, thought Fred. Fred told her, "Tell your boss that the person they are staking out on Pelham Parkway wants to come in. Tell him to call me."

Within a few minutes a man called. This one Fred was sure was the agent in charge. "Mr. Summers, my name is Agent Bloomberg, and I am in charge of the investigation you referred to in your conversation with my colleague. Why don't you bring Nikolai Sastachov in, and we can resolve this."

"Niki, you sure you want to do this?" Fred asked his client.

"Yes, Fred. I can't think of any other way, so let us do it."

FBI office, New York
Nikolai and Fred walked into the offices. Fred informed the front desk that they had an appointment with Agent Bloomberg, and almost instantly he appeared from a side door and received them. "I am Agent Bloomberg, and you must be Mr. Summers, and this I presume is Nikolai Sastachov; this way gentlemen."

He escorted them to an interview room. Both Fred and Nikolai were familiar with these rooms, though they had never been in this particular one. All interrogation rooms looked the same: a two-way mirror on the wall, behind which some agents would be watching the show and analyzing; usually one table and two chairs—one for the suspect and one for the interrogator; and a camera, either in the ceiling or in some other strategic position to record the interview. This room was no different, except this had three chairs.

Mark sat down on one; Fred and Nikolai sat opposite him. Mark opened a folder and took out a picture of a man talking on the phone and using the ATM. "This is you, Nikolai. We have matched this with our database and that of the bank. Tell us, who are you talking to on the phone here?"

Nikolai stared at the picture in amazement and disbelief. Fred jumped in, wary that Nikolai might implicate himself by saying the wrong thing. The fact that his client hadn't immediately denied the allegation was enough of a cue for him to take over.

"This is nothing. You can't tell who is in that picture, and since when it has become a crime to talk on a cell phone and to take the money out of an ATM at the same time?" Mark ignored him; his eyes were fixed on Nikolai. He could tell Nikolai was not afraid. Maybe a little amused, but why, he could not figure out.

"That is not me," he simply said.

"Okay, where were you on May 29, around 5:30 p.m.?"

Fred jumped in again. "And precisely what is my client accused of?"

"Mr. Summers, this is a matter of national security, and if you keep this up then I may have to pull you in for inquiries too, so why don't you shut up?" It was not the threat or the words used, because Fred was used to both and much worse, but the cold and calculated manner in which they were delivered that unnerved Fred. Fred looked at Nikolai tentatively. who was completely unaffected by the threat.

"This is not me. I can help you find this man, but you have to give me something first," Nikolai said.

"Listen, who do you think you are talking to? This is not your local precinct or the assistant district attorney's office, where you bargain. This is national security, and unless you tell me what you know, you are going down for aiding and abetting terrorism, and this is all you are getting." Mark spat out the words. Still the Russian was not moved; he sat there calmly.

"I want to be in the witness protection program. I want a new identity and enough money to start over." He made it sound like a normal business conversation in a coffee shop.

Fred, realizing his client had something up his sleeve, decided to earn his keep. "Unless you are prepared to charge my client, we are leaving."

Mark looked at Fred with pure venom. "You are not going anywhere except to jail, unless I say otherwise." He got up and left.

Fred wanted to ask his client what was going on but knew better, because the Feds and whoever else was there were listening and watching.

Mark went back to the observation room, where his team and two agents from the FBI were watching the show. Mark looked at Nikolai Sastachov's file. The guy had worked for the KGB and had served in Afghanistan, so he was no spring chicken. He had apparently sought asylum in the United States around ten years ago and had not made a nuisance of himself since then, till now.

"So what do you guys make of him?" he asked to no one in particular.

Junior was the first one to respond. "Nothing to it; let's send him to Gitmo—we'll get the truth out of him soon enough."

Mario differed. "This guy has something. You can tell by his composure he has something up his sleeve. His lawyer is right: we have nothing, and the ID won't stand up in a courtroom. But he's not the least bit rattled. And he has asked for something very specific: witness protection. This guy has a plan, and we have just become part of his plan. I think we should talk to him." The two Feds said nothing. They were here just as observers, for now.

"Okay, I have to talk to the boss." Mark left the room, went to an empty meeting room, and called Deputy Director Simmons on his direct line.

The DD answered on the first ring with a question. "What do you have for me, Mark?" Mark briefed him on the events up till now. "Okay, dangle witness protection in front of him, but let him know we will decide that on the basis of the information's quality. Otherwise, he can go to Gitmo. And Mark, get me some results."

Mark went back to the interview room and sat opposite Nikolai. "Okay, we can talk about witness protection, but only after you have delivered and we're satisfied with the quality of the information and the results."

"Within the next twenty-four hours, I will lead you to this man. After that it is up to you. After I do this I want my new identity and other papers, including money to start over again. Fred will draw up an agreement that should be signed by either a senior officer of the bureau or of DHS. When I have that, I will deliver," said Nikolai.

"Well, Counselor, I suppose you have work to do. Come with me, please. And Mr. Sastachov, you please wait here."

Fred was taken to an empty office and given a laptop to type the agreement. He was also told not to use his phone. Fred had a basic draft ready within half an hour, which was read and approved after some suggestions by Nikolai. The district attorney was called in to sign the agreement, and wasn't pleased at not being told of what was going on. Nevertheless, he signed in the interest of national security. The phrase seemed to have universal appeal and influence, mused Mark. Three copies of the agreement were given to Nikolai. The original he couriered to his mother; then he gave a copy to Fred and asked him to leave. The third copy he folded and put in his own pocket. Fred left, realizing that this was the end of his client, at least as far as Fred was concerned.

That done, Nikolai turned to Mark, who was sitting across the table from him, and who still seemed angry with him. Nikolai said, "The man you are looking for is Sasha Chernovitch. You can find him just about now at the Razzle Dazzle nightclub at this address. The nightclub is owned by a former Russian colonel who served in the K division of the KGB. His name is Yuri Gangosky. Yuri and his gang are mercenaries—they will do any job if the price is right."

"Nikolai, you will stay here until we tell you otherwise," said Mark, and left the room.

Mark met his team and a senior agent of the FBI, Agent Polanski, along with Hutch and Johnson, in the conference room on the same floor. Garcia had printed a folder containing pictures and detailed biographies of Sasha Chernovitch and Yuri Gangosky, and a brief on the Razzle Dazzle nightclub.

Polanski took over. "First thing tomorrow morning, I am putting in place six teams. They will work around the clock in two shifts. One team will keep Sasha under surveillance, another will keep tabs on Yuri, and the third team will watch the club. I have put in for authorization for phone tapping of all three as well. Given their backgrounds that should not be too difficult to come by. We will keep you people informed of everything." Thus, the operation got underway.

Mark had another thought. He had noticed in the background information for the Razzle Dazzle nightclub that the club had been designated as a hotspot for drug trafficking. Mark called his boss, Simmons, who in turn called his counterpart in the DEA, the Drug Enforcement Agency. Within a few hours, Mark was told he would hear from someone who was working undercover at the Razzle Dazzle club for the DEA.

Mark decided it was time to visit the club. He decided he would go there alone and see how things developed.

He found the Razzle Dazzle easily enough. The evening was still young, but the club was popular and had already attracted a good crowd, mostly local executives and businessmen stopping by to get a drink or two before heading to wherever they were going. There were the usual crowd of single men trying to get lucky and the usual assortment of hookers looking to pick some customers.

Mark sat down at the bar and ordered a beer. He noted that there was a door in the far corner. The lighting in the bar was arranged in such a way as to almost conceal the door, but it was there, and it was only used by the club employees. Mark had observed this was not a kitchen or service door, because that was on the other side of the bar and was constantly being used by the waiters.

Mark positioned himself at an angle so that his back was to the inner door, but he could watch the door through various mirrors without having to turn his head or look in that direction. After careful but subtle observation for almost an hour, Mark had learned that the door gave access to a hallway that appeared to lead to a basement door.

Mark had not spotted Sasha or Yuri, so if they were here, they must be in a separate part of the club, somewhere more private.

As he left the club, his phone started vibrating. It was Garcia.

Amir had not left a number for Yuri to contact him. Their arrangement was that Amir would call the club in the afternoon, and he would be told if the meeting was on. The code phrase was "I have got two tickets for tonight's game." When Amir called, he told the guy who picked up the phone he was "Danny," the name he had agreed on with the Russian for this phone call. He said the code phrase and was told to call back in four hours for further instructions.

The FBI had missed this call because they had not yet implemented the phone taps.

Amir called back in four hours and was given some numbers, which he jotted down. During their meeting Yuri had given him an old map. Amir unfolded the map and checked the numbers he had been given, identifying the location on the map. The meet was preset for one hour after the call, so Amir had less than one hour to get to the rendezvous.

This call was picked up by the FBI's listening team, but they had nothing to go on. They didn't know who the caller was or what the call was about—only that someone had called and had been given a set of numbers.

The information was passed on to Special Agent Polanski, who asked Hutch to pass it along to Mark and his team.

Garcia was still at his desk in the FBI office. Hutch handed him the numbers scribbled on a piece of paper. Garcia took one look and knew these were coordinates from a map; however, he had to have the same map to know what the grid reference pointed to.

Mark answered the phone and got an update from Garcia on the possible map coordinates. A map meant a location, and a location could mean a meeting. If the call had come just now, then maybe the meeting was on tonight, Mark speculated. He got in his rented car and started off for his hotel. As he approached the T junction to turn onto the main road, he saw two vehicles whizzing past. Mark got a good look at the driver and recognized him. The driver of the front car was Sasha, and he decided he would follow the two cars at a distance. Mark turned in the road and started following the Russians.

Mark picked up the phone, called Agent Polanski, and told him what was going on. Polanski took the details from Mark and told him to keep a safe distance, while he sent two teams to back him up. He next called Garcia and updated him, with instructions to keep other members of the team in the loop.

Suddenly both the cars turned in different directions. Mark was taken by surprise; he had a split second to decide, so he followed the car that had turned right. He had no way of knowing if he was following the right car.

The driver of the second car, Mike, Mikahel Leonosky, who had turned left, noticed that Mark had not followed them. He called the driver of the first car, Sasha. Sasha answered, "Yes, we have him," and closed the phone.

Mike had noticed Mark's car at the intersection. He had also seen the flash of recognition on Mark's face and realized Mark had recognized someone in the vehicle driven by Sasha and was now following them. Mike had told Yuri, who was seated behind him. Yuri was pleased. Mike had not lost his touch; he was still the best man he had on the team, especially when it came to surveillance and counter-surveillance.

Yuri had told Mike and Sasha to follow the split routine. It had worked; Sasha was to take the tail to another nightclub and keep him busy. Yuri had called one of his people in the police force and given him the license plate of the car the man was driving, to find out which agency he worked for.

An Old Warehouse in the Docks Area of New York
Yuri arrived at the warehouse. Mike had made sure they had no one else following, and Sasha had confirmed that the man was still with him. He had called up for backup, which had arrived as Sasha updated them.

Yuri and Mike went in the warehouse. There was a staircase that led to a raised office in the corner of the warehouse at the mezzanine level. Yuri had used the warehouse from time to time for his "business" meetings; the company that owned the warehouse had gone into bankruptcy, and the creditors were still fighting, so there was no one to pay the security company. As a result the warehouse was available to anyone who had the muscle to use it from time to time, and Yuri had plenty of muscle.

Mike turned on the security cameras, which had been installed by the previous owners and which covered all the entry and exit points to the warehouse to ensure that no unauthorized movement of staff or stock took place. This system had served Yuri well, and he had had it serviced occasionally to ensure that it was in good shape when he needed it. There was also a PA system in the security office where Yuri and Mike had settled down for the meeting.

After fifteen minutes they saw a car drive up in front of the main entrance of the warehouse. Mike pressed a button, and the main doors of the warehouse opened. The driver of the car hesitated only a moment, and then the car drove in.

Amir alighted from the car. The two men keeping watch outside had confirmed that Amir had arrived alone. Nevertheless, they allowed Amir to wait for another ten minutes. Finally, Yuri spoke on the PA system. "Why don't you come up, Mr. Khan."

Amir obliged and made his way to the staircase at the far end of the warehouse. He arrived at the office door and was received by Mike, who thoroughly frisked him. When they were satisfied that Amir was carrying neither weapons nor wires, he was allowed inside the room. Yuri was safely ensconced behind the large desk in the old security office. Amir sat down opposite him. Yuri took out two cans of iced tea—he knew his guest didn't consume alcohol—and placed them on the table between them.

Mike left the room, leaving the two men alone. Amir took a flash drive from his pocket and put it inside the laptop Yuri had set up. The laptop was hooked into a portable overhead projector that Mike had brought along with the laptop. Amir loaded his files and opened one called "Courthouse."

The screen showed a picture of the courthouse where the hearing for Aafia's appeal was to take place in four days' time. Amir clicked the mouse button, and next came the image of the room where the hearing was to be held. Another click focused on the ventilation system outlet in the ceiling; yet another click showed the inside of the ventilation system.

Amir paused and, pointing to the image, said, "This is where the gas tank will be placed by your people, the night before the hearing. The tank will be wired to a timer that will be set to trigger it at 9:30 a.m.; that is thirty minutes after the hearing starts. The gas will knock out everyone, not just in the courtroom, but in the whole building, so your team will be equipped with special goggles and masks to be able to see and breathe without hindrance, and execute the plan.

"The gas clouds will trigger the fire alarm and the sprinklers. This cannot be allowed to happen, because water will not only dilute the effect of the gas, but the alarm will bring the fire brigade and cause pandemonium outside, which may make the getaway complicated. So at exactly 9:29, one minute before the set-off time, the fire alarm will have to be disabled.

"Once everyone is unconscious, your team moves in and picks up Aafia. She only weighs around ninety-five pounds, so that should be easy.

"Your team will have seven people: six men and one woman. The woman I will arrange for; she will be a double for Aafia. You and Mike will take Aafia and go down in the basement. There is a drainage system there, which I have marked here on the map." Amir highlighted a map of the basement on the overhead projector. "Through the sewerage system you will come out here." Amir showed a spot on the street map that was two streets behind the courthouse. "There will be a van parked here, which will have an open bottom. A ladder will be lowered from the van into the manhole and you, Mike, and Aafia can get inside the van undetected. You will drive Aafia to the airport, where she will board a flight for Houston. You will travel with her to Houston, where I will meet you and collect her. Once you deliver her, you will get your balance payment."

Yuri was impressed that the Afghan had done his homework. Everything was meticulously planned and outlined. Yuri waited patiently, though, because he knew Amir was not finished.

"The second team, let's call it the B-team, will escape through the main entrance in full public view. They will drive through town, causing some havoc to ensure that the police are able to follow them. Their job will be to head for Canada. They will cross the Canadian border at Fort Erie. Their objective is to board the double on a flight from Toronto to Dubai. My man will give them all the papers for travel from Canada to Dubai, including the ticket. Once the double is delivered to Pearson Airport in Toronto, your second team's job is done, and they can disappear after that. You have to take utmost care to ensure that the double team does not know that there has been a switch and they have a double; otherwise they will get slack, and that will jeopardize everything.

"In this flash drive there are maps of the building and a map of the basement and the sewerage system that will lead you to the waiting getaway van. Also, there is a map of the route the double team should take; it is critical that they take the planned route because my associates will set up many ambushes, diversions, and booby traps along the way to ensure that the second team gets away. You will have to arrange papers for your people to get in and out of Canada. I will provide papers for the double. Her papers, incidentally, will be genuine, so there is nothing to worry you there.

"This flash drive also has details of the security at the courthouse, the security detail for Aafia, and profiles of all the known security people in the immediate area of the operation.

"We will meet in Houston on June 5 at the Bush Intercontinental Airport. You can go back on the same flight if you wish, after delivering the package to me." Amir fell silent.

Yuri smiled. "My friend, this is a lot more work than I had bargained for, but a deal is a deal. I will see you in Houston." Amir got up, shook hands with Yuri, and left without another word.

Amir had been instructed to make no contact whatsoever with anyone once the operation was in motion. There was to be complete communications silence till the operation was complete.

Mark was watching the club where Sasha had gone. Junior and a female FBI agent had gone in as casual customers, and they were keeping an eye on things inside the club. Suddenly the earpiece in Mark's ear came to life. It was Junior. "Target is coming down the stairs. He has a briefcase with him. He is heading for the exit." Mark saw Sasha and his partner, another burly Russian, emerge from the club and get into their car.

They had decided to arrest Sasha here and pull him in for questioning, hoping that Sasha would reveal some details of what was being planned. The DEA's source had confirmed that there was a drug deal going down today, so Mark had teamed up with DEA, who would carry out the bust.

Suddenly searchlights came on, illuminating the street and the area where Sasha and his partner stood, frozen in the glare. A voice on the megaphone said, "This is the DEA. You are under arrest. Put your hands up." Sasha and his partner did as they were told. The DEA team quickly moved in and cuffed the suspects, who had made no move to resist or escape. FBI and DHS watched while the arrests were made. Junior and the FBI agent were covering the club door with their guns drawn. This was easy, thought Mark. Way too easy. He didn't like it but could not complain. The operation had gone smoothly, and there had been 100 percent cooperation from everyone.

Sasha and his partner were taken to the DEA's interrogation center. The search of the suspect's car and briefcase had revealed nothing except $50,000 in cash. The DEA figured that Sasha had made a delivery and was taking the cash back. Both Sasha and his partner had weapons, but they were properly registered.

Sasha and his partner refused to answer any questions. Their lawyer was waiting for them when they got to the DEA offices. The DEA decided they didn't have enough to make a case, so they had handed over the suspects to the FBI and DHS, who had not been able to extract anything from the two. They seemed to have become dumb ever since their arrest. They only spoke to their lawyer, in Russian.

Eventually their lawyer kicked up enough fuss to force the FBI and DHS to let his clients go. By midnight Sasha and his partner were on their way back to Razzle Dazzle, laughing.

Mark had argued with Deputy Director Simmons to keep Yuri under surveillance. After much debate, the DD had given in. The other teams watching Razzle Dazzle and Sasha were pulled back.

Mark decided that he and his team would head back to Washington.

Amir arrived in Houston by an early-afternoon flight; he took a taxi to Carlos's garage. He headed straight for the office where Carlos had told him to come. Carlos's office looked the same, and Carlos himself still sported the image of an overweight and underpaid bookkeeper, but now Amir knew better.

Amir sat across the desk, facing Carlos. He took out a folder and handed it to Carlos. Amir opened his own copy of the folder while Carlos picked up his folder. "On the evening of 5 June," Amir said, "I will deliver the package to you at George Bush Intercontinental Airport. You have to deliver her to Turkey. This is how the plan will work: tomorrow at the Mexico City airport, one woman and two children will be arriving from Turkey. The woman will be carrying four passports: one for herself, one for each kid, and the fourth one for the package. You will arrange for the woman and kids to be collected as VIP guests, and their four passports will be taken by your contact in immigration for stamping of the visas. They are all traveling on valid tourist visas. This folder has the pictures of the woman and two kids and copies of the passports they will be traveling on. Once their passports are stamped, your people will escort them to Mexplus Hotel downtown, where a suite has been booked for them. Two of your men will act as their guards round the clock. While in Mexico they will be sightseeing, which has already been arranged with local tour operators.

"On the evening of 5 June, after collecting the package, you will escort her to Mexico through the land border at San Antonio. You will not stop to rest until you have crossed into Mexico. Once you are in Mexico, you decide on the best way to go forward. The package is to be put on a flight to Istanbul on June 6 in the afternoon. You will arrange for her and her family's smooth transition through Mexican immigration. Once they arrive safely in Istanbul, you will get the second half of your payment. One of your men will have to be on the same flight and follow them through Turkish immigration; it will be your job to make sure that any problems at Turkish immigration are resolved. You have to make sure that she gets into Mexico and out of there without any problems. It is that simple."

Amir paused and opened a water bottle that was sitting in front of him and took a few sips before putting the bottle down. "This folder contains all the details of their incoming and outgoing flights and hotel accommodations, and copies of their IDs. Is there anything you need?"

"Nope, amigo. I will see you in Istanbul," replied Carlos. Amir realized that Carlos had committed himself to accompanying the package to Istanbul and that he expected to meet Amir for the remaining payment. This was good, thought Amir.

Yuri and his team, eight people including himself, had assembled at the same warehouse in the docks area where Yuri had met Amir a week ago. They had rehearsed their plan, wearing masks and with smoke blowing all around. In addition to the team, Yuri had employed a young black kid who was around twelve years old and weighed ninety pounds, to simulate the package. The boy was carried by each member of the team many times for fifteen minutes at a time, because this was the time Yuri had calculated it would take them to retrieve the package and get her into the underground sewage system.

Yuri had placed two people outside the courtroom every day for the past week. Their job was to report everything: movement of police, traffic wardens, arrival and departure of prisoners' vans, the security provided for the prisoners by the US Marshal's office, and arrival and departure of the judges, lawyers, court staff, and media people. Yuri had decided that these two people would keep watch outside the courtroom till the operation was over. They were not part of the team that was going to carry out the operation; their specialty was to watch and to merge in the background so no one noticed them.

Two members of Yuri's execution team had visited the courthouse a number of times during the past week and taken a good look at the ventilation, firefighting, and electrical systems of the building and various other points of interest, like the location of toilets and possible places to hide weapons and masks. A gas tank had been placed inside the ventilation system, and it was timed to trigger the gas at precisely 9:30 a.m. The team had identified and prepared for disruption of the power supply and the fire alarm system, so everything was in place.

Both of the vans that would be used in the getaway were ready, their drivers briefed and trained for the job. They would not be part of the team that snatched the target. Weapons for the operation had been issued and tested by each team member for reliability. Everything was set. Yuri, like a military commander, went over every little detail with his team. They had dinner together; he had ordered takeout food from one of the finer Russian restaurants in New York, and it was accompanied by the finest vodka available. After the meal, the team turned in for the night. Yuri had decreed that until the operation was complete, the two teams had to stay together.

Yuri and Mike were to dress as lawyers; the other members of the team would have various costumes. Two would be dressed like cops, two like court workers, and two like media men. Everyone would have false IDs supporting their personas.

Yuri was satisfied that he had not overlooked anything and decided to turn in for the night.

The Prisoner

Aafia woke up in her cell. She had been placed in solitary confinement; there was a small window in the door where food was delivered, but other than that, there was no contact with the outside world. She could see dark sky through the small one-foot-by-one-foot window of her cell. The window was around ten feet high and had a grille on the inside and mashed wire on the outside. None of this bothered her; this was her ninth year in captivity since she was picked up from her parents' house in Karachi in the middle of the night. She had spent half of that time in an Afghan jail, where she had become known as the "gray lady." It was a book written by another prisoner that talked about the plight of her and her children in the Afghan jail at Batgram that had forced the Americans to stage their drama, as a result of which she was here now serving eighty-six years for committing no crime. Her only crime was she was a Muslim and had married another Muslim who was accused of terrorism. For this she had paid with nine years of her life; the life of her youngest child, who had died in captivity for lack of medical treatment; confinement of her children; and now her own prolonged separation from them, maybe forever.

She weighed around ninety pounds; she only ate once a day to make sure that she stayed alive for the sake of her children. Her health, for what it was, was very frail, and she was sure she looked more like a sixty-year-old than a woman in her late thirties—or was it early forties? she thought and then shrugged to herself. It did not matter. Nothing mattered anymore. She was reconciled to living her days in this prison, accepting it as God's will.

She rose from her bunk, which she called it because it was not a bed, not in any sense of the word. She walked to the small sink in the corner and performed ablutions, washing herself in the manner prescribed: she washed her hands up to her wrists first; then she washed her face, followed by her hands up to her elbows; then she rubbed wet hands over her hair, behind her neck, inside her ears, and through her fingers; and finally she washed her feet. Once she finished her ritual, she stood in one corner, away from where the toilet was, raised her hands to her ears, and folded them on her chest, reciting verses from the Holy Quran. She spent a good part of the hour in prayer, kneeling on the cold naked floor because no prayer rug was allowed. She no longer cared; it only mattered to her that she was praying to her Allah, who didn't need a prayer rug or even a set direction, because he was everywhere, ever present, the omnipotent. She stayed in meditation until her cell door was opened and she was told to come out.

She slowly rose from her place on the floor. Her legs were cramped so she had difficulty standing for a few moments, but then the blood started flowing and she regained her balance. She came out of her cell, and two prison guards put handcuffs and foot restraints on her. They'd had to have these made to measure for her, because she was so tiny that the standard issue had easily slipped off her hands and feet. She was walked, wearing the restraints and in a lot of discomfort, through the prison block, passing through many corridors, turning corners. Eventually, after what seemed like forever, they arrived at the exit door. There she was handed over to US Marshals for her transportation to the courthouse, where her appeal was being heard.

She was allowed to enter the prison van on her own. She was placed in a cage-like compartment of the van. The front of the compartment had a small window with bulletproof glass and a grille that allowed the guard in front to look inside. The rear of the van was divided into two compartments, one for the prisoner and one for the marshals. There were two of them, both armed and looking dangerous—each of the guards was over six feet tall and weighed more than 250 pounds. Aafia thought mischievously that if one of the guards were to fall on her, she would probably die of the impact, but they still needed guns—a shotgun in their hands and a Magnum on their belts, and probably a third one around their ankles, as the cops did in movies, all to guard against a frail woman who weighed around ninety pounds.

The rear compartment was separated by a window and a door from the prisoner's compartment. Aafia settled down for her journey, which she knew from experience would take almost an hour and a half. Well, the good thing was, she had no other appointments today. She chuckled to herself silently.

The van arrived at the courthouse as expected, in exactly ninety minutes. Four separate teams put in place by Amir's predecessor had followed the van separately, each taking turns. Each team had two volunteers; they had been told this was to keep a vigil for Aafia's safety. This routine had been followed for the past two years, ever since the general started working on the plan that was underway today.

Yuri and Mike arrived at the courtroom wearing suits and carrying briefcases, looking every bit like hundreds of lawyers present around the courthouse. They got through the security at the entry without a hitch, since they were not carrying anything but some photocopies of obsolete law suits. They headed straight to the second floor, which was far less crowded and where their gear had been stashed away.

The men's room had a big "out of order" sign discouraging any visitors. This was part of the plan; undeterred, Yuri and Mike entered the toilets, where other members of the team had already assembled. Once inside, the outer door was firmly locked.

Yuri went over the plan one more time with his team. The double who was to be snatched by the team was not allowed to join the team, but was to remain in the courtroom from where she would be taken by the B-team. It was approaching quarter past nine, and they all set their wristwatches to stopwatch mode, counting down to zero hour.

Yuri and Mike were the first ones to leave the men's room, this time dressed in workers' overalls, carrying a ladder, tool box, and clip board. The overalls were a copy of those from the company that did maintenance work in the building. Four members of the team were dressed in the uniforms of the service that provided security for the building, carrying weapons and walkie-talkies.

Yuri and Mike positioned themselves outside Courtroom 1, where Aafia's hearing had already started. As planned, the circuits to the lights just outside the courtroom door had been cut. This was where Yuri put down the ladder and Mike climbed up to "fix" the problem. The time was 9:25. In four minutes the fire alarm was to be cut by the team, and one minute after that, the gas would be released.

The four security guards had split into two pairs, and one pair was on the same floor as Yuri and Mike, while another pair was on the staircase between the two floors.

The first pair walked toward Yuri and Mike, positioned themselves around the ladder, and asked Yuri to show his work order, ostensibly checking the authentication of the work being done. As they handed the papers back to Yuri, their stopwatches started flashing. Time was up; zero hour had arrived. The gas started filtering through the vents. Mike pulled out four masks from the ceiling and handed them to the team, who quickly placed them over their faces. The guard at the courtroom door saw this and started reaching for his gun, but it was too late—he had already taken a whiff of the gas. The two members on the staircase also took out their masks, which had been hidden there, and, placing them on their faces, they walked into the corridor to join the rest of the team. It was 9:31 in the morning.

Four of them entered the courtroom; two stayed outside to cover them. Inside the courtroom, Mike headed to where the prisoner was slumped over, next to her lawyer. He quickly lifted her. At the same time, Yuri identified the double, Sonia, who had covered her face with a cotton handkerchief, a makeshift mask that was coated with a chemical to prevent the gas from affecting her. Yuri lifted

Sonia and handed her to the two waiting by the door. All four of them, carrying the two females, exited the courtroom. Mike and Yuri headed for the staircase and the basement. The B-team, led by Karpov, headed for the main entrance carrying Sonia.

As a matter of standard policy, two marshals always stayed outside with the security vehicle. However, also as a matter of usual practice, both had decided to take a leak and get some coffee, so when one of the marshals inside the courtroom realized the gas attack was underway and yelled, "Code red!" into his walkie-talkie, the two guards outside took a full five minutes to turn around and enter the courthouse from the back entrance, where they had been stationed. By the time they reached the courtroom, everyone was unconscious, and the prisoner was gone. In their panic the marshals had not grabbed any gas masks, which were part of the standard kit they carried in their cars; however, one had covered his face with a handkerchief. He survived the gas, while his partner, having inhaled some residual gas, went down just outside the courtroom. The one remaining marshal, Joe Brad, sprinted out of the courtroom and on to the main entrance. There was no sign of the prisoner or her abductors. Then he saw a traffic warden, a middle-aged lady who had moved behind a van. Joe ran to her and simply asked, "Which direction?" The lady was smart enough to point in the direction the fugitives had gone and made a right turn, indicating they had gone straight and taken a right turn.

A courier had just stopped outside the court building and was dismounting his motorbike. Joe shoved him aside, grabbed his bike, and was gone before the biker had even finished falling and hit the road. Joe took out his cell phone and called the emergency number for the US Marshals office. He briefly told them what had happened, giving his own location and the fact that he was trying to pursue the escapees.

Natasha's job was to do surveillance for Yuri's team. She had witnessed the escape, and after five minutes saw the marshal chasing the team on a motorbike. She relayed the information on her cell phone to Yuri and Abrahamovich. Abrahamovich's job was to provide support to the B-team. Abrahamovich instructed one of his removal van drivers, who was between the marshal and the getaway van, to bring the biker down and check his progress. About that same time, Joe got his first visual of the getaway van moving very fast through the New York traffic, and he quickly transmitted the location and direction on his mobile phone to the marshals' office. As Joe navigated through traffic, a van reversed in front of him, not giving him enough time to stop or avoid a collision. Joe instantly realized he had to let go of the bike if he was to survive the collision. He did, and the bike went shooting from under him, crashing head on into the van. Joe, flying through the air, landed on the ground, putting his hands under his head to prevent any serious injuries. He got up with scraped elbows and knees and one side of his face badly bruised, but still very much in his senses. He took half a minute to update his office, went around to the front of the van, pulled the driver out roughly, tossed him on the ground, and got in the driver's seat.

Joe was back on chase, but the van in front had gained ground and was not visible. Joe looked for gaps in the traffic that had been created by the fast-moving van ahead, and like a good tracker he followed the gaps—which were really like footprints for an expert—and the traffic disarray. Joe saw a traffic helicopter up ahead and realized that the getaway van had been spotted from the air. He could also hear the sirens heading in the direction of the helicopter. He started to relax and then suddenly his van lifted from the road, six feet up in the air, and he felt a sudden intensity of heat. His last thought before he passed out was that somebody had rigged the van with explosives.

The traffic helicopter was chasing the getaway van from the air. The police cars were still a few minutes away when the van entered a public garage. Within three minutes, four different vehicles exited the parking garage, all heading in different directions. The van was abandoned inside the garage, and team B had driven out in one of the four vehicles.

They arrived at Teterboro Airport, in New Jersey, thirty-eight minutes from the time they left the courthouse. If they hadn't switched cars, they would have saved four minutes.

At Teterboro airport there was a small plane waiting for Karpov and his team to fly them to Rochester Airport near the Niagara border crossing with Canada. Karpov and his entourage, including Sonia, were all dressed in black suits, white shirts, and colorful ties. They all carried bags with the insignia of a top Wall Street firm, and looked every bit the part of a team of investment bankers going to a meeting.

They arrived in their chartered plane at Rochester and went into the rest rooms to change clothes. Then they rented a car and left the airport. Their next stop was the Greyhound bus stop, where they bought tickets separately and waited to board the next bus to Toronto via Niagara. Karpov and Sonia were traveling as a couple, while the other two were traveling individually. All of them had genuine papers. Now they were all dressed in casual attire and looked like ordinary Americans or Canadians crossing the border.

The Greyhound coach pulled in at the border checkpoint. Sonia and Karpov were the first to come off and headed for customs, arm in arm, like a steady couple with a lot of love between them. They were first to arrive at the customs counter, and both were met with intense scrutiny. Both their papers were genuine and in perfect order, their fingerprints were a match, and nothing about them raised an alarm. They were allowed to cross into Canada. They came out on the Canadian side, where a car was waiting for them. As soon as they got in, the car whisked away.

The White House

The president had been informed about the breakout and had immediately summoned the CIA, FBI, and DHS.

The president turned to FBI Director Robert Bruce. "Bob, tell us what you have."

"Mr. President, we have limited information, which has already been shared with you. Prisoner Aafia has been abducted from the courthouse in New York and is currently escaping in a car. We have deployed every resource at our disposal to track her and her abductors to bring her back."

"Mr. President." This was David Balham, head of DHS. "For the past few weeks, we have been tracking the movements of a Pakistani who has been in New York and had called a special dedicated line in the Pak embassy here with a coded message. The message was then relayed to the foreign minister's office in Pakistan."

"So, David, do you have an ID on this man and his whereabouts? Do you think he is the mastermind behind this operation?" asked the president.

David Balham found himself in a tight spot. "Mr. President, the man was too careful and took adequate precautions to ensure he evaded detection and identification. So, no, we don't have an ID, but based on some work done by our team at DHS with the full support and cooperation of the FBI, we believe that a gang of Russians is somehow involved with the Pakistani."

"So let me sum it up for you: we have a Pakistani suspect we don't know the identity or whereabouts of, and he may possibly have connections to a Russian gang? Is that right, David?" The lawyer in the president had taken over, and David Balham was feeling like a witness under scrutiny on the stand. "And where is the Russian gang now, David?" the president asked.

"Mr. President, as of two days ago they all went underground and have not been seen or heard of," replied David Balham.

"Okay, gentlemen, it seems like it is not just your colleagues in Pakistan who have been caught napping. It seems to be an infectious disease going around. Here is what I suggest: use every ounce of the US government's power, influence, and resources, and find the Russians and the Pakistani." The president rose, signaling the conclusion of the meeting.

The president asked the CIA director to stop for a private word. When the others had left, the president asked him, "John, how is the work on your project going?"

"Mr. President, we have started putting teams and resources in place. We will be ready when you order us to launch," replied the director.

"John, I have a feeling that we are approaching the red line rather quickly," replied the president.

"Understood, Mr. President; we will be ready."

In Washington, Mark got a call from Deputy Director Simmons and was told that he and his team would be responsible for bringing the prisoner back. Mark, Mario, Garcia, and Junior boarded a plane in Washington for New York. They arrived in New York within an hour and decided to use the airport security offices as their base camp. They were patched into the FBI and the US Marshals office.

The latest status was that the van had been abandoned in the parking garage.

Garcia plotted the time of the change from van to another vehicle, the speed of the vehicles moving in the garage, and the time required to get in and speed off, and came up with a three-minute window in which the alternate vehicle must have gotten out of the garage. During that three-minute window, twelve cars had come out of the garage. There were no vans.

Mark immediately called the FBI and gave them the license numbers of all twelve cars, and asked for their help in tracking them down. Garcia had also calculated the speed at which those cars might be traveling and had given possible present locations for the twelve cars.

While the FBI was working to track the cars, Mark and his team identified the owners of all twelve cars, tracked down their cell phone numbers, and started calling them. On the first try, six answered and were told to immediately stop and report their location on the given cell number. The cars' drivers were told they were in imminent danger of a terrorist attack. Karpov also received the call, though he was not the owner of the car. The car had been snatched with the owner's mobile phone only an hour ago and had not been reported yet; in fact, the owner was being held prisoner by his gang and would remain in their custody for the next few hours, until the car had served its purpose.

Karpov called one of his gang members who was in the vicinity and asked him to go to a 7-11 and call the FBI, confirming to them that the car had stopped. Karpov had no intention of stopping, but he needed to avoid detection for as long as possible.

When Mark got a call from Karpov's associate giving the car license number and the location, he quickly dispatched a local police patrol car to go and check it out, while he and his team concentrated on the other six cars.

Karpov stopped at a service station, tossed the car owner's cell phone inside another car, and quickly resumed his journey.

It took Mark and his team another half hour to track down the other five cars. That was a total of eleven cars. One was still missing, a white Toyota Camry—a car favored by many Indians and Pakistanis. Mark put out an APB on the white Camry.

It took two hours for the patrol cars to get to all eleven cars, which had stopped at various locations, and check them out. Only ten cars checked out. The eleventh, which was supposed to be at a 7-11, was not found.

Mark heard this news with some dismay. This meant that he had two cars to find now. He put out an APB on the second car too.

Mark and his team tracked down the Camry, which was parked outside a motel near La Guardia airport. A quick phone call to the motel confirmed that the car's driver had checked in with a lady and was presently in his room.

Mark dispatched a SWAT team to the motel and waited.

The SWAT team at the motel broke into the room and found a man and woman in a compromising position. Before the couple realized what had hit them, they were handcuffed and a bed sheet was thrown over them to cover their nudity. The man was an Asian, most likely Korean, and the woman appeared to be of Hispanic origin. The SWAT team relayed the description of the couple to the DHS team. Mark realized they had stumbled upon an illicit affair, and the woman's description, a voluptuous brunette, did not match the escaped convict. Mark instructed the FBI agent on the scene to interview the couple and release them after putting the fear of God in them, just to make sure they didn't get any ideas of suing the department.

Once across the border in Canada, Karpov called his boys in New York to release the owner of the Town Car. As soon as the Town Car owner was released, he took a cab to the nearest police station and reported the incident. The duty sergeant had heard about the escape from the courtroom in the morning and had dispatched patrol cars to identify some vehicles at the DHS's behest. He looked at his desk, where on a pad he had noted cars that were to be checked, and sure enough, one was a Town Car that never showed up where it was supposed to. The duty sergeant walked into the captain's office and informed him of the theft and his own conclusion that the theft was somehow related to the DHS operation that was underway at present.

The captain called the FBI and informed them. The FBI asked the captain to interview the car owner personally and relay whatever information he got to the FBI. In the meantime, a team of DHS agents was dispatched to collect the car owner.

The captain interviewed the car owner and found out that his cell phone had also been snatched and that the car was equipped with GPS tracking. The captain called the FBI and relayed the information. Within minutes, Mark had received the information, and GPS device was activated to find the vehicle. The results were immediate. The Town Car was parked at Teterboro Airport.

When the team arrived at Teterboro Airport, they learned that four people had arrived in the Town Car—three men and a woman. They had a plane waiting for them and had taken off almost immediately. The information was relayed to Mark, and while he was getting the information, he walked out of the airport security building, motioning for his team to follow. While he was still on the phone, they hurriedly boarded a plane.

The team at Teterboro Airport found out from Flight Control that the small private plane had taken off for Rochester Airport. Mark asked the pilot to fly them to Rochester. He informed the control tower, and they were cleared for immediate takeoff. Mark called Deputy Director Simmons on the phone and gave him an up-to-date status report, asking him to liaison with US Customs at the Niagara border and to be on the alert for the suspects trying to enter Canada.

The deputy director asked his secretary to get the US Customs supervisor in Niagara on the line, and the supervisor assured Deputy Director Simmons of his full cooperation. He personally alerted his team, who were all given a photo of Aafia. The officer who had cleared Sonia and Karpov approached the supervisor "Hey, Jack, a couple passed through here a while back. The woman looked a lot like the picture, but much better kept and healthier. I thought you should know."

Jack cursed under his breath. That was all he needed—a suspect crossing undetected on his watch. Not enjoying the prospect, he called Simmons, who took the news rather well, thought Jack.

Simmons told Jack that Mark would be there shortly and to put the entire facility at his disposal. Some forty-five minutes after Jack's conversation with the Deputy Director, Mark landed in a helicopter at the Niagara Falls border.

Mark hustled to customs; he had already received a heads-up from the deputy director and had requested for customs to review the footage of the time when the couple crossed the border, and have it ready for him.

As soon as he entered US Customs at the Niagara border, he was received by the duty supervisor, Jack, who played the video footage of the couple's exit from customs. The car that had taken the couple was identified, and an APB was put out through the Canadian police.

Karpov and Sonia were just approaching Mississauga, traveling on the QE Expressway, and were less than fifteen minutes away from Pearson Airport, Toronto.

In fifteen minutes they arrived at the airport; the car dropped them and took off. Karpov and Sonia were met by another Russian waiting there with all their documents, boarding passes, and luggage. They headed for the gates.

As the car that had dropped Karpov and Sonia was coming out of the drop-off bay into the lane to exit, another car driven by a Chinese woman rammed into its side. Karpov's driver, in his haste, had not looked over his left shoulder before pulling out. There was a police car up ahead, so Karpov's driver decided to play it cool. He took out his cell phone and told his contact of the mishap. The contact relayed the information to Karpov, who quickened his pace through airport security. Their flight to Dubai was already boarding, so with a bit of luck, he and Sonia would be on that flight before anything else developed, thought Karpov.

The policemen, Sam, walked toward the accident, and radioed the car number plates to his colleague, Steve, who was still in the patrol car. The numbers were punched in, and immediately an alarm flashed, identifying one of the vehicles as "most wanted," with an "approach with caution" warning. Sam got the message on his walkie-talkie and stopped in his tracks. His partner had called for backup, and to have all exits out of the airport blocked. Steve also came out of the patrol car, and both of them unholstered their guns, aiming at the driver of the suspect car. Sam yelled at the top of his voice for the suspect to step out of the vehicle with his hands raised. The driver did as he was instructed. Sam walked toward him very slowly, wary of any sudden movement. When he reached the driver, he asked him to turn around, frisked him roughly but thoroughly, and quickly handcuffed him. Only then did Sam and Steve start breathing normally. They jostled the suspect to their vehicle; in the meantime other police cars arrived and started clearing up traffic and taking a statement from the Chinese driver who had caused the accident.

Mark got the good and the bad news: good news that the car and the driver had been captured, bad news that the passengers had already left and were probably on their way to the boarding gates.

Mark called the airport security office and sent them the latest pictures of Karpov and Sonia (Aafia, he thought). By the time the pictures made it to the boarding gate, Emirates had already completed boarding, and the plane was pulling out of the gate.

Mark asked the airport security to scan the cameras and video recordings for the past half hour from the nearest point to where the accident had taken place, and work from there on. This was done, and soon Karpov and his charge were identified—the cameras followed them to the Emirates flight boarding. The security supervisor checked the clock—the flight had taken off over forty minutes ago. This information too was relayed to Mark.

Mark asked airport control to contact the captain of the Emirates flight and ask the flight to divert to JFK International Airport. Mark wanted the couple arrested on US soil, under his jurisdiction. The captain received the instructions with dismay and turned the plane toward New York. He estimated arrival time in just over an hour.

Team A
Yuri and Mike went down to the basement of the court building, through the basement into the sewer lines, and came out under the manhole exactly as planned. In another five minutes, they removed the manhole cover. The van was parked above it. Yuri pressed a small button on his key ring. The floor of the van opened, and a small ladder was lowered. Yuri was first to climb out, followed by Mike, carrying the prisoner.

As soon as they were aboard, the manhole was covered, and the van moved off. Their destination was Pier 6 on the East River in Manhattan, where a helicopter would be waiting to take them to the airport. Aafia's handcuffs and foot restraints were removed. She was still unconscious, so she was given an injection to bring her around.

Yuri knew that within ten minutes they had to be inside the airport building, and within another twenty-five through the airport security. It didn't matter which flight or to where, but the top priority was to get out of New York. After thirty minutes an alert would have gone to all airports, seaports, and train and bus stations. The only description they would have would be of a frail woman.

Aafia slowly opened her eyes and was immediately alarmed, seeing that she was surrounded by white men, for all those on Yuri's team were Russians. Her first impression was that she was in an ambulance with paramedics, and then she realized that the men wore suits and not paramedics' uniforms. None of them had beards, so they were not Muslims who had come to save her. She was being abducted, or maybe this was another drama to kill her off in a staged escape.

"We are taking you to your people. You will not be harmed, but you must cooperate with us," Yuri told her.

Now Aafia was sure she was going to be killed in a staged escape attempt. Another trick by the CIA, she thought bitterly. She said nothing and just stared at her captors. Yuri produced a tape recorder and played it to Aafia. "Sister Aafia, we have sent these people to bring you to us. Remember Maymar." That was it. The message was in Urdu, her native language, and the accent was of someone from the same family origins as herself. The mention of the word Maymar was the code, because Maymar was the housing estate in Karachi from where she was abducted by Pakistan's security agency, where her ordeal had started. Aafia pressed the "stop" button, and the tape gave a tiny explosion and destroyed itself. Fortunately, Aafia had just tossed the tape recorder toward Yuri, so she didn't get hurt. Neither did anyone else. Yuri cursed. These bloody Afghans or Pakistanis, whoever they were—they used explosives like *miswak*.

Yuri continued, "In a few minutes we will be arriving at the airport. We need to change your appearance, because everyone will be looking for a frail woman in her thirties. We have to shave your head; your papers will show that you are a cancer patient and have lost your hair in chemotherapy."

"Give me a blanket," she said. A blanket was produced from under the seat, and she wrapped herself in it.

Mike took out a trimmer and said very gently, "I am going to use this to shave your head, okay?" She said nothing, so Mike decided to take that as a yes and slowly started running the trimmer over her scalp. Within minutes her hair was gone. Next, a first-aid kit was taken out and some marks were made on her scalp to make it look like she had undergone chemotherapy.

The van stopped, and Yuri and Mike got out. They gave Aafia a makeup kit and some clothes: a pair of jeans, a T-shirt, flat shoes, a pair of glasses, and a cap. "Please change and use the makeup. You have three minutes." Aafia was out of the van within two and half minutes.

The distance from lower Manhattan to JFK is twelve miles; however, due to notorious New York traffic and the ongoing chase between the B-team and the law-enforcement agencies, Yuri had decided to take a helicopter, which should get them there in a matter of minutes.

Once at JFK airport, they headed for the boarding gate for the next available flight to Houston. One of Yuri's men was waiting with the tickets and boarding passes and a wheelchair for Aafia, to help with her disguise and expedite their way through the security checkpoint. Within fifteen minutes they had cleared security and were seated on the plane.

The plane took off on time and arrived at Houston on schedule. Yuri met Amir in the shadows at the arrivals, collected confirmation for the transfer of funds and headed straight for his departure gate. He was taking a long vacation.

Carlos was also present at the airport, but he didn't see the exchange between Amir and Yuri. Amir met Aafia and greeted her with the customary Muslim greeting. "*Salamalaikum*, sister Aafia, I am honored to receive you and to give you good news that soon you will be united with your people."

Aafia, still dazed from the events of the day, smiled feebly and nodded to Amir. "Sister, these men will take you to where you need to go. Put yourself in their hands and trust in Allah. Soon you will reach your destination."

"*Jazakallah Khair*," replied Aafia, meaning, "May God reward you for your good deeds."

With the exchange thus concluded, Carlos and his men whisked Aafia in a wheelchair to the waiting van. Amir, too, headed for the departure gates. He didn't know he was going to be sharing a flight with Yuri, because both were heading to Mexico.

El Paso, Texas
Tunnel passages across the international borders into the United States had become a real problem. There were forty such tunnels that had been discovered since 9/11, and the bulk of them were on the southern border. Large-scale smuggling of drugs, weapons,

and immigrants was taking place through these tunnels. One tunnel, running from San Diego to Tijuana, was distinguished by its inordinate sophistication. It was a half mile long and eight feet tall, and went sixty to eighty feet deep. It had a concrete floor. It was wired for electricity. It had drainage. What was interesting was that the California entry into the tunnel was a very modern warehouse—a huge warehouse, compartmented but empty, and kept empty for a year. In one office there was a hatch in the floor. It looked much like the hatch in which Saddam had secreted himself in Iraq. But lifting that hatch disclosed a very sophisticated tunnel. It went under other buildings, all the way across the double fence into Mexico and up into a building in Mexico as well.

Carlos planned to use just such a tunnel that stretched from the Mexican side under the Rio Grande to El Paso. The 130-foot-long tunnel was used for smuggling drugs into the United States. Officially the tunnel had been sealed off upon discovery, but Carlos had had Mexican contractors working underground to create a passage large enough for an adult to pass through.

But the first thing was to get to El Paso, and Carlos had decided to keep things simple. He had chartered a small plane to take him from Houston to El Paso. The flight took almost two hours, and when the passengers arrived in El Paso, night was falling. This was perfect from Carlos's point of view. He had all the arrangements in place to transport his cargo into Mexico undetected, in the dark of night. On the way to the final exit point in the United States, they picked up some food. Carlos had been advised that his passenger would only eat seafood, so Carlos's men had picked up the best seafood available in town and had it waiting as soon as they boarded the van from the airport.

Carlos had decided that he would only have one person accompany him and the passenger through the tunnel. They had packed shovels, dry rations, a large coil of wire, and a small first-aid box for their travel through the tunnel. As an additional precaution,

Carlos had also an oxygen cylinder for each person, complete with a mask. Carlos didn't want to find himself trapped inside a collapsed portion of the tunnel. Regardless of the success of the mission, he had no intention of dying inside that tunnel.

Carlos had had a crew do a dry run through the tunnel twice in the last week, and both times there were no major problems, so he was quite confident that the crossover would go smoothly. They started their journey through the tunnel at a little after midnight, and in an hour had arrived inside Mexico. Once in Mexico, Carlos had a makeup team ready in a van to alter the appearance of the lady passenger to match her photo on the passport and to put some hair on her head. Carlos hated women with shaved heads.

By early the next morning, using a combination of private planes and SUVs, Carlos had brought Aafia to a villa that had been rented by Amir's people in the suburbs of Mexico City, where Aafia was reunited with her two children and her sister.

When Aafia saw her children standing there in the living room of the villa, she finally believed that she had indeed escaped the Americans and by some miracle was being reunited with the only love of her life, her children. She just collapsed in a hug with her kids and her sister, sobbing uncontrollably. The emotional scene was too much for Carlos, who decided to leave them alone for a while. Amir was present in the villa too but had decided to let the family have their time together.

Eventually the family ran out of tears and settled down, sitting in a tight circle on the living room floor. They started talking, catching up and trying to come to grips with the miracle of their unexpected reunion.

The Emirates flight made an emergency landing at JFK. The passengers were informed that there was a technical fault and were asked to remain seated. As soon as the plane came to a halt, a team of DHS agents burst into the plane and immediately took Karpov and Sonia into custody. Both of them protested vociferously, but that was of no use.

One of Karpov's colleagues, a member of the Yuri gang, was also on the plane. He sent a text message to Yuri informing him in code, "The fish is caught." Yuri didn't get the text message because he had boarded a flight to Russia.

Karpov and Sonia were taken to a DHS detention center for interrogation. Mark decided to take over the job himself. He interviewed Karpov first, who completely denied any wrongdoing and stuck to his story that he was traveling with his girlfriend to Dubai for a vacation. Karpov demanded his phone call but was ignored.

The girlfriend also proved to be a cool customer. She repeated the story she had been given by Karpov that she was going on vacation with her Russian boyfriend and had done nothing wrong. A thorough check on both their identities confirmed they were who they said they were. Sonia bore some physical resemblance to Aafia, but was overall in much better physical condition than the prisoner who had been brought to the courthouse and had escaped.

Mark got Deputy Director Simmons on a video conference, and they were joined by the top people from the FBI, CIA and NSA. The group concluded that the couple was a decoy, and the real Aafia was still at large, so the manhunt must resume. It was decided to arrest Karpov and Sonia on charges of aiding and abetting terrorism and assisting in the escape of a prisoner.

The DEA agent who had worked at Razzle Dazzle was called in and identified Karpov as an active member of Yuri's gang. He further confirmed that Yuri had not been seen at the club for the past two nights, and Sasha was running the show in his absence.

Mark was getting a clearer picture now. Yuri had planned the escape, probably at the behest of some Afghan or Pakistani group. He had used Karpov and an Aafia lookalike as a decoy, and had managed to keep all the agencies occupied with a well-lit trail to ensure that the real prisoner escaped while the lookalike was being chased.

Yuri's picture was sent to Interpol and every other agency domestically, to collect whatever information there was about him and his movements in the past forty-eight hours.

Mark asked Mario to work with the FBI team to go over the escape and figure out how the real prisoner escaped.

It took Mario and the FBI agents a couple of hours to figure out how the escape had been executed. They started tracking the A-team's movements through street cameras, and after another day's labor, they did establish that Yuri and his gang had taken Aafia to Houston. There again the trail was picked up using the airport surveillance cameras. It took yet another day's work for the FBI and DHS team to track the movements of Carlos, who had been identified from police records, and his passenger to El Paso. There again the trail went cold, but the conclusion was obvious: Carlos had been hired to get Aafia into Mexico.

The White House

The president was briefed on the escape of Dr. Aafia and given confirmation that the Russian gang was indeed responsible, though a Mexican human smuggling gang was used to smuggle her out to Mexico. From there she had probably been flown into Pakistan and was now safely in Pakistani custody.

"Okay, gentlemen, the Pakistanis have crossed the red line. Now we must do everything we can to not only bring the escaped convict back to the US legal system, but also to remove the Pakistani leadership from power. John, you have my approval to launch the project. Thelma, throw everything at them, apply every economic and diplomatic measure to put maximum pressure on them. Matt, Thelma has briefed you on the progress we have made with Iran, so you better get prepared to shift logistics from the Pak route. David, put together a team to go into Pakistan and bring the prisoner back, no matter the cost or the consequences. We will not let some third-world country humiliate and defy the United States of America." The president paused, having rattled off instructions to each team member.

"Mr. President, if I may?" This was CIA Director John Deskovanci.

"Yes, John," said the president.

"I would suggest that the CIA be allowed to bring Aafia back to the United States. With all due respect to DHS and the commendable work they have done in tracking it all down so far, this is really now a task for the CIA. We already have a team—or rather, various teams—on the ground. We know the country, and we have an extensive network. We can do the job."

"Okay, John, you run with it, but I want results, and I want them fast." The president then turned to the SecDef. "Matt, this has gone beyond a simple difference of opinion between the two governments. We have to prepare for an all-out campaign against Pakistan. Please get a plan put together as a contingency.

"And, John, why don't you see what cooperation we can get from London."

The CIA director understood that the reference was to MI5 and their links to the man from Karachi in the Northern London area of Mill Hill. "Certainly, Mr. President."

London, England

"Sir Timothy, I have the CIA director on the line for you," Sir Timothy's secretary said.

"Okay, Lyn, put him through."

The head of MI5 picked up the phone and greeted his American counterpart instantly. "Good evening, John."

"Good evening, Sir Timothy. You have, of course heard about the escape of the Pakistani prisoner from the courthouse in New York," said the director of the CIA.

"Yes, dreadful business. Your president must be going ape," replied Sir Timothy.

"Yes, and we were wondering how you are handling things at your end, what with the threats to close down your embassy and other harassment of your diplomatic staff," said the CIA director.

"Well, the cabinet decided to sit this one out while we prepare for any eventualities," replied Sir Timothy, not wishing to tip his hand.

"Sir Timothy, we think the time has come for your guest in Mill Hill to turn the heat up. We are taking all measures at our end to ensure that the threat posed by that country is contained and eliminated," the CIA director said.

"I hear you, John, and let me assure you we will do everything at our end to ensure that our mutual goals are achieved," replied Sir Timothy. A few other snippets of information were exchanged, and then the conversation between the two spymasters ended.

"Lyn, call Number 10, and tell them I am coming through to see the PM." Sir Timothy rose from his chair and left the office.

The British Prime Minister's Office

"Mr. Prime Minister, we have just received a call from the CIA director. They want us to help by activating our man from Karachi. I thought you should know," Sir Timothy informed the PM.

"Go ahead, Sir Timothy, but make sure we remain in control, and let us get a better sense of what our American friends are planning," said the PM.

MI5 Headquarters

"Lyn, call Ferguson and ask him to come on the double," Sir Timothy said to his secretary.

"Ferguson is here, Sir Timothy," announced the secretary after a few minutes.

Ferguson had been assigned for the past two years as the liaison for the man from Karachi, who had arrived in England some eighteen years ago, fleeing an attack on his life by the government-sponsored thugs at the time. Ever since his arrival, he had become the British government's cherished asset, providing a network to MI5 that was far better than the CIA's network, combined with street power that had no rival. "Ferguson, pay a visit to our friend in Mill Hill and tell him to turn the heat up in his old city." That was all Ferguson needed to hear and Sir Timothy needed to say. Both were fully aware what this entailed.

Mill Hill, North London

Ferguson was received by the secretary to Bhai. This was how the man was known in his party circles. (Bhai simply meant brother and sometimes referred to an older brother. In India, this term had come to signify a local Mafioso or gangster.)

Ferguson was shown in and was received by Bhai, who was warmth and sweetness personified. "Mr. Ferguson! Long time no see, but I know you are always seeing us, he, he, he." The man laughed at his own joke. The reference, of course, was to MI5 keeping an eye on the comings and goings at the man's residence.

"Mr. Tariq, we seem to be having a bit of bother from your government," said Ferguson.

"Yes, yes, I know. That madman you allowed to reach Islamabad has made everyone's life miserable, but right now he is popular and he has a lot of support. You know he has Afghan gangsters doing his dirty work. Those Afghan thugs killed many of my party workers during elections," Bhai went on.

"Mr. Tariq, we think the time has come for your party to show your government who controls Karachi and who is really in power there." This was a carefully crafted challenge and ego boost delivered by Ferguson.

"Mr. Ferguson, we are not wearing bangles." This was a reference to the Indo-Pak custom of women wearing bangles, implying they were not defenseless women. "Soon you will see my party launching protests against the massive rigging in the elections. We are issuing a white paper, and very soon you will see how uncomfortable these people find their bed of roses."

"I am glad to hear that, Mr. Tariq, and thank you for meeting me on such short notice," said Ferguson, and he rose to leave.

Bhai picked up the phone and asked his secretary to summon the governor and the party leaders from Karachi to London for a meeting.

Aafia and her family were flown to Istanbul, and from there they were flown to Islamabad. It had been decided by the general that it was best to reduce the risk of road travel. Upon arrival in Islamabad, after a brief reunion with her parents and other family members and having made a video of her freedom with a short speech, she was put on a plane to China, where she was sent as a member of the diplomatic staff with a new identity, based in the Pakistani embassy in Beijing. She had been instructed not to travel or deal with any member of the public for the next few months. She was to live inside the embassy compound, and her kids would be admitted to a school where Pakistani children of the diplomatic staff went. Her official job would be to carry out research on business opportunities for Pakistanis in China.

Pakistani Prime Minister's Office, Islamabad
"So, General, tell me, has your new deputy councillor reached Beijing?"

General Bhaya knew the reference was to the recently freed Aafia Siddiqui. "Yes, Prime Minister, she has reached Beijing and, after getting her kids settled down in school, she will start her duties."

"Good, we should now get ready for the next phase," said Sultan.

"Agreed" was the short reply from the general.

The PM's secretary knocked and came in. "Mr. Prime Minister, the cabinet members have arrived for the meeting." Sultan and the general rose and left to attend the cabinet meeting.

Federal Cabinet Meeting at the PM's Secretariat in Islamabad
Sultan began, "Ladies and gentlemen, as you are aware per our manifesto and our pledge to the people to rid the country of Americans, their puppets and foreign influence, we are taking some measures. I am going to take you all into confidence on these measures.

"We are announcing an embargo on local suppliers and service providers, to stop any further expansion of American operations inside Pakistan by denying them any services for their expansion projects. The Americans have already been put on notice to stop expanding their embassy and consulates in my inaugural speech. The British have been told to pack up and leave, but they have not complied. We propose to give them final notice and force their evacuation." Sultan paused and looked at his cabinet colleagues. For once they were all quiet; there was no desk or table thumping or any expression of happiness. I wonder why that is, thought Sultan. After all, everything he had said was part of their election agenda, so these people should be happy.

Sultan went on, "IMF and World Bank have been told to wind up their missions, as have all the international rating agencies. The rating agencies were given seven days to pack up and leave the country. The foreign exchange control regime that was in use before the foreign exchange reforms of 1991 is reinstated, and free exchange of rupees and free movement of currency has been done away with." A member coughed, and Sultan paused and looked at him.

As their eyes met, the minister said, "Prime Minister, we fully support your policies, and of course this is all part of our election manifesto, but some of us were wondering, what is the hurry? We have five years to deliver—that is, till the next elections. I think we should consolidate our power and make sure we have control of all the institutions before we take on the whole world."

"Mr. Malik, we are popular right now. We have a fresh mandate, so people will accept whatever we do, and we have five years to repair any damage and rebuild. So my friend, the sooner we start the better." With that, the PM read on.

"The biggest problem we face is of ill-gotten wealth in the economy and lack of documentation. So we are demonetizing—all the old currency notes are to be discontinued and new notes issued. This move will bring hundreds of billions into the banking system and formal economy, and improve our tax collection." Sultan knew this was bitter medicine and directly affected some ministers and their constituencies, so some opposition was to be expected.

"Prime Minister, we all support your policies, but I agree with my colleague Mr. Malik that we need to move cautiously. We are antagonizing the foreigners who are our biggest financial donors, and we are going to upset the local wealthy class at the same time. We must not open too many fronts at once." This was one of the ministers Sultan expected opposition from, because his business was undocumented and his industry, the transport industry, was going to be affected.

"Mr. Sardar, if we don't take these measures now, then we will never be able to. If General Musharraf had taken harsh measures within the first three months after his military coup, then perhaps we would not be here today. Same goes for General Zia before that. Ali Bhutto took drastic measures just like we are doing, and the people supported him. If he had not lost his way, he would still be alive and leading this country. My friend, fortune favors the brave." Sultan closed his folder, thanked everyone, and rose.

These announcements were to be preceded by the airing of the video of the American ambassador's threats, taken in the Blue Room a few weeks ago, when he was threatening the newly elected government with dire consequences. The videos, Sultan expected, will incite public hatred against Americans and divert their attention.

⊷+ +⊷

"Prime Minister, we are getting reports on most TV channels of people protesting in the streets, and crowds are moving toward the American and British missions." This was the prime minister's secretary, Altaf.

"Get me the interior minister on the line" was Sultan's brief reply.

"Prime Minister, Interior Minister Chaudhry is on the line," his secretary informed him.

"Okay, Altaf, put the extension down. I don't want you to take any notes on this conversation." Sultan waited for Altaf to put the phone down. Interesting, thought Altaf, but he knew the interior minister's secretary would be taking notes, so he told his assistant to go over to the interior minister's office and get a transcript of the conversation.

"Chaudhry, what is the latest?"

"Prime Minister, in Karachi, there are street battles between our supporters and our rival parties' workers. A group of our party supporters is marching toward the American consulate on Mai Kolachi. In Islamabad, the diplomatic enclave has been cordoned off," reported the minister.

"Well, why don't we avoid a confrontation between our own people and our security agencies? There is no point in losing our blood for foreigners, is there?" suggested Sultan.

"Okay, sir, understood. I will convey the message to the provincial government," said the minister.

"Minister, the Sindh Province chief minister is on the line, sir," Chaudhry's secretary informed him.

"Chief Minister, I hear there are protest marchers heading toward the American Consulate in Karachi?"

"Yes, Minister. I was about to call you myself. What is the federal cabinet's policy? How much force can we use to stop the protestors?" Chief Minister Sindh asked.

"None. No force is to be used against the protestors. Chief Minister, we do not want to pit our forces against our people. We don't want a civil war," concluded the federal interior minister.

"But, Minister, if we do nothing, then the enraged mob may burn down the American consulate," the chief minister said, forcing his point home.

"Chief Minister, our information is that the protestors will chant slogans, burn the American president's effigy, and then disperse. If your government takes any violent action, then let me be very clear: WE WILL NOT BACK YOU UP."

The CM stared at the phone, on the other end of which there was no one, as the federal minister had slammed the phone down.

"Minister Chaudhry, I have the Commissioner of Islamabad on the line," the minister was informed by his secretary.

"Minister, we have cordoned off all the roads heading into the Blue Area and the Diplomatic Enclave, but more and more people are gathering at the barriers, and I fear the situation may get worse. We will have to use force to disperse the crowd, or they will break through the barriers," the commissioner of Islamabad reported.

"Commissioner, remove the barriers. This is a free country; people have a right to demonstrate. Just make sure that security around the prime minister's house, the presidency, and the National Assembly is not breached. People need to vent their anger, so let them. They will shout, throw a few stones, and burn a few tires, and then they will go back. Under no circumstances are you to use force against people. Is that understood?" The commissioner looked at the phone in his hand in disbelief.

"Yes, Minister, I understand perfectly." The commissioner put the phone down at his end and called his secretary into the office.

"Jamil, take notes, and send this memo by email, fax, and courier to the interior minister and the prime minister. Also, send copies in plain unmarked envelopes to the American embassy.

Address it to the interior minister:

'Dear Sir, as per your explicit instructions, we have removed all the barriers at various entry points to the Islamabad Blue Area and the Diplomatic Enclave. In your assessment, the protestors will turn back after minor protests; however, I beg to differ with that assessment and consider the risk of the demonstration turning violent very high, resulting in loss of property and lives of both Pakistanis and foreigners. In view of the foregoing, I tender my resignation with immediate effect.'" With that, the commissioner dismissed his secretary, lit a pipe, and started puffing on it.

The White House

"Mr. President, this is something you need to see." The president's chief of staff turned on the TV in the Oval Office.

It was the Al Jazeera TV channel out of Qatar, and the anchor was saying in an excited voice, "We have just received this video from one of our sources inside the Taliban organization. It shows Aafia Siddiqui, who was until recently in the custody of the American government, serving eighty-six years of prison time. It seems like Ms. Siddiqui is free and happy with her children. Taliban commander Maulvi Dareywala's group has taken responsibility for releasing this video. We would like to mention here that the Maulvi Dareywala group is closely associated with Dalbadin Maarmatyar, who is one of the top Taliban commanders and leaders."

"Call the CIA chief, foreign secretary, and defense secretary for a meeting," the president said.

"They are already here; I took the liberty of calling them as soon as I found about the video. They are in the cabinet room," replied the chief of staff.

Cabinet Room—White House

"Gentlemen, this has gone far enough; we cannot let this pass. We need to bring the prisoner back to the United States and punish those who are responsible," the president said.

"Mr. President, I have spoken to the foreign secretary of Pakistan, and he is denying any involvement of his country," Thelma, the foreign secretary, said.

The president's secretary walked in and whispered something to him. He nodded and she left. "John, there is an urgent call from your office. You can take it here," the president said to the CIA chief, who was surprised at this.

He picked up the phone and listened intently for a few minutes, and then looked at the president and said, "That was our station chief in Islamabad. He just got a call from Dalbadin Maarmatyar, who is presently in Iran and swears that none of his people were involved in this. He further conveyed that he was offered the job by General Bhaya, the Pakistani foreign minister, days after they took over power, but he declined and moved to Iran to stay out of the way."

"So it looks like the Pakistanis have betrayed us again," observed the president of the United States of America grimly.

"Mr. President, the media is calling for retaliation, and opinion polls are suggesting the same about the public. We need to give some kind of response before it is too late," said the president's chief of staff.

"Well, we can always attack Pakistan and teach them a lesson," said Matt Clapton, the defense secretary.

Yeah, the military and defense contractors would really love that, thought the president bitterly. Another war and another half a trillion expense in the defense budget. No one seems to care that the country was living on borrowed money, and a lot of it was coming from China, who was Pakistan's best friend and neighbor. I want four more years, and I intend to see those through without a direct war involving the United States, concluded the president inwardly.

To the defense secretary he said, "Matt, we cannot go to war against a country that has nearly one hundred nuclear warheads and a leadership that is the most unstable we have seen in that country's history. And I don't think China is going to sit by idly and watch. Direct military action is not an option; but I agree we need to show some action to contain the PR damage domestically."

The president turned to the CIA chief. "John, we need a location on Maulvi Dareywala, and for now we just hit him. We will feed the media on that while we work on a more indirect action plan against Pakistanis."

"Okay, Mr. President, I will get right on it," replied the CIA chief.

White House—Two Days after the President's Order to Find Maulvi Dareywala

"Mr. President, we have a location on Dareywala. We talked to our friends in PakMil, and they have assured us of full cooperation starting with the location of the Taliban leader," said the CIA chief.

"So the Pakistanis continue to play double games," the president said to no one in particular.

"Mr. President, the sense we are getting from PakMil is that they are not on the same page with their political leadership on many issues, especially on US-Pakistan relations. They want to keep channels of communication open with us," said General Cowlon, who had been invited for this meeting, as he was responsible for all military action in the AF-Pak area.

"I hear you guys. For now we hit Dareywala and his people, let the heat simmer down on the domestic front. Then we will decide what to do about the Pakistanis," the president concluded.

Khyber Agency Tribal Area in Pakistan

In the shadow of the Safed Koh Mountains, on a moonless night, darkness had descended, the weather was hot and clammy, and chatter could be heard from the mosque, where some people were gathered in darkness.

"Control, Maulvi Dareywala is sitting, along with half a dozen of his men, in the forecourt of his seminary," said Wali into his transmitter. Wali and Firoz were hidden about five hundred meters north, camouflaged on a small hill. Both worked for Pakistani intelligence agencies; both were wearing tribal dress, spoke fluent Pashto, and had papers showing them to be from a nearby village.

"Wali, how does this make sense? We are guiding an American drone attack against this guy, while our government and political parties are protesting against these attacks. For God's sake, we trained this guy in Akora Khattak seminary," said Firoz in some frustration.

"Firoz, you now work for an intelligence agency; stop thinking like a soldier. The first rule of the intelligence business is, what is, is not, and what you see is not what you see. Everything is an illusion. We work in and deal in shadows. Our targets are constantly shifting, but our objective remains unchanged," replied Wali.

Firoz thought this was all poppycock, but in order not to displease Wali, who was his senior, and to kill boredom, he asked, "And what is our objective, and why do we want this guy dead?"

"Our objective, my young friend, is to defeat the Americans and make sure they never get out of Afghanistan. And if they do, they must leave everything behind so our army can use it. Our objective is to fight for oppressed Muslims everywhere in the world, be it Bosnia, Kashmir, or China. About this guy, you are right—we trained him and he fought for us, but now he is a mercenary selling his services to the highest bidder, and his new masters are sitting in New Delhi. He carries out attacks on Pakistani assets on New Delhi's orders."

"Hang on a second; I am confused. I thought we wanted the Americans to leave Afghanistan," Firoz said.

"We got the Americans into Afghanistan in the first place," said Wali, enjoying himself. "Mulla Omer was ready to surrender Osama, but we made sure he didn't. Our country's budget cannot support the army and pay for the weapons we need to fight the Indians. The Americans have paid us over fifteen billion dollars in cash, and what we have learned in terms of weapons technology and other tactical benefits is priceless. Our Afghan friends have reaped tens of billions of dollars in hard cash and other benefits, and they invest most of their money through our banks and in our economy. So it is a win-win for us. Once the Americans leave, we will get nothing from them, and neither will our Afghan friends, and we will have millions of Afghan refugees making their way back into Pakistan. Who wants that? Tell me, would you let a goose laying golden eggs leave? No one will. The Americans must stay in Afghanistan, otherwise India will start dictating to us, and that we will never let happen. Why do you think we keep blocking the ISAF route? They are trying to leave and take their stuff back. We don't want them to, the Afghans don't want them to, the Indians don't want them to, and the Saudis don't want them to. The only countries that want the Americans to leave are Iran and China."

Wali's earpiece crackled. "Confirm target location."

Wali whispered back, "Target location confirmed."

"Let's get out of here," Wali said, and Firoz followed him, slowly crawling down the other side of the small hill. They had bicycles hidden a hundred paces down the road, behind the bushes. Those cycles would be abandoned after covering three kilometers to the place where two motorbikes had been hidden. They could not risk the Taliban hearing the sound of their motorbike engines.

As they mounted their bicycles and raced away from the seminary, they heard a whirring sound in distance. They knew from past experience that the drone was above them somewhere, ready to fire. This was followed by a swoosh sound. Both pedaled hard, but in thirty seconds they were flying through the air after the missile fired from the drone hit the seminary, and the impact forced their bikes off the road. Somewhat dazed, they remounted their bicycles and got away as fast as they could.

"Prime Minister, the cabinet is waiting for you." The words from his secretary brought Sultan out of his reverie. He rose and headed to the cabinet room.

"Good afternoon, ladies and gentlemen. General, will you please recite a few verses from the Holy Quran to start the meeting?"

After the recitation the finance minister cleared his throat. "Prime Minister, if I may?"

Sultan was relieved that someone was willing to move the meeting forward, because his own mind was on the threat looming on the horizon. The Americans had just hit some Taliban in the Federally Administrated Tribal Area of Pakistan; this group was hit because the Americans were led to believe that they were behind Aafia's release. This had been engineered by the general, through his influence within the intelligence community in the country. The message from the Americans was clear: they were going to eliminate anyone implicated in the escape of their prisoner Aafia. But Sultan's biggest worry was that there might be a coup from the military, and all his hard work would be wasted.

"Prime Minister, the IMF has suspended aid. Asian Development Bank, the World Bank, and Japan's EXIM Banks have announced the suspension of various projects' funding that had been previously committed. As a result, our country's credit rating has been downgraded to 'junk' status, and we are seeing over a hundred million dollars net outflow every day. The Ministry of Finance fears that within a month, we will be looking at a default scenario," concluded the finance minister gravely.

The minister for industries, who belonged to the business community, added, "Prime Minister, the EU has withdrawn the duty exemptions they had given to us and have imposed antidumping duties on Pakistani textile products. The top three American buyers who, combined, purchased over a billion dollars of Pakistani textile exports, have canceled their orders. We are likely to see the closure of many textile factories if this trend continues."

"All of this is expected," Sultan replied, trying to sound relaxed and in control. "If you look at our policy discussions before the elections, we had anticipated these moves, so there is no need to panic. We need to stay the course. Certainly there will be pain, but no pain, no gain."

The interior minister reported, "Prime Minister, there have been violent demonstrations in Karachi; the ethnic party there is galvanizing its supporters. Opposition parties are forming an alliance like that of the 1977 PNA movement that ousted Ali Bhutto."

Sultan tried to reassure his cabinet members. "Let us get our media machine dealing with it. We have documents and plans all laid out for these scenarios; we need to get on the box and educate people about what's going on. I want every member of the cabinet and most of our senior elected members to be on TV. Don't say no to any journalist, to any show. You need to tell people that the CIA and their partners are planning political assassinations, which they will blame on the government. You need to inform the public that foreign agents will be carrying out terrorist attacks and will create panic everywhere. Get out there and spread our message, that all of this is as expected, as planned. Each of you will be given media kits that will give facts, figures, and evidence of past such conspiracies by the CIA, along with questions you will face and answers you may give." Sultan noticed that General Bhaya had kept quiet throughout the meeting and continued to stare at his writing pad. Was the general distancing himself from these discussions and decisions? Sultan wondered. As soon as Sultan got back to his office, his secretary gave him a short report, which showed that the stock markets were in a free fall and the rupee had depreciated 10 percent overnight.

Sultan's intercom buzzed, and the secretary informed him that General Bhaya was coming through. "You were very quiet in the cabinet meeting, General," Sultan said as the general walked in and took a seat.

"There can only be one leader, and it is you. If I had jumped in, it might have seemed like undermining your leadership, and this could have created the wrong impression," the general replied smoothly. He went on. "We need to discuss serious defense issues."

"Yes, that we do, but first tell me: what's the news from GHQ?" Sultan needed to know how secure his flanks were.

"They are engaged in a dialogue with the Americans. We know the army and the Pentagon are very close—in some ways closer than we are—to our own army. But the high command is still trying to grapple with the fast-changing scenario. There is a lot of support for our policies from soldiers and officers below the colonel rank. The colonels and senior officers all see this as a path to destruction, but they will not take any action unless there is support from below, which will only happen if we do something that is perceived to be against the army. That we are not planning to do, so we should have enough time to execute our plans. Let us meet later today for a game of golf." The general rose and left.

Sultan was peeved. The general had not even waited for his confirmation; he had simply assumed Sultan would show up as ordered. How dare he! The general's wings needed to be clipped, Sultan decided.

Later that evening Sultan, with a driver and two guards, left the prime minister's house in a white Toyota Land Cruiser, a vehicle very common in Islamabad, and arrived at the golf club. Sultan had deliberately arrived half an hour late, just to keep the general waiting.

Sultan asked his guards and driver to wait with the Toyota and walked toward the area behind the ninth hole. There was a secluded spot there, and a picnic bench had been set up there by the club management for the members. The air was cool and pungent with the fragrance of wild flowers; mosquitoes and dragonflies were buzzing. Most of the golfers had gone home for the day, so it was quiet. There was a rustling of branches and a sudden movement in front of Sultan. As he watched, a couple of monkeys jumped across his path and disappeared into the woods on his left. Sultan looked sadly after the monkeys; his people were far less fortunate than these monkeys and just as intelligent. Sultan shook his head and moved on, arriving at the picnic bench in a few rapid strides.

General Bhaya was sitting, and facing him was a man in his early seventies, with a full head of gray hair, bushy eyebrows, and a perfect set of teeth that he barred at Sultan as he rose to greet him. Sultan recognized him of course; this was the famous Dr. Q, who was known to many as the father of the Islamic bomb. It was called Islamic on the misguided notion that should any Muslim countries need it, they would be welcome to it! This was nonsense, of course; Sultan had read before coming to power that there was an agreement with the Saudi government to allow them access to nuclear weapons should the need arise, but Sultan had not seen any official paperwork on it. There was Pakistani cooperation with Iran and Libya in nuclear technology for military purposes, of which this man, Dr. Q, had been accused. Iran and Libya had of course spilled the beans to achieve their own goals, leaving Pakistan to face the international music, which had led to incarceration of the doctor under General Musharraf.

Sultan accepted the extended hand of the nuclear scientist with a smile, nodded to General Bhaya, and joined them at the table.

The general started speaking. "Doctor, you are aware that a year ago, during the planning stage when various scenarios were 'war-gamed,' it was concluded that once Pakistan embarked on an independent course, the Americans would come after Pakistan with everything they had in their arsenal. There is no way Pakistan's defense forces could take on the Americans in a full-scale confrontation. We certainly don't want Pakistan to turn into Baghdad of 1990. And now that we have put the Americans under pressure, the likelihood of such a scenario emerging is very high. Therefore, we need you to help us in delivering a nuclear package that will deter the Americans from attacking Pakistan."

"I agree, General; the United States must be checked from waging a full-scale war against Pakistan," replied Dr. Q. "To do that, they must face a credible threat of nuclear devastation on her own soil. It is out of the question to deliver nuclear bombs by air at targets inside the United States. Therefore, the only solution is to arrange for nuclear bombs to be smuggled inside its borders."

Sultan's mind went back to how Dr. Q had demanded that he would only cooperate once the elected government had crossed a red line—i.e., freeing Dr. Aafia from American custody. Thus, Dr. Aafia's release had become a central plank in the nation's future defense. He hoped now that Dr. Aafia was freed, Dr. Q was satisfied that the new government and leadership were indeed serious, and he was not going to be made a sacrificial goat as he had been by General Musharraf's government some years ago.

"Prime Minister," Dr. Q said, turning his attention to Sultan, "let me share with you a brief tale of how deeply the Americans have penetrated us, before we move on to our discussion at hand. Rest assured this story is not the ramblings of an old man but pertinent to the issue at hand," Dr. Q went on, smiling condescendingly at Sultan.

"In the mid-1980s, I had purchased some highly technical computer equipment for calibration, to be used in our nuclear program. The Americans had gotten a whiff of it, but the shipment was destined for Tokyo, Japan, where a façade setup had been created to make it look like the equipment had been installed there. In reality the equipment was loaded on a PIA flight to Tokyo, which stopped in Pakistan where the equipment was replaced with some relatively cheap computers. The CIA followed the consignment to Tokyo and was fooled into buying the story that the equipment was actually in Tokyo. But the most senior Pakistani bureaucrat of the time was on the Americans' payroll; he had tried to prevent funds from getting to suppliers to thwart the nuclear program at the behest of the Americans. Sadly, we had to publicize a scandal about his son-in-law's corruption to ensure compliance by the bureaucrat. When I say 'we,' I of course mean the intelligence agencies and the security establishment of the country, which was then headed by the good general here. Oh, those were the good days, weren't they, General?" said the doctor with a dreamy look in his eyes, reliving his past glory.

General Bhaya cleared his throat to speak, but the doctor beat him to it. "Prime Minister, have you been given a tour of our nuclear facilities?"

Sultan was a bit taken aback at this line of enquiry. "No, Doctor, I have not been," he replied, a bit uncomfortably.

"Well, rest assured you will not be given one," said the doctor. "You see, our military leadership believes that it is the only institution that can be trusted with the security of strategic weapons, and even elected prime ministers are treated like enemy intelligence agents. Your father may have initiated the nuclear program and been hanged for it at the Americans' behest by our military, but you will still not qualify for a tour." Dr. Q paused. Sultan gathered the reference was to the hanging of Ali Bhutto and his daughter Benazir Bhutto, who was twice prime minister of the country.

"But if you are a military general and have come into power by committing treason, bending the constitution and usurping power, the same military will keep mum, even if you allowed Americans to occupy a facility within ten minutes' drive of the country's most cherished nuclear asset. This is how our military operates, and make no mistake: when I say military, it's not the navy, who are scoffed at as a bunch of sailors, or the air force, which is considered a bunch of glorified drivers and mechanics by the army. No, sir, I mean the Pakistan army, and more specifically the army chief and a few of his buddies, foremost and most influential among them the chief of ISI." Dr. Q paused and took a sip of water.

"Doctor, it is the Pakistan Army. It is our army," Sultan said.

Dr. Q laughed. "It is not the Pakistan Army; it is the army's Pakistan. Let me correct some misconceptions you may have. There is the ISI, which is the most powerful institution in this country—yes, even more powerful than the army. And then there is the Pakistan Army. The rest of the country is there to serve them. Anyway, more to the point, the Americans have had enough access to Pakistan's nuclear arsenal to know all our nuclear secrets. Therefore, it will not be possible to move enriched uranium for covert weapons development without their detection." Sultan gave a sigh of relief, hoping that the whole idea would fall apart, and he could make some kind of deal with the Americans and move on with putting the country back on track.

Dr. Q perceived this as disappointment rather than relief and went on. "But there is another way, and this is where the general's network can yield results. Our nuclear weapons are constantly moved, and you know one thing the army can't keep straight is paperwork; the boys in khaki hate paperwork. So it is very easy to manipulate this weakness to get hold of some nuclear weapons for what we have in mind."

Then why do we need you? Sultan thought bitterly.

Dr. Q looked into Sultan's eyes, seeing shades of disillusionment, and smiled inwardly. He had made the release of Dr. Aafia a condition for a very simple reason: he wanted to make sure that the new government had been put in a position where they simply could not turn back. Dr. Q knew that the Americans would come after his country with everything they had; they would try to take Aafia back. The ensuing confrontation would make sure the United States and Pakistan could never be allies again. Only by making that happen could the process of cleansing the Muslim community from the American influence begin. This was Dr. Q's firm faith. He knew he would not live through this, but he had no regrets. He'd had a great life and had done more for his country then any man alive or dead. This was his reward.

Dr. Q went on. "I have a blueprint for our plan. NLC, the army's transport arm, regularly moves nuclear weapons to a facility in the west of Karachi. The next shipment is due in a few days. En route to their destination the weapons will be switched with duds, identical-looking weapons but with no nuclear load. As these weapons are to sit in storage at the air force facility, there is very little likelihood that the switch will be discovered until it is too late. Besides, the general has assured me that the person in charge at the storage facility is under our influence and will fully co-operate and keep us informed of any negative developments.

"The nuclear weapons will be moved to a ship, which has been bringing wheat from the United States. The ship has been modified at Karachi Shipyard according to the design prepared by the navy engineers the general assigned to the job. The hull of the ship will now carry twelve nuclear missiles, which can be fired from a mobile launcher. The ship sails in seven days and will dock in the United States six weeks after that," concluded the doctor.

After a lot of deliberation, the doctor had decided to keep the plan very basic and simple. Dr. Q and the general both knew that the simplest plans had the best chance of success, so it had been decided to use a team of navy engineers to craft a holding space inside the cargo vessel for transporting missiles. Neither the engineers nor the navy had any clue as to what they were doing or why they were doing it; they were simply given the dimensions of the hold and the design. No one from the ship's crew had any idea of the secret hold. The plan was to load twelve missiles with nuclear tips onto the ship without the knowledge of the crew or the captain. These missiles would then be unloaded covertly in a US port. From there they would be transported to twelve different locations.

Twenty-four men had been recruited and trained to carry out the mission of firing these weapons and then blowing themselves up. All the recruits had been head-hunted from the Federally Administrated Tribal Area of Pakistan. All the recruits had one thing in common: they had all lost family members, and some had lost whole families, in the US drone attacks. They all wanted revenge and had no desire to live on or fear for losing their lives.

Getting these men into the United States and positioned was the responsibility of the general. The doctor was responsible for the technical aspects of the project.

Dr. Q and the general had spent a considerable amount of time identifying the twelve potential targets, but the final list was only known to the general.

General Bhaya decided it was time for Amir to get back into action. He called Amir on his cell phone. Amir, after bringing Dr. Aafia to Pakistan, had decided to take some time off and sojourn in the port city of Karachi. This was where he was now.

Amir instinctively knew that the caller was his old mentor, the general, and responded instantly. "*Salam walaikum, Moaalim.*" Amir had always looked upon the general as a teacher, and the general had always treated him like a cherished pupil. This was also a code of sorts between them.

"Bacha, how are you?" And without waiting for the answer, the general went on. "Let us meet tomorrow for breakfast."

"Insha'Allah, I will be there." Amir understood that the general did not trust mobile phones or any kind of electrical communication devices, and kept his conversations as short as possible. Amir didn't need to be told that the meeting would be at the general's house in Islamabad, and that he would have to get there before dawn.

Amir arrived in Islamabad in the early hours of the morning. One of Amir's old comrades was at the airport to pick him up and drive him to the general's house. Amir was aware that various other intelligence agencies and police operatives had witnessed his arrival, as it was routine to watch the airports, and it would be reported in due course to the higher authorities. Amir also knew that because of his past, the information would be passed on to the CIA, who had an extensive network inside Pakistan. But this is where the trail would go cold; no one would dare follow Amir and his comrade because this town was owned and run by the intelligence agencies, and Amir was still considered one of their own, especially after the general's elevation to the higher corridors of power.

It took Amir half an hour to get to the general's house, which was in a locality called Chak Shahzad. Amir entered the house through electronic gates that had swung open as their car drove up. Amir got out and waved good-bye to his comrade, who reversed the car out of the still-open gates.

Amir walked to the part of the house known as *hujra*, which was designated for male guests of the general, and entered without knocking, because that was the custom. The general was sitting on his prayer mat absorbed in early morning prayers. Amir performed ablutions in the bathroom, which was at the far end and designed for this purpose, and joined the general for the predawn prayers, the fajr.

After the prayers, a servant brought a tray that had two breakfasts and left the host and the guest. After the usual greetings and a little bit of small talk, the general moved to the real issue. "I want you to travel back to America and arrange for getting twenty-four men to enter the United States without detection. You have to leave immediately; the passengers must reach the United States within a week." The general handed Amir a briefcase that had Amir's ticket, his passport, cash in US dollars, and a few other things.

They finished breakfast, and Amir rose to leave. The general got up and embraced him tightly. The general's tight embrace and its length of a few extra seconds alerted Amir to the great danger he was undertaking. He had worked with the general for three decades now and was used to carrying out orders without much explanation, because he knew that both he and the general shared the same mission. The prospect of danger didn't bother Amir, and he knew that the general had sent countless men on missions that were more dangerous. It was the general's tension that made Amir realize that this might well be his last mission for his country, and maybe even of his life.

Amir took the next flight to Houston via London and arrived in Houston the next day. During his research for recruiting Carlos, Amir had come across another human smuggler, Chikko, but for the Aafia project, Amir had opted for Carlos because Carlos was greedier, smaller, and therefore suited the mission more.

Amir met Chikko and told him what he wanted. It was agreed that a group of twenty-four college students would arrive from Pakistan on a tour of Mexico, and from Mexico Chikko's team would smuggle them into the USA. Chikko wanted US$25,000 each, which meant a total price tag of over $600,000. Eventually they agreed on a total package of $250,000, a quarter of a million dollars. Amir insisted on paying only $50,000 up front, another $75,000 when the "students" arrived in Mexico, and the balance upon their arrival inside the United States. Nice bit of business, Chikko thought.

Chikko was aware of the tunnel Carlos had recently used, though he didn't know the details except that the tunnel was in good condition. Ironically, he was thinking of using the same tunnel to bring his group of tourists into the United States.

Amir headed to the airport. He planned to take an Emirates flight to Dubai and connect to a flight for Islamabad from there. He hoped to be back in Islamabad the next day.

The Coastline between Karachi and Baluchistan
In a secluded area of the Arabian sea, on the border of Karachi and Baluchistan, two boats pulled up in a place known as Sonmiani, which had no public access and a warning sign telling trespassers that this was a restricted military area. Both the boats were manned by sailors wearing navy uniforms. The receiving party on the small dock quickly loaded four wooden boxes into the two boats, and within fifteen minutes the boats had left.

It took the two boats another hour to make the journey to Karachi Shipyard. It was 3:00 a.m., and the whole city was enveloped in darkness because of a major power failure. The boats were directed to a designated area where another team of navy sailors unloaded the cargo. The whole process was completed without a single word being spoken. The team bringing the cargo had no knowledge of what it was, and neither did the team receiving it.

The boxes were taken to a predesignated part of the boat, which was in the aft, close to the hull. A third team was waiting there. These were engineers from the army and scientists from the Atomic Research Center in Kahutta. Together they opened the boxes and with great care ensconced the nuclear-tipped missiles in the cavities specially created for this purpose.

The whole exercise was completed in three days, during which, except for the engineers and the scientists, all the other teams were changed. No one sailor was allowed to work twice on the delivery, and after their task was achieved, they were posted to remote places.

On the fourth day, when all the engineers and the scientists had left, Dr. Q and the general arrived for final inspection. Dr. Q was satisfied with the arrangements and confirmed to the general that the cargo was ready for the journey.

The general would inform the CEO of the shipping company to sail the ship in the morning, to bring her cargo of wheat from the United States.

A few hours before departure, the captain was given orders from the defense minister authorizing one additional crew member. Amir handed his papers to the captain and headed for his bunk. The general had informed him that others were already onboard ship under the supervision of Imroz, an old confidante of the general who had retired from the navy some ten years ago.

Thus, the ship sailed the next morning, its crew and captain unaware of the deadly cargo they were carrying.

The Terror Plot

The US president was meeting with his CIA chief. "John, now that we have the Taliban who claimed responsibility for freeing Aafia out of the way, we can focus on our plans to teach the Pakistanis a lesson. Tell me what you have."

"Mr. President, we have a plan ready and can put it into motion once you give the order, but given the extreme nature of the project and the outcry that is bound to ensue in its aftermath, I strongly advise you not to get into details. Your verbal instructions will be enough for me to proceed, as we will be using non-American assets for this project," replied the CIA chief.

"Okay, John, proceed. Just make sure we make such an example of them that the world will not forget, and no one will ever again dream of playing such games with the United States of America." The president rose and walked out.

━◁┼ ┼▷━

Yehudi, for that was the name by which he was known to the Americans, walked into the Library of Congress in the Thomas Jefferson Building in Washington, DC, and headed for the Local History and Genealogy room. It was near Second Street, SE, and very close to the exit, should the need arise for him to get away in a hurry. He was disguised as a seventy-year-old man with a slight stoop, bushy eyebrows, thick spectacles, long white hair, and a flowing white beard.

He was meeting his handler from the CIA; after retiring from Mossad, Yehudi was now a freelance security consultant, mostly working for the CIA and Mossad, though he had at times taken "assignments" from unlikely clients, like clandestine services for some Persian Gulf countries. Yehudi was born in West Gaza to Christian parents and spent his early life in refugee camps in Lebanon. At the age of twelve, he was recruited by the Lebanese Front, Jabhat al-Lubnaniyya, and from there he was spotted by Mossad and eventually joined that organization. He was sent as an Arab fighter to Afghanistan to fight Russians while gathering intelligence about the Afghan war theater and various players operating there. He became proficient in Darri, Pustho, and Farsi. After the Russians left Afghanistan, he moved to the Levant region of the Middle East and operated there until 9/11, when he left Mossad and became an independent contractor. Since then he had done many assignments in Pakistan, Afghanistan, Iraq, and Libya.

Yehudi knew his handler, but his handler didn't know what guise he would appear in. A "Temporarily Closed" sign had been placed outside the Local History and Genealogy room, and the room had been sterilized by the CIA. His handler was already there for the meeting. He watched warily, until Yehudi smiled and took out a cigarette case. This was their signal, and the handler relaxed.

"We want you to carry out an operation in India," the CIA man said.

"This envelope has details of the results we want; you can decide on operational details and resources. I have also included details of a bank transfer for the project, already executed to your designated account for your usual fee and expenses."

Yehudi took the package and left. He had not spoken a single word, so there would be no voice recording or voice matching, and he was in disguise, so there was no way of making a positive identification. The money he was receiving would be moved by his banker as per standing instructions and would disappear in a financial labyrinth.

Later the same evening, he took a flight to Dubai, where he maintained several apartments, all rented out on short-term leases but available to him anyway because he had keys to each one of them.

After getting over jet leg, he flew to Kabul, and from there traveled by road to the North Waziristan Tribal Agency in Pakistan.

Though technically in Pakistani territory, this was Taliban country, and the government of Pakistan had no control here. He had avoided coming through Islamabad or Peshawar, because the Pakistani intelligence agencies would have been on his tail.

His destination was in Razmak, a small town between north and south Waziristan—a seminary called Jamia Islamia Arabia Razmak. The fact that Razmak was home to a military cadet college didn't bother him; after all, some of the top Al-Qaeda leaders had lived for years right next to the biggest and most famous military academy of the Pakistan Army, in a town that was virtually owned and occupied by the army.

It was early morning; prayers had just ended when Yehudi entered the seminary. He was greeted by a guard at the gate. "*Salam walaikum,* Abu Yahyah." Here he was known as Abu Yahyah; Yahyah was the name of his son from an Afghan wife who lived in these parts. Yehudi didn't see them anymore; his wife and son lived with her parents, and he sent them money through Afghan money changers out of Dubai. As far as his Afghan family knew, he worked for the Taliban and was away on jihad; he couldn't come home to visit them because that would put his family at risk.

"*Walikum salam, wali jan.* How is everything?" he replied without stopping. He took off his shoes, entered a small room, and sat down facing the only occupant of the room. The short, stout Egyptian doctor looked at him from behind his bifocal spectacles and greeted him in Arabic, then leaned forward to embrace him and kiss him on the cheek in the Arab fashion of affection. This man had been Yehudi's commander from the early days of Afghan jihad and now believed that Yehudi was running his own cells of Al-Qaeda all over the Middle East.

Two hours later he left and retraced his steps back to Dubai.

Yehudi had, through the Egyptian, recruited Lashkar for the job; Lashkar was a local Taliban outfit in Pakistan that had changed its name many times, from Lashkar to Hizb to Jamaat, and many other variations.

Lashkar was to provide two men for the job, both in their teens, and who would have been brainwashed into believing anti-America and anti-India propaganda. Lashkar was given US$100,000 for expenses. No details of the actual operation were given; the two men were to be delivered by Lashkar to the Egyptian's contact, who would arrange to smuggle them over the Lahore border into India, not far from New Delhi.

The Wedding That Was a Funeral
New Delhi, India

Yehudi arrived at the wedding venue dressed in the uniform of a porter. What he saw in front of him was a small estate set on five acres in the heart of India's capital. The house was more like a palace, and for all practical purposes it was a palace: the family that occupied it had been the de facto royal family of India for the past sixty years. The wedding was ten days away, but for the next ten days, there was going to be a party every night. These Indians certainly knew how to celebrate weddings, Yehudi thought.

Yehudi observed that the place had been frequented by every kind of supplier and their workers for the past month, so it was really not difficult for him to prepare a detailed plan of attack, nor would it be difficult to bring his recruits inside the venue well before the wedding day, along with weapons and explosives. The security was overbearing but not really that effective, given the magnitude of the event and the sheer number of people involved. TV cameras and teams of journalists had been frequenting the place like rats all over a garbage bin.

Lashkar's men arrived in Delhi as promised by Yehudi's contacts. Yehudi spent a great deal of time with the two men, and ensured they were ready for the task. A few days before the wedding, he brought the two men to the house through one of the service entrances, dressed as porters bringing in decorations for the functions. The three men, Yehudi and his two wards, stayed hidden for the next few days on the grounds of the big mansion.

Wedding Day

It was a lovely Sunday afternoon. The wedding ceremony for the second son of India's most powerful family was to start at 7:00 p.m., and there was a party afterward that would continue well into the night. The preparations had been going on for six months—anybody who was anybody was going to be here. Today would be a new chapter in India's who's who, and those who were not there would soon find themselves crossed off the most elite invitation lists.

After the guests started arriving and the waiters were all over the place serving food and drinks, Yehudi decided to come out of his hiding place. He and his two operatives were dressed in waiters' uniforms. They had showered and shaved inside their hideout and looked every bit the part of service staff milling around the wedding party. Both operatives, Ismail Khan and Ishaq Wazir, were wearing suicide vests and had been pumped up with sermons about paradise and the beautiful women, *hoors*, waiting to welcome them with open arms once they detonated their bombs. Ismail Khan was a few months older than Ishaq Wazir, and a rather handsome young man.

The time was coming up to 7:00 p.m., and even though the sun had not set, the tall trees surrounding the property blocked the remaining sunlight.

Yehudi placed both men in the front rows with their trays, and told them to move very slowly until the bride and the groom arrived. That would be the time when both were to press the switch. Both young men started circling through the crowds with their trays. They were mesmerized by all the glitter and glamour, by fashionably and often scantily dressed beautiful Indian women. They felt like they were on the set of an Indian movie with actors and actresses all around; in fact, there were some famous actors and actresses present.

As the clock chimed seven, the bride and groom entered the stage that was set for them. Ishaq, correctly reading the signal, jumped toward the stage and detonated his vest. As Ismail turned toward the stage, he saw Ishaq leaping toward it. At the same time, an Indian woman in her midforties, passing very closely to Ismail, gently rubbed her hand on Ismail's trouser zip. Completely thrown off by this act, Ismail was momentarily delayed from exploding his vest, and he was knocked out by the impact from Ishaq's blast.

Yehudi had moved to a vantage point toward the gate of the palace and was watching everything. He saw Ishaq leaping forward, saw Ismail collide with an Indian woman and the surprise on Ismail's face, saw Ishaq exploding—and then there was complete mayhem. Yehudi realized Ismail had not detonated his vest. This posed a problem; Yehudi could not leave loose ends. So, much to his dislike, he moved inward toward the carnage and soon located Ismail, still knocked out. Yehudi turned the timer switch on the suicide vest to one minute and quietly left the venue. Within a minute there was another explosion.

The world media had captured the act of terrorism live on camera; over two hundred million Indians had watched their social elite blown to pieces in real time. It was too soon to identify the dead, but the worst was assumed.

Al Jazeera TV in Qatar received an email from a Taliban group based in Pakistan's Waziristan area, claiming credit for the attack and vowing to carry on the fight against the Indians, the Israelis, and the Americans. The email had two photos of the suicide bombers attached, thus there was no doubt that the email was authentic.

Cabinet Room, Indian Government
Prime Minister Dev, who was on his way to attend the fatal wedding, had been delayed by a protest that forced his entourage to take a different route. A few minutes before his arrival, the bombs went off and the prime minister immediately returned to his office. All the ministers, defense chiefs, and the head of the intelligence agency, RAW, had been summoned to the PM's office for an emergency meeting.

By the time Prime Minister Dev returned to his office, the media was fully covering the terrorist attack on the wedding in Delhi. It was feared that scores of ministers, some senior military officers, many members of the most important political family in India, and many show business personalities were killed or wounded in the attack.

There were already demonstrations in many parts of the country, and the PM feared violence that would inevitably and rightly target Muslim communities.

Two hours after the attack on the Delhi wedding, the cabinet started the meeting to discuss the situation. By now Al-Jazeera had already telecast news of the Lashkar email with the photographs of the two terrorists, so there was no doubt about the perpetrators of the attack. This was the same group that had been responsible for many previous attacks on India and was known to have been sponsored by Pakistan's ISI.

The prime minister asked the interior minister, "Dada Bhai, why don't you brief us on the law-and-order situation and the extent of damage in the terrorist attack."

"Prime Minister, soon after the bomb blast, an Indian policeman opened fire on some diplomats coming out of Pakistan's high commission in Delhi. The policeman was arrested and was instantly acclaimed as an Indian hero by the media. In another incident, a Muslim family in Gujrat was massacred by a crazed fan of a movie star who was rumored to have been killed in the terrorist attack.

"Going by available figures, which indicate a surprisingly low casualty count, so far only eleven people have been declared dead. However, this tally is likely to rise. The number of injured was reported to be around eighty-five, with very little information about the gravity of their injuries. The bride had tripped at the fatal moment, and the groom had moved forward, leaning down to rescue her; as a result both the bride and the groom survived the attack unscathed. This information is kept classified as top secret, and the whole family has been moved to an undisclosed location for the time being. However, two movie actors, three ministers, and one general are counted among the dead."

No one really cared about the ministers or the general, but the movie stars were a different matter. Indians worshipped their movie stars.

Next, Prime Minister Dev said, "General Krish, present the army's position in the event hostilities break out."

Chief Krishna, a man of fifty-seven years who had played a key role in developing the doctrine of Cold Start for the Indian military in the past decade, had been preparing for this day all his life. His father had also been in the Indian Army and was killed in the 1965 war at the Sialkot front in a battle against the Pakistan Army.

"Gentlemen and ladies"—he army, air force, and navy have prepared for this day for the past ten years. But every time, diplomacy, international pressure, and the 'give peace a chance' nonsense have prevented us from teaching the enemy a lesson they will not forget. We propose that India attack Pakistan forthwith, and with that I mean that at the conclusion of this meeting, orders are issued for the Indian Air Force to be ready to launch an air assault on Pakistan. We must not give them time to react, because they will keep on denying, and then the Americans, the Chinese, and the Saudis all will jump in to save the Pakistanis yet again. I have here a detailed plan of action if the cabinet so desires." He paused.

"Chief Krishna, do you realize that what you are suggesting can lead to mutually assured destruction of both countries?" asked the prime minister, who was a Hindu fundamentalist and always thought in terms of exploiting the opportunities to cleanse India of non-Hindus.

"Prime Minister, with all due respect, sometimes wars are inevitable, and this is one of those times. As for destruction, there will always be destruction, be it by war or natural disaster. But we should not look at this as a war, but as an opportunity to fix some lingering problems we have allowed to fester for so many decades. Furthermore, we believe that with the element of surprise that we have on our side, we can easily minimize our own loses and inflict maximum pain on our enemy." The army chief glared at his boss.

"And you think that the Pakistanis will sit idly with their nuclear arsenal while we attack them?" retorted the prime minister.

"In the first wave, we take out their air defenses and the maximum number of missile facilities. We follow it up with a ground assault and simultaneously inflict lasting damage on their navy. Then we negotiate a peace treaty," answered the chief.

Yeah, sure, thought the Indian prime minister. This is how General Musharraf had thought when he invaded Kargil in 1998, and had it not been for the Americans, we would have destroyed them. That's the problem with men in uniform: they cannot think beyond war, the bloody fools. But without revealing his inner thoughts and contempt, he went on, "General, you seem to forget that the Pakistanis have defined destruction of their defense capabilities, which you propose, as a red line that if crossed will justify the use of their nuclear arsenal."

"Prime Minister, our intelligence and profiling of the top military leadership in Pakistan suggests that they will not cross the nuclear attack threshold," asserted the chief.

"Thank you, Chief Krishna."

"Mukerjee," the PM said, turning to Mrs. Mukerjee, the foreign minister, "give us your assessment."

The cabinet meeting continued for another hour, and it was unanimously agreed that India would retaliate against Pakistan as recommended by the army chief. Due to national security implications, all the ministers were asked to stay at the PM's house to prevent any premature leaks.

The cabinet meeting was followed by the meeting of the Defense Committee, which included the prime minister, the defense minister, the foreign minister, and all the service chiefs. The committee was briefed on the war plan, which was duly approved.

The Indian military was authorized to attack.

The prime minister informed the speaker of the parliament to discontinue sitting of the parliament for the next thirty days; it was expected that most politicians would either proceed abroad or to their home states. The prime minister and his cabinet moved to a secret location that had been developed as part of the war plans, as did the military high command.

Internal and external security at all critical and important national strategic installations was raised to the highest level. Backup plans for each and every location, hardware, software, and key strategic personnel were initiated.

It was decided that the Indian Air Force would launch their attack on Pakistan at midnight. This would be synchronized with an attack by the Indian Navy, which would effectively lay a siege to the Karachi port, which was the commercial juggernaut of Pakistan's economy and supply line. Within twenty-four hours, key IBGs (independent battle groups) would move into position to invade Pakistani territory.

The war was underway.

HOW IT ALL ENDED

Cabinet Meeting at Muree Hill Station Near Islamabad, Pakistan

The cabinet meeting had been called as soon as the news of the Indian attack had spread. In addition to the elected members of the cabinet, the prime minister had also invited all the service chiefs, provincial governors and chief ministers.

The meeting started with the navy, air-force, and army chiefs reporting damages, which in their initial estimate were devastating. Most of the navy had been rendered ineffective; the air force too had been largely destroyed and a number of the army's forward positions had been completely wiped out.

"Prime Minister, the nation demands we retaliate with full force, and we do so immediately." This was the home minister.

"General Bhaya, what is your assessment of the situation and recommendation?" Some considered the general to be the most powerful man in the country, now holding the dual portfolios of defense and foreign affairs.

"Prime Minister, let us get the facts straight: we had nothing to do with this attack in Delhi. In all likelihood the attack was engineered by the CIA with the help of Mossad and was aimed at igniting a war between Pakistan and India. This is clearly in retaliation to our policy of breaking free from the American and Western influence. The Americans have been very clever; they have stopped all kinds of economic aid and cooperation, which we expected, and they have combined it with igniting a war. We expected this too, but the timing and the speed, I must admit, has caught us off guard. We are now faced with the devil's alternative: damned if we do and damned if we don't. This is not unlike 1998, when India forced our hand by exploding nuclear bombs and we had no choice, in the face of immense public pressure, except to carry out our own nuclear tests, which caused the collapse of the country's economy and subsequent martial law by Musharraf."

The general paused to marshal his thoughts, and went on. "We are in a state of war, and there is no way we cannot react."

The prime minister nodded and asked other ministers to speak their minds. Each one demanded action. When all the members had finished venting their anger, Sultan asked his cabinet colleagues, "Does anyone have any idea how many lives will be lost if we embark on this path?"

There was pin-drop silence. Finally, a minister from the Maulana's party spoke. "Prime Minister, it matters not how many of us or our people die, but it matters that we respond. We are first and foremost Muslims, so we fear not death."

Sultan turned to his finance minister, a Harvard-educated economist who had worked for the World Bank and then moved to investment banking, where he made his millions and then had returned home to serve his country. "Qasim, tell me, can we fight a war? Let me rephrase—how much will the war cost, and given the current state of country's finances, how long can we sustain a war?"

"Prime Minister, before elections we had run various scenarios, and the conclusion we had reached, which has not changed, that we can at best fight a very short and limited war. And even then the cost to the economy will take a few years to absorb. In terms of numbers, by the time the war is finished, we will need a new fleet of fighter planes, which will cost us—if anyone is prepared to sell them to us, that is—around fifty billion dollars, and this is just one item. I would guess that the military hardware and logistics alone will cost us another twenty billion dollars, and that is not counting the cost in human lives or the cost to the economy."

"Okay, a session of the assembly has been summoned for this evening at the Faisal Mosque. Let us meet then and see what our colleagues have to say." With that, the cabinet meeting concluded.

All the cabinet members, chief ministers, and governors rose and left; however, the three service chiefs remained seated. They had been informed that a follow-up meeting would take place after the cabinet meeting.

"Okay, Chief, what is your assessment of the damage and future strategy?" Sultan asked the army chief.

"Mr. Prime Minister, due to our recent policies, we are isolated. No Western country is even prepared to talk to us. Even Saudi Arabia is giving us the cold shoulder. Iran is wary of us because they fear that we are an extremist Sunni government, and China has so far offered no comment. We have suffered massive damage and casualties on the Kashmir and Lahore fronts due to intense bombardment carried out by the Indians before our own air force was even able to take off. It is too soon to give an accurate assessment, but the damage is extensive. Our Multan, Bahawalpur, and Pano Aqil flanks have been nearly wiped out by the Indian Air Force early this morning. We are getting reports from the navy that Indian ships have moved to block all our sea routes.

"We recommend that you give a speech assuring the nation that we will take immediate retaliatory action; we will fly some missions over India and engage India in the Sialkot, Kashmir, and Lahore sectors. We will allow media full coverage of these activities and follow it up with a massive propaganda campaign on every TV and radio channel, to convince people that we have inflicted serious damage on the enemy. We have intelligence agency staff ready to take over each and every TV and radio station in the country. We follow that up with a delegation to China seeking their help in convincing the United States to stop India from committing any more acts of aggression," the army chief concluded somberly.

The chairman of the Joint Chiefs spoke. "Mr. Prime Minister, we all concur with the chief's recommendations."

Sultan spoke. "Okay, gentlemen, we will do what you have suggested and then some. Here is what we will do: the army will open the fronts the chief has suggested, and the intelligence agencies should be given a go-ahead to control the media. The general will go to China, not to open a dialogue with the Indians or the Americans, but to see how far we can rely on their support. The air force will send fighters inside India, and the targets we will strike will be water reservoirs, especially those built upstream of Kashmir; nuclear plants; and their known missile bases. We also want to target Bangalore, their high-technology hub, but given the depth of the target, we may have to go for a land attack carried out by a team of dedicated commandos who will have to be infiltrated into the country, unless we can use assets that are already there. We want to do maximum damage to their economy and areas that foreigners have invested in, which generate billions of dollars in revenue that feed the Indian economy and the military. These must be our priority targets. Given the depth of some targets, many of these missions will not see the return of their pilots, but that is a cost we have to bear.

"We know we cannot fight a long war, so let us inflict as much damage as possible on their infrastructure in the shortest possible time. We are targeting the water reservoirs because these will take years to rebuild, cause massive floods and devastation in their own country, and will restore our water supply for some time, allowing us to recover faster in the aftermath of the war. I want our navy to use as many al-Qaeda-style attacks as possible on the Indian Navy, and let us give complete support to every militant organization that wants to strike inside India—but their targets must be infrastructure, both civil and military.

"I am going to declare a cease fire with the Taliban in the Northern Areas and invite them to join in the good fight against the Indians. If they take up our invitation, then let us push them into the front line on the Lahore and Sialkot fronts. If any Afghan Taliban are willing to join us, then let us allow them to fight on the Kashmir front. We will deploy all the policemen who have been placed in the surplus pool after the elections and in the face of reforms on the front lines too; let them sacrifice for their country. Hopefully, once this war is over, we will have gotten rid of a lot of corrupt and militant people from our society. We will start a massive draft campaign and get every seminary student to join the war; this is of course jihad, what they have been yearning after for decades. The job of our regular army will be to guide, train, and deploy these new recruits."

"Mr. Prime Minister, this is madness. All these inexperienced recruits will be cut down by the Indian forces in no time." This was the chairman of the Joint Chiefs of Staff.

"General Syed, a bullet or a bomb does not stop to ask your age, experience, or bio data, so it is really of no consequence who is on the front. We will take casualties; it is better if we conserve our trained forces for the second round—if a second round comes, that is," replied the prime minister.

"I also want our forces to concentrate on creating two gaps or corridors of attack, one on Lahore and another on the Sialkot front, through which we can send the new recruits inside India in the shortest possible time to cause as much damage as possible. We will send wave after wave of humans and inflict terror in the hearts of the Indians. I expect that within days we will have almost two million volunteers on our borders itching to take up the fight with the Indians. We must give them their fight. This can seriously demoralize the Indian nation, and some of them might even get to Delhi.

"Thank you, gentlemen: please go ahead and prepare. I intend to establish a command post on the Lahore front, and the general will be the acting prime minister if something happens to me. Written instructions to that effect have been given to the speaker of the National Assembly and the attorney general," concluded the prime minister.

"Mr. Prime Minister," said General Bhaya, "thank you for your confidence in me, but I intend to join our forces and would like to be based in the Sialkot sector, where heaviest battles are likely to take place. So I suggest you nominate someone else."

"I appreciate your valor, General, but my instructions remain the same. However, in the same set of instructions, I have taken the liberty of nominating your successor as well." With that the prime minister rose. The general saluted the prime minister out of respect and admiration; the service chiefs followed.

However, the army chief was sick of all this bravado. These fools had no idea what they were getting the country into, and the general had completely gone senile in his old age. But the chief didn't have any choice in the matter—even many of his commanders shared the enthusiasm of the prime minister and the general. Besides, everyone was spying on everyone in this country, so his options were very limited at this time.

Once the service chiefs had left, the prime minister and the general sat down to discuss other options.

"General, where is the ship that left Karachi port a few days ago, headed to the United States to bring back a cargo of wheat for our people?"

The reference was to the wheat cargo ship with concealed nuclear weapons. "Prime Minister, the ship is in international waters and is beyond the naval blockade the Indians are trying to enforce. I have already instructed the captain to stay in international waters within a short distance of India's shores. I had also taken the liberty of loading on the ship two mobile launchers and a crew of six who are trained in launching missiles from the mobile launchers, so we have nuclear missile launching capability we can employ without any detection."

"Okay, General, why don't you call the Indian ambassador and ask him to convey to their PM our message that we had nothing to do with the attack, and if India does not cease forthwith, we will have no choice but to take extreme measures. We don't want to use the nuclear word. Also talk to the UN secretary. Convey the same thing and ask them to call an immediate session of the UN Security Council, condemn the Indian aggression, and ask India to immediately cease fire or we will have no choice but to use any and all measures to deal with their naked aggression. I will talk to the Americans and see if they will play ball, though I am sure what their answer and attitude will be."

The White House

"Mr. President, the Prime Minister of Pakistan is holding on the line to speak to you," said the secretary to the president, who was running on the treadmill, doing his early-morning exercise routine.

"You mean someone from Pakistan is on the line waiting to put through their prime minister?" said the president.

"No, it is the man himself," replied the secretary.

"Uh-huh; tell him to speak to the secretary of state, and get the secretary of state on the line for me."

"Mr. President, I have the secretary of state on the line," announced the secretary.

"Thelma," said the president, "You might be getting a call from the prime minister of Pakistan. He just called here, and my secretary asked him to call you. Tell him to hand over the prisoner Aafia to our embassy in China. Only after that will we talk. Don't say a word more than that."

US Secretary of State's Home

As soon as the secretary of state put the phone down, she received her second call of the morning, and it was the prime minister of Pakistan, as predicted by the president moments ago.

"Good morning, Mr. Prime Minister," said the secretary of state.

"Madam Secretary, we would like to discuss with your government the naked aggression of India, before things get out of control," said the Prime Minister of Pakistan.

"Certainly, Mr. Prime Minister. Call me as soon as your people have handed over the escaped prisoner, Aafia, to our consular staff in Beijing, China. Then we will talk." The US secretary of state put the phone down.

In Pakistan, the prime minister stared at the phone in his hand and slowly put it down. So the United States had been informed, no doubt by one of their thousands of informants spread all over Pakistani society, that Aafia was safely ensconced in Pakistan's

Beijing embassy. Well, this didn't change anything—this just showed the world how unreasonable the Americans were, and that they were indeed part of the Indian attack conspiracy.

The call was monitored by the PM's military secretary, who reported the conversation to the COAS.

The Army Chief's Office in Rawalpindi
"Osman, get our military attaché in Beijing on the line for me," the army chief ordered his personal assistant, who was a colonel.

Colonel Osman got the military attaché on the line. His name was Rao Bahadur; he was also a colonel in the Pakistani army Baluch regiment.

"Rao, my boy, I need you to do something without a moment's delay. Get Dr. Aafia—use force if necessary—and take her to the American embassy in Beijing. Hand her over to them and then call me," the army chief concluded.

"Yes, sir; right away sir" was the automatic response of the military attaché in Beijing, China.

The army chief knew that only with the mediation of the Americans could a face saving be achieved and the war halted. There was no doubt in his mind that Pakistan was no longer in a position to fight a war, not even for a few days. And there was no question of using the nuclear weapons, even though the Indians had crossed the predefined red line, because that was mutually assured destruction of both countries, which would result in the deaths of tens of millions of people. He was not going to let that happen on his watch.

Next, the army chief called the US ambassador on his secure line. He made sure that this was a strictly private conversation.

Secretary of State's Office, Washington, DC
"Madam Secretary, I have our ambassador from Pakistan on the line," the female secretary informed the secretary of the state.

"Yes, Henry, what do you have?" the secretary of state asked without any small talk.

"Madam Secretary, I just got a call from the chief here." The secretary of state knew that this was a reference to the army chief of Pakistan. "He has assured me that the prisoner, Aafia, will be handed over to our embassy in Beijing within the hour. He wants us to get India to immediately cease fire, after his country has put up a show of attacks on Indian forces and a propaganda campaign has been launched to make them look good. He has conveyed to me that this is not his government's decision, but his decision in the greater national interests and to promote world peace, as well as to save tens of millions of human lives," concluded Ambassador Henry, from the US embassy in Pakistan.

"Okay, what do you make of it, Henry?"

"Madam Secretary, the chief is telling us that he is prepared to work with us but his government is not. So if we can help the chief seize power, we can normalize the relations between the two countries and get back to business as usual."

"Okay, Henry, thanks. I will get back to you," the secretary of state said and put the phone down.

The White House
"Mr. President, we need to help the army chief in Pakistan to restore some sanity. That is our only option," the secretary of state said, briefing the president and his team on developments in Pakistan.

"Okay, people, let's hear what you have to say," the president said, inviting his team to open up.

"Mr. President, I concur with Thelma; we really have no other option. Pakistani leadership, the elected one, poses a clear and present danger not just to the United States but to the whole world. We are at the threshold of nuclear Armageddon, and we must take any and all measures to contain the situation," said Matt Clapton, the US defense secretary. Everyone else agreed, but none ventured any solutions.

"John," the president said, addressing CIA Director John Deskovanci, "what can the CIA do?"

"Mr. President, we have a fleet of drones inside Pakistan. We can fly a drone over Islamabad and take out their leadership with one single strike," replied the CIA director.

"What about collateral damage to civilians?" the president asked.

"There will be a few hundred civilian fatalities, but that is inevitable in such an operation," replied the CIA director.

"Okay, go ahead. Let's get rid of these madmen and make the world a safer place." The president rose and walked out of the conference room.

Islamabad—Faisal Mosque

After the destruction of the parliament building in the Indian attack, it was decided to hold today's meeting at the largest mosque in the country.

The prime minister and the general, in his capacity as foreign and defense minister, were seated in the front row facing the majority of the assembly members belonging to the ruling party. However, none of the service chiefs were present, being occupied with the defense of the country.

Evening prayers had just concluded, and the mosque was empty except for those who were authorized to attend the parliament.

Speaker after speaker called for the government to retaliate, using nuclear weapons to settle differences with India once and for all. One member of the assembly who was on the CIA's payroll was carrying a device that was relaying the audio of the meeting live to CIA headquarters in Virginia.

By now the Pakistan Air Force was on full alert, and they immediately detected a drone taking off from Shamsi air base, an air base that Pakistan had loaned the Americans. Immediately a call was placed to the coordination officer in the American embassy, who calmly explained that the drone had been ordered to survey the damage caused by the Indian attack so the Americans could come up with appropriate measures to help Pakistan. Surprisingly, this load of cow dung was swallowed by the duty officer without question. The duty officer reported the matter to the air force high command in Chaklala, close to Islamabad.

The base commander at Chaklala decided to take no chances and ordered a MBIDA Spada2000, a low- to medium-altitude air-defense system consisting of radar with a sixty-kilometer range and four six-cell missile launchers to follow the drone. The Aspide 2000 missile could intercept enemy missiles and aircraft at a range of over twenty kilometers.

As the drone was flying over Islamabad, it fired a single missile. MBIDA pilot Zafar, seeing this, immediately shot down the drone and reported to the base commander, who asked him to return to the base.

The missile fired by the drone hit the Faisal mosque and wiped out most of the parliament of the country, along with its leaders.

GHQ Rawalpindi

The army chief got a call from a local police chief informing him of the attack on the parliament's session at the Faisal mosque and the complete destruction of the mosque, with the fear that there might be very few survivors.

Army Chief Pervez, without any hesitation, ordered the 111 Brigade to move to Islamabad and take over the city.

Within the hour the army chief appeared on national TV and made a moving speech about the enemy attack on Islamabad that had wiped out the national leadership, leaving him no choice but to take over the country to save it from complete chaos and destruction. The chief vowed to avenge every loss of life and property, and asked the nation to remain calm.

When the army chief got back to his office, he had a very worried navy chief waiting for him.

"Ajmal, tell me, what is worse than what has already happened to our country?" asked the army chief.

"Pervez, we have a bigger problem," said the naval chief. "I have just learned that last week a ship was modified at the naval shipyard under direct orders from the general, may he burn in hell, and loaded with six Shaheen III missiles. As you know, the Shaheen III has a range of three thousand kilometers and can deliver either a conventional or a nuclear payload much faster than liquid-fueled missiles because it does not need to be fueled before launch, reducing deployment time significantly. Six of those with nuclear payloads are sitting in international waters just off the coast of India."

The chief, without a word, reached for the phone and got the American ambassador on the line. "Mr. Ambassador, I need to urgently speak to your president. This is a matter of averting a nuclear war."

"Chief, I will see what can be done." And with that the line was disconnected.

The White House
"Mr. President, we have our ambassador from Pakistan on the line." The president's first reaction was to tell the ambassador to talk to the secretary of state, but he realized that Henry was a veteran and stickler for discipline. If he was calling direct, then there must be good reason.

"Okay, put him through" said the president.

"Mr. President, I just spoke to Army Chief Pervez, who has taken over in the aftermath of the missile attack that killed his country's elected leadership. He says he needs to speak to you urgently and directly on the matter of averting a nuclear war," said the ambassador.

"Okay, Henry, let me take it from here." The president put the phone down.

"Jeanne, get Army Chief Pervez of Pakistan on the line and patch the secretary of state into the conference," POTUS said to his secretary.

"Good evening, Mr. President, or rather good afternoon," Pervez said. It was evening in Pakistan but afternoon in Washington.

"General Pervez, I believe you wanted to speak to me. I am listening," the president replied curtly.

"Mr. President, as you are aware, I have just taken over in a national emergency resulting from the death of our entire elected leadership. I have come into possession of some very disturbing information that I must share with you to avert a nuclear catastrophe." After a brief pause the Pakistan Army chief continued. "Mr. President, the MV *Badr,* flying a Liberian flag, is currently in international waters five hundred kilometers off the coast of Mumbai. The ship's cargo contains six medium-range ballistic missiles loaded with a nuclear payload."

"Holy shit! What were you guys thinking? Have you lost your minds completely?" yelled the president.

"This was a clandestine operation planned and carried out by General Bhaya, our late defense and foreign minister, who we believe is now dead in the missile attack. We fear that the ship will launch the missiles and cause a nuclear holocaust. We want you to incapacitate the ship before it is able to fire and do any more damage," said Pakistan's new leader.

"Okay, we will see what we can do," replied POTUS, and put the phone down.

The president looked at his wristwatch. It was 1:00 p.m. in Washington.

"Jeanne, get everyone in here on the double." His secretary knew this meant the whole cabinet and the military high command.

2:00 p.m., Washington, DC

"Gentlemen, an hour ago I learned that the Pakistanis have a cargo ship with nuclear weapons hidden on board waiting off the coast of India in international waters, loaded with six nuclear missiles. The acting chief executive of Pakistan, Army Chief Pervez, called me with this information and wants us to neutralize the ship. It is almost twenty-four hours since the first Indian attack on Pakistan, and almost six hours since the ship may have had any contact with its planners in Islamabad. Suggestions?" POTUS looked around the table.

"Mr. President, let us just call the Indians and tell them to take out the Pakistani ship. That should settle it without us getting any more involved." This was coming from the secretary of state.

Ignoring the SecState, the president asked, "Can someone tell me how much time we have before the *Badr*, the Pakistani ship, fires the nukes?"

"No time, sir. If the ship is loaded and waiting, theoretically they could fire any time, so worst-case scenario, we are already out of time," replied General James.

"Options?" POTUS asked of his military chief.

"Calling the Indians and getting them to react in a limited way—to just confine themselves to neutralizing one ship—may take too long, because the Indians may be tempted to launch a wider strike of their own. So that's not really an option; we have to use our own attack capability in the Indian Ocean to take out the missile ship," replied General James.

"How long will it take?" POTUS enquired.

"If we give the order now, our birds should be in the air over the Indian ocean within thirty minutes. Another hour to locate the ship, so give or take two hours, and the Indians or any other air force in the world cannot beat that," General James replied proudly.

"Okay, General, give the order. Let's not waste any more time," POTUS ordered with a sigh.

Onboard MV *Badr*
Captain Ghanchee had imposed a complete communications blackout on his ship after hearing of the Indian attack. He didn't know what was in the secret cargo but feared the worst, and he didn't want any panic reactions. He patiently decided to wait for further orders.

Amir had arrived on the ship just before it was due to leave the port. He had been given papers as a sailor, but in addition to that he was also given a sealed envelope that he was to open when something untoward happened or when they reached their destination. The general had also asked Imroz, who was a former navy lieutenant, to accompany Amir.

Amir had his own radio equipment, which he used without the knowledge of the captain. Apart from the communication gear, loaded onto the ship were sufficient weapons for some dozen sailors, who were handpicked by the general. All were trained commandoes.

Amir checked the time; it was 11:00 p.m. in Pakistan and 1:00 p.m. in Washington. He went into his bunker and checked for the latest updates. He was shocked to learn that his mentor, the general, and the whole elected leadership had been wiped out in a missile attack suspected to be from a US drone. Amir already knew of the devastation caused by the Indian attack early that morning and was eagerly waiting for some news from the general. The wait was over; there was not going to be any news from the general. The time had come to open the sealed instructions.

Amir opened the envelope. First was his guideline, which instructed him to launch the missiles in any manner he saw fit if there was an attack on Pakistan and his contact with the general was lost. This had already happened. The second letter was from the office of the naval chief and was endorsed by the defense ministry, declaring Amir captain of the ship, MV *Badr*, and putting ship and crew under his command.

Amir got out his duffel bag and put on the uniform of a naval officer, which he had been asked to carry. Thus attired, he sought out Imroz and told him to do the same. Both men, attired in their uniforms, rounded up the commandos and unlocked the weapons box that had been loaded onto the ship. Four commandos, with Amir and Imroz, made their way to the bridge. The remaining commandos were posted around the ship to maintain order.

Amir handed his papers to a dumbfounded captain, who silently stepped aside. Imroz took off the captain's shoulder stripes and put them onto Amir's shoulder. Thus the command of the MV *Badr* changed hands.

The captain and first officer were taken to their quarters and confined there, with a sailor guarding their cabin.

It was 11:15 p.m. in Pakistan and 1:15 p.m. in Washington, DC.

Diego Garcia Naval Base, Indian Ocean
The orders were received from Admiral Mullen at 2:30 Washington time, to launch a search-and-destroy mission in the Indian Ocean. The target was a Pakistani cargo ship, MV *Badr*, suspected of carrying nuclear warheads.

Captain Connor was given the mission. Connor was rated as top gun at the air force academy on completion of his training; he was the best pilot around by a long shot. At thirty, he was still unmarried and was considered to be something of a ladies' man. Captain Connor was to be accompanied by Captain Junas, who was five years older, but still rated as one of the most competent pilots around.

Both were to fly newly inducted F-35 Lightning II stealth fighter planes. The F-35A carried AGM-158 joint air-to-surface standoff missiles, or JASSMs), a type of cruise missiles.

Operation Foxhunt was launched at 3:00 p.m. Washington time.

Onboard MV *Badr*

Amir handed over the bridge to Imroz, who had spent his life in the navy, and headed for the secret compartment where the missiles were stored. With the help of a dozen regular sailors, under the watchful eye of the commandos, the missiles were brought onto the main deck of the ship. Next, the mobile missile launchers were taken out of their boxes and set up on the main deck. There were two launchers and six missiles, so it would have to be three rounds of launches.

Amir left Firoz, one of the commandos, in charge. Firoz, Amir knew, was the most senior of the six technicians who could load and launch a missile. All six were stationed around the missile launchers.

The time in Washington was 2:30 p.m., and in Pakistan, 12:30 a.m.

Amir had no target list, so he had to improvise. He summoned the pilot of the ship and, using his laptop and GPS system, got a map of the Indian Ocean on the screen. He figured that Mumbai and Gujrat were within firing range. He searched for coordinates for major Indian cities in those areas, and fed them into the missile's guidance system.

The missiles were armed and ready. The first two had the targets Mumbai and Gujrat.

With a deep sigh and an ominous feeling, Amir ordered the missiles fired.

The time was 4:00 p.m. in Washington, and 2:00 a.m. in Pakistan.

Captain Connor's onboard computer showed that two missiles had been launched; Connor immediately realized that the launch pad must be their target, and fed the launch pad coordinates into his flight computer.

Connor decided not to waste any more time, and fired two missiles at the launch pad coordinates.

The time was 4:05 p.m. in Washington, and 2:05 a.m. in Pakistan.

It took the American missiles twenty minutes to reach the target. The time was 4:25 p.m.

Amir's team had loaded two more missiles, and as Amir gave them coordinates to feed into the guidance system, he saw a light in the sky coming toward them. That was the last thing anyone on board MV *Badr* saw.

The missiles hit MV *Badr* at 4:26 Washington time, and 2:26 Pakistan time. Within the next fifteen minutes, the ship had gone underwater.

Captain Connor radioed Diego base and informed them of the good news and the bad news: the bad news was that two nuclear missiles had been fired; the good news was the ship had been sunk, so there were not likely to be any more missile launches from that ship.

The White House, Washington, DC, 4:45 p.m.
Admiral Milken said, "Mr. President, our boys have sunk the Pakistani ship, but before we got to it, the Pakistanis managed to fire two nuclear missiles on India."

The president and the cabinet members had stayed in the war room at the Pentagon to monitor developments.

The president said to the secretary of state, "Thelma, call General Pervez and inform him. Jeanne, get me Prime Minister Dev of India on the line."

"Mr. President, I have Prime Minister Dev on the line."

The president took the phone. "Mr. Prime Minister, I have some terrible news. A rogue Pakistani ship has fired two nuclear missiles at India. We have eliminated the ship and any further threat from there. We received this information from General Pervez of the Pakistan Army, who is presently the chief executive of the country after the death of their leadership. This was an act of the past Pakistani regime. We believe the new regime under General Pervez is amenable to a peace arrangement. I urge you to use extreme caution in dealing with the situation, and take all measures to defuse the missiles headed your way."

After a shocked silence, Prime Minister Dev said, "Mr. President, thank you for the information. We will do whatever we need to defend our country." He hung up.

The Indian prime minister turned to his cabinet members, some of whom had turned ashen, having heard the president of the United States on the speakerphone talking about an incoming nuclear attack on Indian soil.

The Indian Air Force was ordered to intercept and destroy the incoming missiles. The missile heading for Gujrat was successfully intercepted, but the missile heading for Mumbai had already gotten through the defense net and landed on Mumbai in the early hours of the morning.

Three million people died instantly, millions more would die in the coming days, and the effects of the nuclear attack would last for decades.

The Morning after the Nuclear Attack on Mumbai
The president of the United States called the Indian prime minister and told him that his country must stand down; there must be no more aggression, and the two countries must sit down to work out a peace agreement.

The Indian cabinet wanted to retaliate with nuclear weapons, but in the end better sense prevailed, when they were faced with the direct threat of American intervention on Pakistan's side.

Pakistan agreed to dismantle its nuclear arsenal under international supervision. An agreement was reached with India to resolve the Kashmir dispute by accepting the existing line of control as the international border. Siachen Glacier was vacated by both the armies under UN supervision, and other smaller disputes were also settled.

THE END

Lightning Source UK Ltd.
Milton Keynes UK
UKOW06f2054280617
304300UK00008B/377/P